"I loved Ten Low. Combining the taut characterisation and clever wit of Stark Holborn's sp**___** Western with some splendidly inclusive and innovative **___** of Firefly and Joanna Russ, with a **___** JOANNE HARRIS, BEST-SELLING AUT**___** OF LOKI AND MANY MORE

"A fantastic, punchy SF action story, full of blood and grit and bitter pasts." – ADRIAN TCHAIKOVSKY, AWARD-WINNING AUTHOR OF CHILDREN OF TIME, DOGS OF WAR AND MANY MORE.

"Stark Holborn continues to impress. Great characters and a blistering pace." – GARETH POWELL, AWARD-WINNING AUTHOR OF THE EMBERS OF WAR SERIES

"Ten Low showed me the most vibrant desert world since Dune. [It] leaves the old guard masters in the dust." – ALEX WHITE, AUTHOR OF THE SALVAGERS TRILOGY

"Stark Holborn's writing is clever, original and thrilling." – R. J. BARKER, AUTHOR OF THE BONE SHIPS AND AGE OF ASSASSINS

"An action-packed SF adventure with an intriguing majority female cast? OH, HELL YES!" – STINA LEICHT, AUTHOR OF PERSEPHONE STATION

"I loved this from beginning to end. Stark Holborn grabs you by the throat on page one and never lets you go!" – CAVAN SCOTT, BESTSELLING AND AWARD-WINNING AUTHOR

"A gritty space western that fans of The Mandalorian should lap up." – PAUL CORNELL, AUTHOR OF THE SHADOW POLICE AND WITCHES OF LYCHFORD SERIES

TEN LOW

STARK HOLBORN

TITAN BOOKS

Ten Low
Print edition ISBN: 9781789096620
E-book edition ISBN: 9781789096637

Published by Titan Books
A division of Titan Publishing Group Ltd
144 Southwark Street, London SE1 0UP
www.titanbooks.com

First edition: June 2021
10 9 8 7 6 5 4 3 2 1

This is a work of fiction. All of the characters, organizations, and events
portrayed in this novel are either products of the author's imagination or are
used fictitiously. Any resemblance to actual persons, living or dead (except for
satirical purposes), is entirely coincidental.

A CIP catalogue record for this title is available from the British Library.

Printed and bound by CPI Group (UK) Ltd, Croydon, CR0 4YY.

For N.E.D.

ONE

THE
BOOK
OF
THE
GENERAL

HUNCH CLOSER TO the sputtering fire. The darkness is vast, hiding countless lives, but down here the wind just coughs dust into my eyes. I close them against the grit, against the light of the struggling flames, against the emptiness around me, knowing I should sleep but afraid of what I might dream.

My thoughts have a habit of coming loose. The more I keep to myself, the more they seep from my head, catching on the stubble of my scalp and trailing out behind me like cotton. Unless I'm careful, I won't get them reeled in again before I make Redcrop. I can't afford that. Single words, single thoughts: no doubts and no questions.

I tug the scarf further towards the brim of my hat. Sometimes I wish for hair, thick and curling as it once was, to cover my ears and warm my scalp. I feel for the pouch at my hip. It is slack, the beads inside cold and too few. Breath. I hold one to my lips and try to believe it is what people say: a sphere of pure air from the forests of Prosper.

The bead clacks against my teeth before I bite down. The splintering plastic cuts my trailing thoughts and stops me from leaking into the night, even though there is no good oxygen within; just an empty orb and a dusting of dex-amphetamine. Enough to ease the fatigue caused by the thin air, even after all these months.

I swallow, the noise loud in my ears. Beyond the tiny fire there's nothing. Just the wind. Some folk say the wind is alive, that it coils between the stars like a snake. Who am I to say they are wrong? Too long out here and you begin to hear the wind speak. An endless sigh that started a hundred thousand cycles before I was born.

Carefully, I drag my bag closer and bring the notebook into the firelight. The cover is peeling, and there aren't many blank pages left, but I turn to one and take the pencil nub from the crease.

Hafsa Gellam, I write, and see her face again, eyes heavy with exhaustion as she gripped my hand. Beneath her name I draw a line and label it *Child Gellam*. Another line, another name: *Child's Child?* I draw on, tracing four imaginary generations, until the pencil scrapes the bottom of the page.

So much potential… Life in the Barrens is hard won and easily lost, but Hafsa is a strong woman, and the child seemed healthy when I left. If the child lived, and went on to produce a child of their own and so on… I close my eyes. What if just one of those newly possible people saves another, with a word or a deed or a single, unthinking act? How many futures could that tiny, bloodied newborn carry within? How many lives could I add to the tally?

When I open my eyes I know at once that I'm no longer alone. Something is out there, beyond the firelight.

It's *them*.

I can't see them, but I sense them, clearer than ever before. The hairs bristle on my arms. They've surrounded me.

'What do you want?' I whisper.

The wind howls; whips out a tongue to lick the moisture from my eyeballs, cat-slinks around me. But that's just the wind. *They* haven't moved.

'What do you want?' I ask it again.

Useless to talk. They would not listen to anything I have to say. I'm not even sure they speak. Words are a skin to keep fear within the body, and they have no bodies, have no fear.

Whether they understand me or not, there is a shift, a change in the air as if they are pressing closer, and my heart starts to beat madly. They seize my attention, stretch it far beyond my normal capacity, stretch it out to the east where something waits, hot and sharp and urgent.

My mind rebels, catapulting me back into myself, into a confusion of images: cold metal piercing skin, pain on the wings of black birds, a figure gloved in blood...

I open my eyes. I'm lying in the dirt, the hat fallen from my head. Beyond the fire there's nothing, just the night. Have *they* gone? Impossible to tell. They're never truly gone, just as they are never truly here.

But they have left a feeling behind them: the conviction that past the plateau to the east, something waits.

I look up to see the ship fall flaming to the earth.

•

It takes me the rest of the night to reach the crash site. The glow lights the horizon pink as raw flesh. I travel as fast as I can, but the mule is sluggish, jostled by the wind, sand-scoured and grit-loaded. By the time I smell the smoke, night is losing its fullness and the wind is weakening, dragged to another hemisphere by the darkness.

I've seen wrecks in my time, in their many stages of tragedy, but never one like this. The destruction is total, every inch of metal a flame, every flame so hot it has scorched the sand to glass. There's no telling what the ship once was, no telling how many souls it carried to this bright and violent end. I scrape at the dirt with my boot. Can't linger here. A wreck like this will attract scavengers like the Seekers within hours.

What's a ship doing out here, in any case? There are no ports, only the scattered townships of the Barrens. A navigational error? I squint up into the lightening sky. From how far has the ship fallen?

The impact crater is still hot enough to sear my face, and as I peer down I see that it's useless. There's nothing left, only blackened streaks and shards.

I start to walk away when my gut lurches, as if it's trying to drag itself east. The images come on fast again: a bird with black wings, cold metal, bloodied hands… Spitting, I straighten up. *They* are obviously not finished with me.

I get back on the mule and drive away from the wreckage, towards the rising sun.

Morning in the Barrens is beautiful, but it comes with an asking price of hunger and cold, loneliness and near-insanity. A price that almost no one is willing to pay.

I have paid, many times over, but I don't spare a glance at that hard-won beauty. Instead, I stare at the track that has carved its way through the dirt. At the end of it, beside the twisted remains of a lifecraft, two figures lie motionless on the sand.

In the few seconds before I reach them, I think about turning the mule aside, leaving the bodies and continuing on, into another future.

But I won't, and *they* know that. *They* know my choice was made long ago.

Twenty paces away I stop, reaching for the knife at my belt. Gangs like the Seekers or the Rooks sometimes use bodies as bait. I edge closer.

The downed lifecraft is dull silver, new-looking, with no markings or badges to suggest what kind of ship it might have come from. That isn't unusual. Ever since the war it has been standard practice to strip all lifecraft bare, in case of a landing in enemy territory. Not that Factus took a side; no one wanted it anyhow. Even the Free Limits had little use for a waterless wasteland where the enemy was everything and nothing.

Wisps of smoke coil from the ruined craft, and the whole thing stinks of hot metal and melting plastic. Gripping the knife, I lean over the figures. They lie huddled, so close together it's difficult to tell them apart, covered in sand as they are. The larger one is a man, I think, cradling a smaller one. I nudge the man with my boot. When he doesn't move, I pull off my ragged gloves to reach in through the smashed helmet of the flight suit.

His face is cold but there's a pulse, faint and faltering. The helmet of the smaller figure is raised, a little. I worm my fingers through the gap and feel that the flesh there is warmer, the pulse stronger. The man's arms did their job.

I brush the sand away from the suits, searching for identification. But they too are plain: no labels even. The man is solid and muscular and at least seven feet tall. It takes all my strength to roll him away. As soon as I do, a weak groan emerges from the shattered helmet. I ignore it, and ease the smaller of the two into a position better suited to breathing.

As soon as I touch the body, I feel slackness within the sleeves. Whoever is wearing the suit is small and slight. The man is undoubtedly an adult – could this be a child?

Swearing, I unclip the helmet from the suit. A child: what might that do for my tally? I don't dare think about it as I wrench the helmet free.

Black hair tangles around a small face grey with blood loss, the features lost beneath a cake of dried gore and sand. Desperately, I check the skull, searching for wounds. When I find the contusion on the scalp, three inches long and bleeding sluggishly, I let out a breath. If that is the only damage – and if the child regains consciousness – they should live.

Just as I bend to pick the child up, something strikes me hard in the side, sending me sprawling. Choking on dust, I scramble for my knife, cursing myself to falling into an ambush…

But no. There are no other blows, no figures emerging from

foxholes dug into the sand, no swooping crafts. Reddened eyes stare back at me. The man is awake.

He croaks a word, blood staining his teeth, and his eyes go to the knife, then to the child. He tries to rise, only to fall again with a gurgle of pain.

'No harm,' I tell him, holding up my hands. 'No harm. Medic.'

'You... touch her,' he says, in an accent I can't place. 'You die.'

He is not in a position to be making any kind of threats, but I nod. 'I need to fetch my kit. I have supplies. I can treat you both.'

'Where?' He half lifts his head to stare around, ropes of strain in his neck. 'Where is here?'

'The Barrens. North of Redcrop.'

He raises his eyes to the sky, losing its beauty now, turning flat white. 'Where?' he insists.

I follow his gaze up towards Brovos, pinkish-red and just visible in the sky. The last planet in the system, and beyond its orbit, nothing but the Void. Has he fallen from so far he doesn't even know which moon he is on?

Above, invisible in the air, *they* sway and shift the lights of other worlds.

'Factus,' I tell him, turning away. 'We're on Factus.'

•

The man's eyes follow my movements as I haul the tarp from the back of the mule. He's more alert now, but that does not mean he will live. Folk often have a wave of consciousness before the end. I once read about forest trees on Earth, and how they did much the same: used the last of their strength to send their life force through the roots and into the soil, giving it to others. That was what this stranger had done, in all likelihood, for this child. So be it. One life is better than none at all.

I set up a shelter from the rising sun, stretching the tarp from the post anchored on the mule across to the wreckage. I try to work fast, my eyes on the child, not yet conscious.

'You,' the man croaks. 'Woman. Your name.'

'Hafsa Gellam,' I lie, as I tie off the tarp.

I feel his eyes travelling across my sunburned face, half-hidden by the scarf that wraps my neck from collarbone to chin, across my shorn head, my old jacket, my hands, roughened by the winds.

'Which side?' he asks.

I open the medkit to check its contents which, in truth, are pitiful. I haven't been able to bring myself to stop at a trade post for some time and here is the evidence: two rolls of squashed bandage, a bottle of cleaning fluid, a few ampules of analgesics and tranqs and boosters, needles, thread.

'What does it matter?' I say, searching for my cleanest rag. 'War's over.'

'Which side?'

'I didn't fight.'

'Everyone fought.'

'Not here.'

He grunts, as if to say *that's something I can well believe*, but when I take out a roll of bandage, his eyes narrow. The bandages are black market, lifted long ago from a consignment headed for the First Accord. At the sight of the double yellow triangles stamped upon the wrappings, he seems to relax.

Whoever he is, he's given himself away. One way to find out for sure. Kneeling, I unclip the shattered helmet from his flight suit and work it free. As the man gasps in relief, I see the tattoo on his temple, half-hidden by tangled copper hair. The same double triangles that mark the bandages. Beneath them is a thick line. A lieutenant, then. I glance at the ruined craft – a defector? I start to unclip the rest of the suit.

'No.' He knocks my hands away. 'Her.'

'Your injuries are worse.'

His face is a bad grey colour but he lifts an arm to hold me off. 'Her first.'

I shrug. Whoever he is, whatever trouble he's in, it's likely I won't be able to do much more than make him comfortable. Either way, I have to be fast. Desolate as this place is, Seekers have sentries, and even the heat won't keep them at bay.

When I release the child's flight suit, I see that I was right; she is a lot smaller than the garment implied. I would guess at around twelve or thirteen years old. She wears a beige thermal shirt and trousers, like pyjamas. The collar is soaked with blood, and a tear at the elbow and smears of oil speak of a hasty escape. Had she been sleeping when the ship's distress call went out, whisked from her bed into an escape craft by this man?

Perhaps. Though something tells me he is not her father. A bodyguard, then? A kidnapper? Whoever they are, they aren't new settlers, or farmers from Brovos. They look too healthy for that and rich folk don't venture out this far if they can help it. The modern lifecraft and brand-new flight suits could have come from Prosper, or Jericho, or some inner-system enclave.

I test the child's limbs. They are all mobile, no sign of trauma. The blood pasting her face seems to come only from the scalp wound, which is ragged, though shallow. But when I wipe the mess away, I see something that stops my hand.

Beneath the blood, a tattoo stands out dark on her temple. The same double triangle.

I draw back. 'Who is she?'

'She needs help.' The man looks at me, half-desperate, half-hostile. 'You said you'd help her.'

He's right. I grit my teeth. No matter what tattoo she has, she is a child, she is hurt and I am the one with the medical kit. I clean her head with some of the bandage and stitch the wound as best I can through her hair, hoping for her sake that she doesn't wake before I am finished. When I pull the last stitch tight, she stirs and bares her teeth, but her eyes remain closed.

The man doesn't make a sound while I work, only keeps his eyes fixed on the child's face. Too late, I see what the effort has cost him. The redness has vanished from his skin, leaving it blue-white, drained. He is dying.

His white military-issue vest is sodden with blood. A dark,

shining snake pulses from the wound between his ribs. A piece of shrapnel from the crash is embedded there, dug deep. He must have turned on his side at the moment of impact, and taken the brunt, sparing the child.

'Leave it,' he gasps, when I touch the piece of metal. His voice is full of liquid. 'I know it's bad.'

I nod. Little use in lying to him.

His eyes find mine. 'She will live?'

'If she regains consciousness, and if there's no damage to her brain, and if the wound does not fester—'

A bloodied hand grasps my sleeve. 'She can't die.' He hauls himself towards me, using the last of his strength. 'If you hurt her, you'll pay with your life.'

'I will not hurt her. I told you, I'm a medic. You have my word.' I stare down at him. 'Are you going to tell me what's going on?'

For a moment he can only heave breaths. The stink of gore and sundered flesh fills my nose.

'What's the nearest town...?'

'Redcrop. A day's ride. Mining township.'

'The Accord – have authority there?'

I laugh, humourlessly. 'They like to think so.'

He sags back. 'Take her there. Find a wire. She will know— what to do. She must...'

A noise catches my ears and I stop him with a gesture. In the distance, but coming closer, something is droning: the distinctive, double-cough of an overhauled engine. I swear and spring up.

'What?' the man asks, as I rip the tarp free and bundle it onto the mule.

'Seekers, most likely,' I say, piling everything into the medkit, 'coming to scavenge the site.'

'Seekers? Bandits?'

'More like a cult.'

I see a light in his eyes, and know what he's thinking; even a cult can be bribed, can be traded with.

'Forget it,' I say, 'the Seekers are crazy. If they see you are hurt, they will kill you both and take your organs before they listen to a word you say.'

I bend to retrieve the unused bandage. For the space between breaths we are eye to eye. I see myself reflected there, and it's a face I hardly know, the eyes shadowed and squinted tight, the skin wind-whipped and scar-peppered. The engines grow louder. A dust cloud appears in the distance.

'Go then,' he chokes, 'take her, and remember your oath.'

I don't argue. The options are two living and one dead, or three corpses, plundered by the Seekers. I know which one I prefer, and anyway, no matter who the child is, the tally doesn't lie. I lift her awkwardly and wedge her among the bundles on the back of the mule. Then I'm in the driver's seat, pulling the scarf over my mouth.

'Tell her I died for her,' the man's cry comes over the noise of the dirt mule's engine. 'Tell her I didn't know their plans. Tell her she must fight.'

I don't answer, just take off towards the horizon.

•

I ride for Redcrop. There's nowhere else. Much as I dislike being in a settlement, it is as safe as anywhere and at least I have a few contacts. As for the girl… I glance back to where she lies, slumped upon the mule.

Tell her I didn't know their plans.

A shiver ripples across my skin, despite the heat. No child should have military tattoos, no matter how patriotic her family. They couldn't be real.

Perspiration collects beneath my hat, dripping from my scalp into my eyes, so I stop the mule in a strip of shade cast by a boulder. The child mumbles as I lift her down, her eyeballs swivelling back and forth beneath the lids, as if reading from some giant book. Her skin is hot and dry, her breathing shallow. With a sigh, I feel for my pouch of beads. Don't want to waste one, but it might be enough to wake her, and I need answers.

The instant it shatters between her teeth, her eyes fly open.

They are bright hazel-brown, the whites bloodshot. For a second they roam the sky, contracting in pain at the brightness, before settling on me. Something like fear crosses her face, still a mess of dried blood, and she opens her mouth to cry out, but chokes.

I grab the flask of water from my belt and hold it to her lips. She swallows greedily, stale as it is, until I take it away.

She gasps for a few breaths. 'LaSalle?'

'The large man with the red hair? He is gone.'

'Gone?'

'Dead. He was badly injured in the crash. You remember the crash?'

The child winces, raising a hand to her head.

'You were hurt,' I tell her warily. 'But I have stitched the wound. I believe you'll live.'

The child blinks hard, her lips trembling – on the verge of tears. I sigh, relief surging through me. So she is just a girl, hurt and afraid, no matter what the tattoos imply. A military ward, perhaps?

'There's a cut on your head,' I say, trying for simpler words. Alone for so long, I've forgotten how to speak to anyone, let alone a child. 'And I think the crash may have bruised your brain. You will probably feel sick, for a while. Do you understand?'

She seems to see me for the first time, taking in my face, my clothes, the dirt mule behind us.

'You won't hurt me?' Her voice is high and frightened. 'Or sell me in a market?'

'No.' I sit back. 'I'm just a medic.'

She sniffs and nods. 'Help me stand up?'

'Be careful.' I lean down to take her arm. 'If you do have a concussion—'

In a flash, my arm is twisted and I'm flung off balance, landing face down into the dirt. I roll onto my back, snatching out my knife by reflex, but a small fist knocks it from my grasp. I try to cry out when something slams down on my throat.

It's the girl's boot. She stares down at me, her lips curled into a snarl.

'You won't kill two of us, carrion.'

As blue and yellow stars start to fill my vision, the wind blows, brushing sand across my face and for a second, less than a second, I feel *them*.

They are like a creature with a thousand eyes, hungrily tracing every outcome, showing me innumerable realities, too many for my mind to bear.

I am dead in the desert, the child driving the mule away. I throw her off with such force that her head strikes a boulder. I am dead, the wind drying my corpse to leather. I drag her across the sand, me, her, each of us the victor, the victim…

I shoot out an arm and I see every conceivable movement gather around it, a blur of limbs and chaos, impossible to track, until – like a clear signal from static – I see my own hand grab a fistful of dust and fling it into the girl's face.

She falls back. Before I can get to my feet she lunges again, this time with the knife in her hand. I scramble away, body a mess of adrenalin and not enough air as she attacks in frenzy, aiming to kill.

But *they* have shown me this path, and as I crash into the dirt mule, I know what to do. I reach behind me, groping for the medkit. Metal meets my fingers and the moment the girl leaps, I strike.

The knife falters two inches from my heart. The girl's lips twitch in a snarl, before a convulsion shakes her body and she glances down at the syringe protruding from her neck.

23

'Y—' she begins before the knife falls from her grip and she crumples, lifeless, to the ground.

•

I don't allow myself to sit and breathe until the child is restrained and tied as securely as I can manage, even though she won't wake for hours. In my panic I gave her enough tranquilliser to suppress a grown adult, and there's a chance that it could kill her.

Her small face twitches as the drug makes its way through her system. Cursing myself, I fetch the canteen of wastewater from the mule. My brain thuds with questions, with the thin air and the ebbing adrenalin and the lingering horror of *their* presence. Wetting a rag, I begin to wipe the dried blood from her face.

At first, her features appear unremarkable: skin sallow with blood loss, round cheeks, pointed chin. But as I clean the mess away, I see the undeniable evidence of what she is. Although she's young, thirteen at most, her face is deeply lined. Between the heavy brows and around her mouth are creases usually seen on someone who has lived through years of hardship. Her physique too, is unnatural. She's lean, but not through malnutrition and labour and ill health, like most on Factus, but sinewy, with hard muscles beneath the skin of her arms and legs.

Some part of me still hopes that I am wrong, that she's just a poor sick child after all. But when I clean the last of the blood away from her temple, there's no denying it. There's the tattoo – the double triangle and three thick lines – proclaiming what she is.

I shove myself away. My own temple throbs, as if the skin there – a faded pink scar now – is reverting to newly seared flesh; as if my hand has only just dropped the hot iron. Covering my face, I try to find some control, try to wrest myself back from the woman I once was, the woman who only a few years ago might have taken up the knife and used it without question.

I close my eyes. The Free Limits are finished. The woman who fought and killed for them is gone. Now, the tally is all that matters and it demands that the child, whoever she is, *whatever* she is, must live.

Besides, I have a promise to keep.

•

I make sure to arrive at the trade post in the twilight, when the winds are picking up and no one cares to look too closely at the shape on the rear of my mule, covered with the tarp. It's reckless, but there's no way I'm going to take the child into the settlement until I have some answers. Too much attention. Some bad part of my brain whispers that she might wake and escape on her own and so spare me a decision I don't know how to make.

The trade post is outside of Redcrop proper, separated from the settlement by fields of sickly-looking century trees and ghostly agave. Townsfolk prefer it this way. It keeps uncertainty out of their lives, along with scratchtooth drifters and wreckers, bandits and scavengers, the desperate and the damned who come trailing suspicion and violence from the Unincorporated Zone.

Redcrop is a faithful, fearful town: they take no risks and brook no questions. Questions lead to uncertainty, uncertainty opens the door to doubt and so, to *them*.

Different in the cities; there, hundreds of people make thousands of choices, every day. It's enough to keep *them* at bay, people reckon, gives them enough to feed on. But out here in the wastes people are few and choices are scarce, and if you let yourself doubt – if you let chance into your life – you'll shine out like a beacon through time and space and *they* will come to feed.

Or so it goes. All folk ever have are stories. Farms too near the Edge destroyed utterly by one bit of bad luck after another, brawls that somehow turned into massacres, folk who ran, maddened, into the desert and were never seen again. No proof. Just thin-air superstition – the Accord said – stoked by mercenary peacekeepers and vice wardens for the purpose of extracting money from the fearful.

Only people with choice but to ride the wastes alone told stories of meeting *them* and surviving. People like me.

With a sigh, I climb off the mule. I have no intention of lingering, not with an unconscious and murderous child bound and hidden on my vehicle. Another dose of the sedative sent her under when she began to kick and twitch at dusk. I didn't like it, but neither did I want my throat cut.

The post is already ringed with vehicles; dirt mules in far better condition than my own, old delivery quads and charabancs, even a battered ex-army transport painted silver and black, the words

VALDOSTA'S VIPERS emblazoned on the side. A travelling sideshow, no doubt. At least people will be distracted.

I whistle. The shadows move and a shape comes forwards: a teenager with a bald, patchy head, wearing huge, tattered gauntlets.

'I will be an hour,' I say, digging beneath my clothes for a bead. 'I want the mule guarded well.'

The boy nods and drags a piece of gristle from a pouch to hold up in the air. A skeletal vulture sails down from the veiled sky to land on the front of the mule. I leave the boy securing the bird to the handlebars, while it stabs, oblivious, at its payment. Shouldering my pack, I hope that – for the sake of her eyes – the girl-child doesn't wake.

Hat down, I duck between the sheet metal gates and into the trade post compound. It's the dinner hour, and pungent century smoke mingles with the hot smack of planchas, and the odour of boiled onion powder and protein cooked in whatever sort of fat can be spared.

Folk sit in tight groups around the food station, smoking or chewing, picking crickets' legs out of their teeth and gawking at each other's plates to check they haven't been cheated on their meal. The sight of the food, basic as it is, is enough to make my stomach yawn with hunger, after weeks of old field rations.

But business first. Glancing over my shoulder, I approach the door of Sorry Damovitch's place.

Inside, it's quiet, just those who can't afford to eat and instead pummel their guts with mezcal. Sorry himself is at the edge of the room, shoving leaf fibres about the floor with his foot in an attempt to clean up some spill.

As I walk to the bar, one of the drinkers looks up: a large individual with a mottled pink face that speaks of hard drinking. Their straw-coloured hair is dark with grease, in a military cut short enough to show the three-dotted tattoo of a private of the Accord. As I pass, they push their stool back to stop me. Their expression turns sour as they take in my hat and the scarves that wrap the length of my throat.

'Wasss your business?' comes the slurred challenge. Before I can answer, Sorry himself shuffles forwards, his hangdog face drooping further at the prospect of violence.

'Please,' he implores, holding out a hand towards me, 'for your own safety, go outside. I will serve you from the back door. What do you want?'

'Just the usual,' I say.

He lets out a breath.

'Doc. You look—' He shakes his head. 'Next time, take the hat off, yes?'

I nod, though I'd do no such thing. A shorn head like mine gave nothing away, but the scars on my temples certainly did. People don't like not knowing which side you were on. I follow him towards the bar, the drunk continuing to protest my presence with not-so-muttered threats.

'It would be best to avoid Loto,' Sorry murmurs. 'The Accord revoked her pension. She's been drinking snake wine since noon and is not to be reasoned with.'

'How have you escaped her wrath?' I ask, nodding at his neck, where two neat scars from a prison collar were all that remain of his former internment.

His thin lips lift in a smile. 'Such is the luck of the landlord.' He places a tumbler before me. 'Friend to all, while there is a cup to be filled.'

I watch as he takes a bottle from beneath the bar and pours a few fingers of mezcal into the glass. Ordinarily, it's a stupid idea to drink the stuff – who knows what bacterial horrors have been stuffed into bags and thrown into the vats to hurry fermentation – but I know Damovitch keeps a good batch for those who would not forgive being poisoned.

'It is on me,' he says softly. 'For the last time.'

I drink. It's appalling and makes my eyes sting, but it's better than the jars of snake wine that line the bar; coiled creatures barely visible through the murky liquid.

As I peer at the drowned snakes, Damovitch places a little dish of worm salt and a lump of tinned orange in front of me, giving me time to find my tongue. For a while I just listen to the clang and hiss of the food station outside, to the roar of engines from the stable, the crying of the vultures and the distant desert wind rattling the sheet metal of the fence. I suck the smoky, biting salt from the orange, the combination making my mouth sing, and as always, wonder how much I can say.

He isn't trustworthy, Sorry, but he is at least predictable in his cowardice. He was a Limiter too and in prison had been a

Five, so the story went. He contrived to have his sentence cut by apologising so profusely for his actions during the war, that even the prison chaplain had become irritated and petitioned the governor for his early release just to be rid of him. The governor agreed, on the condition that Damovitch shed his sentence name of "Five", along with the prison collar, and be forever known as "Sorry".

A fair deal, I think, watching him sprinkle more worm salt into the dish. It suits him, and besides, prison governors have handed out far worse names to convicts on release. Better to keep the number. Better to bear the shame and the sneers than allow them to give you a name.

I drain the glass. The girl has a name, one that I'm afraid to discover.

Just dump her here, the woman from the past whispers. *Leave her like the man said. She does not deserve your help.*

'Sorry,' I call. 'How much do you remember about the Accorded Companies?'

Damovitch's face takes on the squeezed, fawning look it does when he's trying to think of an answer that will not get him into trouble.

'Ahh,' he says, grabbing the bottle. 'War's in the past. We're all just citizens, now.'

He tries to pour another slug of mezcal, but I put my hand over the glass.

'Where were you stationed?'

'Nowhere special,' he mutters, 'on Jericho first, Felicitatum, that is.'

'Which faction?'

'The Nightwatchmen.' Glancing at Loto, he raises his voice. 'I didn't fight, not really. I was in logistics, but even for that I am sorry. The Free Limits tricked me into joining, with their promises of open trade and their fancy words. They took the best years of my life.'

I look him dead in the eyes. He shuts up.

'What do you remember about the Minority Force?'

'The war kids?'

I nod. 'The ones the Accord brought up through training camps.'

'I—' He swallows. 'I don't know. FL always said they were monsters, tortured and augmented 'til they weren't even kids no more.'

'The Minority Force were our greatest asset!' The chair falls to the ground as Loto stands, her eyes blazing. 'They were our greatest achievement. And you call them monsters?' A glob of spittle hits the bar, several feet to Sorry's left. Loto's eyes fill with tears. 'Those kids were the bravest of us all.'

'So what happened to them?' I ask, hoping Loto will take the bait.

'War heroes.' She sniffs. 'They're the lucky ones. Set for life, on their pensions. Cushy jobs, easy living on the home planets. Not like the rest of us left behind on these godforsaken rocks among convict scum.'

She takes a step towards me, but Sorry is ready, thrusting a bottle of snake wine into her hand.

'Here now, Loto, have a drink. I know how hard it's been for you.'

'You've no idea,' Loto slurs, grabbing the bottle with its coiled inhabitant, allowing herself to be steered back to her table. 'I *loved* them and they kick me out, treat me no better than one of you damn cons.'

'Listen, Doc, you better leave,' Sorry whispers when he comes back to the bar. 'She is in her cups, and she won't be the only one. Dinner hour is almost over.'

I don't bother nodding. 'Here,' I murmur, digging through my pack. 'Take these for Rowley.'

It isn't much, a couple of tabs of muscle relaxant, but Sorry's face drops into gratitude; the most honest expression I've seen that evening. He might be a coward and a worm, but he loves Rowley – one of a multitude ruined by the munitions factories – and cares for him as best he can. For that, I give him credit.

'May your thoughts be clear, Doc,' he says.

'And mine?'

A figure leans in the doorway, better dressed than anyone I have seen for months in a voluminous grey coat, somehow unstained by road dust. Oiled black curls hang elegantly on broad shoulders. They are heavily made-up with swirls of silvery paint that shine against cool brown skin. Twisted metal rings circle every finger.

'Valdosta.' Sorry grabs at his apron. 'A moment, if you please.' Shoulders hunched, he runs towards the back room.

From the corner of my eye I see one of the drinkers shrink down in their chair as Valdosta walks towards the bar. Even Loto is silent, staring hard at the tabletop. Something prickles at the back of my mind; the reeling sensation that usually signals *their* appearance.

'Care to play?'

Valdosta's open hand rests on the bar. In the centre of their palm is a pair of worn bone dice.

'No.' I look away. 'Those things are dangerous.'

'Only if you fear the outcome.'

When I don't reply, Valdosta breathes a laugh and flicks their hand, sending the dice clattering. My muscles tense. Somewhere behind me a chair squeaks, most likely a drinker wondering whether to run.

I stare hard at my empty glass, willing myself not to see.

'Five and five is ten,' Valdosta says.

Cold sweeps me, scalp to heel.

'Sorry,' Sorry bursts, hurrying from the back room with a paper-wrapped package in his hands. 'Here it is, my apologies, I'll have it ready next time.'

When he sees the dice on the bar his face goes pale beneath the sunburn.

'Thank you, Damovitch.' Valdosta sweeps the dice away, dropping them into one cavernous pocket, the package into

33

another. 'I'd stay, but I have a show to prepare for.' I can feel their eyes, studying the side of my face. 'Perhaps next time, Ten.'

I don't let go of the bar until the door creaks closed, until the ringing of jewellery fades into the sounds of the trade post. Even then, my nerves sing like wire in the wind.

'Who was that?'

Sorry's mouth is a hard line as he scrubs at the bar with a rag, as if the dice have left a stain. 'Valdosta,' he mutters. 'Runs entertainment. And security. Protection from the Seekers, and from...' He stops, staring at the spot where the dice fell, then back at me. 'You should get out of here,' he says.

•

I take Sorry's advice. When I emerge from the bar people are milling about the trade post's square in anticipation of the evening's entertainment. Anything will do: an insect fight, a brawl, a shanking, a drunk falling over their own boots.

Luckily for them, or not, depending on how much protection money they stand to lose, *Valdosta's Vipers* are in camp. I pause in the shadows near the bar, curious despite myself. The sideshows are usually miserable things, cheap tricks or illusions, bits of tech from off-world – common on the home planets but still exciting out here – even re-enactments of famous battles glossed up with fine words that had never been said. There are beetle fights, bird fights, prize bouts between bruisers and strung-out veterans who want to taste blood on their teeth again.

Who knows what these Vipers are. Two performers emerge to set up the stage, wearing tight costumes of silver, their faces smeared with shining paint, like Valdosta's. Catcalls and hollers follow their movements. Not fighters, then. If Valdosta tries to play the dice on a crowd like this, things might turn bad quickly.

I step away when a noise splits the air, high-pitched and wheeling, followed by thunder. Music. I turn back, stunned, as a figure walks out with a drum, and another with a pipe. It's been so long since I'd heard real instruments. A memory returns of sitting in a concert hall on Prosper, surrounded by clean, wealthy people, all of us captivated by the symphony orchestra. I had never heard anything like it but even then, as the beauty of the music moved me to tears, I felt a stab of pain, knowing I was only there to experience it through a lie. I remember holding on to the plush seat, wondering if I could have had a life like that – for real – if I had made a different choice.

But I hadn't. And now, here I am, transfixed by two pedlars with makeshift instruments. All around palms slap in time, voices fill the air, people jostle to see. And I crane alongside them, my eyes hungry, my brain ravenous for a new sight after months of the Barrens.

Valdosta steps out from behind a curtain and raises their arms, commanding quiet. They've shed the voluminous coat for a costume covered with long translucent ribbons that flutter from their elbows, wrists and hair.

'Is this a place of clear thoughts and constant spirits?' they cry.

'Yes!' someone hollers, and the crowd join in.

'Is this a place of the steadfast? The staunch and the unswerving?'

The agreement grows louder. Part of me wants to raise my voice and slap my neighbour and grin. But I can't. If they knew what I was they would cringe from me.

'Then I ask,' Valdosta calls, 'for a volunteer! One brave person to prove that there is no doubt in any soul!'

They clap their hands, and immediately two assistants appear, each holding a battered cage containing a live snake. The noise of the crowd intensifies. They are happy, relieved now that they know what the show will be. An animal show, where someone faces down a dangerous beast to win a prize. It's a favourite in the townships, because everyone knows that the beasts are tame and won't attack; there can be no doubt in the outcome, no danger, though people like to pretend there is. Make something prohibited and it becomes what folk crave, even if that thing is doubt itself.

Shaking my head, I turn away. Valdosta is an ordinary charlatan and racketeer, then, if a glamorous one. I have almost reached the gates when a booming voice stops me in my tracks. The volunteer has been chosen, and it's Loto.

She stands, her arms tucked like a wrestler, her tattooed face flushed with drink. She crouches and – to the approval of the crowd – spits in readiness to face her foes.

Valdosta signals the assistants to open the doors of the cages. I crane to see the snakes uncoil into the night, their tongues flickering. They look the part: pit vipers, heavily scarred and muscular, patterned white and grey like Valdosta's coat. I watch as Loto feints towards them, staggering clumsily.

'Carrion worms!' she slurs. 'Piece of shit Limiter traitors, think we'll just forget?' The crowd roars her on as the snakes jerk and raise their heads. 'I'll kill you both!' Loto screams, her face contorted. 'I'll drink your blood!'

Valdosta's arms shoot up, the snakes rear, and something crashes against my consciousness, too huge to fit inside my skull. *They* are here. *They* are here, and *they* are hungry. Reality stretches and squeezes as every possibility presents itself at once, tangled together. I see flames, I see blood flying, I see the crowd surging towards Valdosta, the decisions of two dozen people happening simultaneously.

Did they follow me here? Did I bring them down upon this place? For an instant something shines through the chaos: a snake's fang, bared and ready to strike. Valdosta's eyes meet mine.

A scream splits the air, and another. Loto staggers, one snake attached to her arm, the other to her ankle, their blunted fangs sunk deep into her flesh. Valdosta still stares at me even as one of the assistants pulls a knife from their belt. All around, people scream that it is *them*: the Ifs, the demons, come to feast.

I run for the gates with the rest of the crowd. The metal judders and shakes as people shove their way outside, stumbling for their vehicles, as if that will help, as if *they* aren't everywhere. Outside the gate I turn, half-desperate to call back to Valdosta. *Do you see what I see? Do they follow you too?*

Nausea churning the mezcal in my stomach, I flee towards the mule, towards the child and the decision that waits there, knowing *they* are watching me go.

•

Across the fire, the girl's face twitches. The fitful light makes her seem old one moment, young the next; now heavy with lines and woe, now untroubled, like any child at rest.

But she is not any child. A bit of scrub snaps and flares and the light catches on her tangled, curling black hair cut into the style favoured by the Accord: longer on one side, short on the other, to display the tattoo of rank to full effect.

I've never seen a child of the Minority Force before. People used to say that they weren't real, that they were just normal children play-acting at being strategists and soldiers, that the whole idea was a propaganda exercise cooked up by the Accord then twisted by the Free Limits to show what the true overreach of power looked like.

I study the girl's face, rolling a bead between my teeth, tasting its dull bitterness before biting down. Considering how she attacked before, I'll need every ounce of wit I have. As the faint buzz of the breath goes through me, I pick up a pebble, take aim and throw it gently. It takes another four before she wakes.

Her eyes are not even fully open before she lunges, only to crash back to the ground. She swears and struggles, but I have tied her well.

'We need to talk,' I say.

She twists, furious. 'I'll slice your belly open, carrion. I'll carve you up for the maggots.'

I sigh and take a syringe from the medkit. Her eyes narrow. Given the doses over the past day, it is remarkable she can even focus.

'Kill me then,' she spits. 'Do it with your little needle, coward.'

'I don't want to kill you. I told you, I am a medic.'

'A medic? You have poisoned me.'

'I have not. The effects will soon wear off. Anyway, I had no choice.'

'You killed LaSalle.'

'I tried to help him. He took the brunt of the crash to save you.' The girl-child only stares. 'He told me to say that he died for you,' I go on. 'He said he didn't know about their plans. That you should fight.'

She spits grit from her mouth. 'He's the one who should have fought. If he had been vigilant, I wouldn't be in this mess. He should have killed you when he had the chance.' After a moment she shifts, grimacing at the cable that binds her. 'Alright, *medic*. Name your terms.'

'Terms?'

'Your terms. What insurgent scum do you represent and how much do you want for my release?'

'You're no hostage. I work for no one.'

'Then release me.'

I shake my head slowly. 'You would kill me.'

She doesn't disagree. 'And so, what? You propose to keep me tied like a beast?' A vicious smile curves her mouth. 'Better to kill me. I'll get free eventually.'

'If I wanted you to die, I would have left you for the Seekers.' I take a steadying breath, pushing away the past self who itches to do what she says, exact my revenge. 'I do not care who you are, or what you've done. I want you to live, for reasons of my own. I don't expect you to understand.'

The child stares at me, her eyes flicking from my hat to my boots, to my swaddled neck. I resist the urge to pull the scarves higher.

'I will release you,' I force myself to say. 'I will escort you to safety and do you no harm. In exchange—'

'You want a pardon,' she sneers. 'I see those deserter scars of yours. You want a slate wiped clean of all your nasty deeds.'

I laugh, a bitter sound. 'You could not pardon me.'

How to explain to this child, who is no longer a child, that the tally is all? That it matters over compassion or fear, that it drives me more than the threat of arrest ever could?

'I want medical supplies,' I say. 'As much as I can carry on the mule. That is my price.'

She is silent, her brown eyes fixed. Above us, beyond us, the winds tear through the canyon: the voices of the dead howling betrayal.

'You will not make it to a base without me,' I finally say, 'if that's what's on your mind.'

She almost smiles, as if in her imagination she has already garrotted me and dumped my body among the rocks. 'Why not? I've survived in worse places than this.'

'Do you know anything about Factus?'

'What does it matter? These border rocks are all the same. And anyway, the Accord will have picked up the distress signal. They will be looking for me.'

'If you set off alone, you will be dead before they find you.' She turns her head away, defiant, unconvinced. 'Alright,' I say. 'Tell me then, which townships are in quarantine for yellowrot? Which mining camps have been taken over in revolts, and why would going to Malady Falco's on the wrong night mean your death? Tell me about the Unincorporated Zone. Tell me about the Edge. Tell me —'

Tell me about them.

I bite the inside of my mouth. *Don't call to them. Don't even think of them.*

'You know who has power here?' I ask instead.

'The authority of the Accorded Nations extends to all known territory.'

'Tell that to the Seekers. Tell that to Hel the Converter.'

The girl regards me with contempt. Finally, she draws herself up.

'Very well. You have your deal. I swear to it by the First and Last Accords. Now, untie me.'

Slowly, as if approaching one of Valdosta's pit vipers, I loosen the knots that hold her, ready for an attack, but she only winces and flexes her muscles.

'Stop cringing,' she says. 'I have sworn by the Accords. That means something to me, even if it doesn't to you.' Grunting in pain, she sits up. 'You have a name, traitor?'

'Ten Low.'

'In the hands of a damn Ten,' she mutters, before shaking back her hair and raising her chin. 'I am General Gabriella Ortiz, Implacabilis, Leader of the Third Minority Force, Hero of the Battle of Kin and Former Commander of the Western Air Fleet of the Accorded Nations.'

High above, beyond the sky, I think I hear *them* laughing.

•

'We were on our way to Landfall Nine, on Prodor. The mining enclaves are showing signs of insurrection, some lingering Limiter sympathies in the camps, and the battalion there is sloppy. I was sent in to burn off the corruption.'

I don't speak, only drive, the burning desert light in my eyes and dust hissing against my face. The General – as she insists I call her – doesn't seem to need the encouragement of a response. Perhaps it's the after-effect of the sedative combined with the analgesic I gave her, but she has turned rather loose-lipped.

'The crash was undoubtedly the work of sabotage,' she mutters. 'But I can't remember it, or leaving the ship. I suppose that's to be expected with a concussion?'

I give a brief nod and she sighs. 'When I return to base, you can be sure there will be a full investigation.' She pauses. 'There were no other survivors, apart from LaSalle?'

'Yours was the only lifecraft I saw.'

'And you're certain that LaSalle is dead?'

'Yes. He was taken by the Seekers.' Her silence is loaded. I sigh.

'They're a gang, or a cult, depending on who you ask. They plunder wrecks, raid townships, wagons. Some people say they are organ traders.'

'And the Accord allow this?'

I let out a snort. 'The Accord control their bases, the Air Line Road, and any bits of territory they consider of use. As for the rest…' I shrug. 'Besides, the Seekers are mad. They live in the Edge. No one's going to follow them in there, and anyone stupid enough to try has never been seen again.'

'The Edge?'

'An area of disturbance. No one knows how big it is exactly. It's…' I shake my head. 'People don't go there.'

She does not question me further, for which I'm grateful. For hours now, my brain has been caught in a spiral, trying to reconcile what I'm doing with what I did in the past. Not so many years ago, I would have driven the mule into a canyon and killed the pair of us and called it victory, rather than let her live.

But that was before. I glance in the mirror at her huddled figure, head bowed against the dust. For all her crimes, she is a child; the

Accord made her what she is, never asking for her consent until the part of her that might have refused was long gone.

And what about you? You were not a child. You followed orders without question. What does that make you?

'What did you get ten years for?'

I blink. 'What?'

'I said, what did you get ten years for? It must have been bad. Desertion?'

'Theft.'

'No one gets ten years for theft. You may as well tell the truth. It's impossible for me to think less of you than I already do.'

My hands tighten on the mule's handlebars.

'For ten years, it must have been *armed* robbery at least,' she continues. 'What did you do to warrant early release? That is why you're here, isn't it? Kicked off the prison hulks with the rest of the petty convicts to make room for real war criminals?'

How many civilians have you slaughtered, how many cities have you burned? I pull the scarf over my mouth and do not speak again.

When the sky bruises with darkness, and the night wind utters its first cries, I slow the mule. The General sways behind me. From the drained look on her face I can tell that she's suffering from Factus's thin air, as all newcomers do before their bodies adjust.

'We will not make Landfall Five without supplies,' I tell her, squinting ahead. 'Over that ridge is a ranch. Word is they aren't hostile to travellers, but that doesn't mean it's safe, especially if they discover what you are. People are not over-fond of the Accord, out here.'

'Do I look like an idiot?'

'Have you ever travelled anywhere without a full military escort?' When she is silent, I shake my head. 'I thought not.'

'I travel as befits my rank,' the child snaps. 'I have been trained to survive in any terrain and environment, to command—'

'Reading about Factus in some Accord propaganda and living on it are two very different things, *ma'am*. And you have to understand, there are certain ways here, beliefs that your spin-doctors will never have reported.'

'Like what?'

Like them. 'Just keep your mouth shut.'

After a mile or so, lights appear in the gloom, faint, pushed at by the wind. On either side of the track, metal fencing stretches across the ground, a huge cage, hammered into the earth.

'What the hell kind of ranch is this?' the General calls over the engine.

'Snake ranch.'

'*Snake?* What lunatic would farm snakes?'

'The kind of lunatic who trusted the Accorded Bureau of Land Development to keep their word,' I say, slowing the mule. 'Steer can't live here for more than a month. Neither can sheep, or goats. Folk learn that the hard way. Snakes are a wise choice. They feed on rats, the meat is substantial, the skins are of good use, and the runts can be sold for wine. As for the venom...'

'Alright,' she grunts.

The ranch house is half-dug into the ground as protection against the wind, its pre-fab metal walls patched with whatever can be found out here. The windows are grit-blasted plastic, impossible to see through, but from within, light shines.

I stop the mule alongside a couple of plough vehicles.

'Here.' I pull off one of my scarves and shove it at the General. 'Wrap your head in that. And for god's sake keep those tattoos hidden.'

'I do not take orders from convicts,' she mutters, but does as I ask, and by the time she climbs down from the mule she looks like any sick, weary child, woken from sleep after a long journey.

The door clatters and a mechanical dog runs jerkily out, uttering its one-note barks. It looks homemade, cobbled together from old craft parts in the vaguest form of a creature. Still, no telling what it has been built to do. I raise my hands. Behind the dog is a figure, carrying a gun. The sight glows like a red eye in the night.

'We are hoping to buy supplies,' I call.

'How many are you?' comes the wary response.

'Just myself,' I hesitate, 'and the child.'

Immediately, the voice yells: 'Skink!' and the dog backs off, tottering towards the house.

A face looms into view. A man with dust-beaten pink skin and watering blue eyes above a wiry grey beard.

'My apologies,' he says, 'I did not know there was a child present.' His gaze goes to the General and he smiles. 'Good evening, little one.'

'Good evening, mister,' the General chirps. She grips the scarf over her face as if shy. 'I'm mighty hungry.'

'I bet you are.' The man laughs. 'I'm Del Kwalkavich, inside is my old ma and my brother's out somewhere in the fields.'

'Tennille Lowe,' I say, 'and this here is my niece.' *General Ortiz, Implacabilis, Leader of the Third Minority Force…*

'My name's Gabi,' the General says sweetly. 'Nice to meet you.'

'Likewise, little lady. Now, you folk said something about supplies?'

•

Inside, the ranch is warm and rank, smelling of cheap biofuel and old fried meat and curing skins. It's cluttered, dominated by a trestle table reinforced with bits of wire, with any conceivable thing that might be of use scattered across it. Snakeskins hang from the ceiling, dozens of them. They brush my hat as we follow the man inside, reminding me, in a horrid flash, of Valdosta's pit vipers.

'Ma, we got customers,' the man says to a huddled shape in a chair by the stove. 'This lady and her little girl.' The man looks at the General, his face bright and pained once more. 'Come say hello to my ma. Ain't often we get visitors nice as you.'

I watch, wary, as the General crosses the floor and stops before the old woman.

'Hello, missus,' she says.

The old woman has half of an ancient pair of headphones pressed to one ear, the wisps of a drama broadcast hissing around the edges. Cataracts cloud her blue eyes, but still they roam the General's face. 'Such a healthy child, so nice,' she murmurs, before looking into the gloom, searching for me.

'A pleasure to meet you, ma'am,' I say, stepping into the light and removing my hat. My scalp prickles; I always feel exposed without it.

The woman frowns. 'But where are the others?'

'It is just the two of us,' I assure her. 'My niece and I.'

'No.' The old woman stares at me. 'No, you are not alone. I heard others. Voices, many of them.' Her rough hands grip the chair. 'Are *they* here?'

My neck prickles. People in places like this never name the Ifs, not if they can help it. Is the old woman mad?

'Alright, Ma,' the man says nervously, glancing my way. 'Nothing's here. We would've felt it. You listen to your stories while I get these folk some food, eh?'

The woman continues to look my way, frowning, until eventually her eyelids droop and her chin begins to bob.

'Don't mind her,' the man murmurs, clearing a space for us to sit at the table. 'She ain't been the same, since my wife died. An accident, out on the trail. But ever since she sees things that ain't there, you know?' He bustles away, searching out plates.

'Mad old hag,' the General mutters. '"Such a healthy child, so nice."' As if she wanted to eat me.'

'Children are rare out here,' I say, still staring at the woman. 'Few live.'

The General grunts. 'I need to wash. I smell terrible. As do you.' She squints into the cabin. 'Will they provide a bath?'

I laugh. After more than a year on Factus, the thought of submerging my body in that much water seems absurd. 'No one takes baths here. Vapour showers, or oil scrapes. Perhaps a basin of wastewater, if you're lucky.'

The General makes a noise of disgust, only to melt into a smile when the man returns, carrying two dishes.

'Here y'are,' he says, clattering the plates down. 'Snake soup with landshrimp. Some of the best meat you'll taste, here to Otroville. Get the warmth back in your blood.'

The soup is thin, filled with long strings of snake meat, blobs of fat floating on top. Ancient peas, dried long ago on some other planet, and other pale shapes bob among it.

'Our thanks,' I tell the man, taking up my spoon.

The man beams, nodding for the General to do the same. I watch as she dips the spoon into the broth.

'Mmm,' she says, without opening her mouth.

'Get you some coffee?' the man asks. 'And for the child?' He hesitates.

'I'll take coffee too,' the General says, with an angelic smile, 'with a little sugar in it? And something to wash my hands?'

The man chuckles. 'Sure, we can spare a spoonful for someone sweet as you.'

'What do you think you're doing?' I hiss, when his back is turned. 'Sugar is worth its weight in gold, out here.'

49

'Didn't you hear? I'm rare.' Her smirk falls as she prods the strings of meat. 'Besides, I need something to get the taste of this muck out of my mouth. What the hell is a "landshrimp"?'

'Woodlouse. You had better get used to it. This is the best we'll get before Landfall.'

'Goddam backward moon.' She grimaces, forcing down another mouthful.

'So,' the man says, when our bowls and cups are empty. 'Y'all said something about supplies?'

I nod. In the corner, the General is carefully washing her face and hands in an inch of cloudy water. 'We're headed to Landfall Five. Need enough fuel to get us there, or at least to the nearest post. Water, too.'

The man rubs his beard. 'Ain't another trade post as far as I know. Though you might meet a vendor coming from the Air Line Road.' His mouth works. 'You can pay?'

'With breath.'

I reach into my clothes and pull out the pouch of beads. My stomach twists when I feel how empty it is. *Think of what you'll get at the end of this. Official army supplies. Not black-market goods, not cut or watered drugs. Good stuff. Stuff that can save lives.* I pick out two beads and set them down on the table. The man's eyes light up.

'Six breaths and I'll fill your mule to the brim,' he says.

'Three.'

'Four.' The man smiles a little. 'You ain't got much choice, Mistress Lowe.'

Clenching my teeth, I add another two beads to the pile. Just as the man sweeps them into a lined box, the front door bangs open. Another figure stands there, holding a flimsy-looking cage. Within it, snakes writhe in knots.

'Who the hell's here?' he snaps, eyes roaming the room. He is younger than the other man, leaner, more alert. My shoulders tense.

'Ralf,' the older man says hurriedly. 'We got guests. This here's Tennille and little Gabi. We just finished trading.'

The man looks me over, sneering at my shaved head, the scars on my temples. Though when he sees the General, his eyes flicker.

'You shouldn't be out here,' he tells me. 'They said on the wire there were a shipwreck, other side of Redcrop, something big. Seekers are out, I've seen their lights.' He stares at me, hard. 'You come from that way?'

I shake my head. 'From Gulch. But we're on our way to Landfall Five.'

'Landfall ain't no place for a child.'

'Nowhere is, on this rock.'

The man grunts, and reaches behind him to close the door. It's pitch dark outside, the desert wind in full voice, roaring over the ranch. And then, without warning, it happens.

Wind whips into the room, guttering the fire, sending the snakeskins writhing. The old woman staggers from her chair with a howl, staring about her.

'*They're* here!' she shrieks. 'They've come for us again!'

'Ma, don't,' Del steps towards her, 'it's just the wind.'

But his voice shakes, terror plain on his face. Because the woman is right. *They* are here. I feel it, the sick, spinning sensation as if the world is being wrung around me.

'Leave us be.' The old woman covers her head. 'We have no doubt. Our thoughts are clear!'

In panic, I turn towards the door only for a gust of wind to blast grit into my face. I stagger back and fight my eyes open to find myself face to face with the woman. Her clouded eyes are huge, seeing far more than what is before her.

'Not us,' she sobs. 'They want *you*. Deathbringer, Troublecrow. Rook, Longrider, Hel!'

Ralf drops the cage with a clatter and pulls out a gun, while the older brother makes a grab for the General.

'No!' I shout. Fear leads to panic, panic to violence, and to any of the thousand blood-soaked consequences that fill the air around us.

'Call them off,' Ralf shouts, even as I see another version of him club me over the head, as another runs for the door. 'Call them off, witch!'

I try to speak, but I can't. It is already too late. I see Ralf fire and hit me in the gut, see the pulse ricochet from the wall into the skull of his brother, into the neck of the General, into his mother's eye, the snakes loose from the crate, their fangs sinking into flesh, the wind fanning the flames in the open stove and the old woman screaming as the hem of her gown catches fire…

'Low!' the General's voice cuts through the chaos, and I see the way: my own hand seizing a metal pitcher and flinging it through the air towards her.

There's the sound of an impact, and a grunt. I turn in time to see Del slide to the floor. The General drops the pitcher, leaping over his body onto the table. Ralf gapes in confusion, swinging his gun around, but he is too slow: the General boots the weapon from his hand, before driving her elbow, hard and sharp, into his temple. He hits the floor like a lump of lead.

The moment he does, I feel a rushing sensation, like being caught in an updraught, and as quickly as *they* appeared, they are gone. Behind us, the old woman begins to wail.

•

The mule's headlamp is weak in the darkness, guttering and flickering at every bump in the ground. Travelling by night is suicide in the Barrens, an invitation to the Seekers, but we have no choice. We have to get away from the ranch, and the chaos we left behind.

I have no idea how long we've been riding when a burst of wind screams us off the trail. I keep control of the mule – barely – gripping the hat to my head with one hand, and steering with the other, into the lee of a huge slab of rock. The wind is so strong it almost pulls the vehicle over as I climb onto the back.

'Hold this!' I yell to the General, dragging out a piece of tarp. 'Get underneath.'

Within moments we're huddled together, the tarp pulled over both our heads – our only chance of weathering the dust storm with skin intact.

'How long will this go on?' the General shouts.

'No telling. But at least it will hide our tracks.'

'What the hell happened back there?'

In the rush of escape, in the frenzy of retrieving my beads and stealing what we needed from the ranch, I'd been able to avoid giving her an answer.

'Just superstition.'

'That was not superstition, that was fear.' The General's voice is hard. 'What did the old hag mean by "them"?'

I let the wind howl for a few breaths.

'People on Factus believe in beings,' I say. 'They call them "Ifs". But I have heard them called other names. Dybbuks, Zabaniyya—'

'*Ifs.*' The General is scathing. 'What are they supposed to be?'

I swallow, trying to unstick my dry throat. I feel as if the wind is listening, its hundred ears pressed up against the tarp.

'People say the Ifs are… invisible demons. Like spirits that make bad things happen.' I grip the tarpaulin tighter. 'People say they feed on possibilities, on doubt, on chance. They say the Ifs are attracted to chaos and influence the world to feed themselves. When they are present, reality changes course…' My voice dries up. 'I have heard it said they can haunt people, follow them, push them into danger at every turn, so they can feed.'

Through the wind, I hear the old woman's cries again, see her terrified face as she stares at me, seeing something I can't through the chaos of possibilities. *Deathbringer. Troublecrow.*

'Nonsense,' the General barks. 'Landgrubber, air-starved nonsense.' She shifts, making herself comfortable. 'Wake me when the storm is over.'

I let her sleep, fearing in my bones that the storm is only the beginning.

•

The General is ill. Almost as soon as she wakes, she spews her guts.

'It's that damn snake stew.' She spits, wiping her mouth.

'I ate it.'

'You're used to muck.'

I check the scalp wound. It doesn't look infected.

'How do you feel?'

'Head pain. Double vision.'

'Some of it will be the air. Your haemoglobin levels will adjust, with time.' I try to feel her pulse, but she snatches her wrist away.

'I don't want nursing. Give me a shot and let's get going.'

Whether through stoicism or pride, she doesn't complain again, just sits on the back and keeps watch as we ride. The sun is burning high when she spots the shape on the horizon.

I squint through the binoculars, trying to make sense of what I'm seeing. It's a wagon, makeshift, with a solar rig and shuttered sides that tell me it's someone's home. It's brightly painted in reds and yellows, adorned with a grey worm shape that coils around the sides.

'Looks like a grubhawker.'

The General grunts. 'A what?'

'Grubhawker. They sell insects, for entertainment, food, pupae for people to breed. Easier to keep alive than animals.'

The General makes a noise of disgust. 'What's it doing out here?'

'Don't know. But something's wrong, if there was anyone home, they would have seen us by now and signalled.' I swing the binoculars around but the wasteland of grey-red dust and boulders is devoid of life. 'If it has been abandoned, it won't stay that way for long. The Seekers will find it and we do not want to be here when they do.'

The wagon is pulled up beside a bluff, two hundred feet from the edge of the trail. From the front, everything looks orderly, but when the rear side comes into view...

It's carnage. The vehicle has been gutted, metal and wires spilling out. It was a grubhawker's wagon, true enough, but now the plastic cases that usually hold maggots and ants and beetles are strewn and smashed on the ground, the insects curled and dead. Anything of conceivable use has been hacked away, down to door handles and seat cushions. As we draw closer, the smell hits me: burned plastic, cold ash, blood-soaked dirt.

The General jabs my shoulder. 'There,' she says, pointing.

A figure lies among the debris. I stop the mule.

'What are you doing?' she snaps. 'I thought you said it wasn't safe.'

'I have to make sure.' I reach into the back for my medical kit.

'Damn fool, that's a corpse, listen to the flies.'

She's right; a distinct buzzing can be heard over the creak and shift of the ruined wagon. The grubhawker's wares, feeding on their master in the end.

'I have to see.'

Slowly, I walk towards the figure. Splinters and shards crack beneath my boots. Perhaps it's the smell of the blood, the way the man lies curled on his side, but a flash of memory returns and for a moment the ground is not wilderness dust but a ruined street, a battleground, and the body is not one but twenty, thirty, all in the cobbled together uniforms of the Limits, their limbs torn, viscera spilling from wounds that will never be healed, some blinded by the strikes, and all of them screaming for me, yelling over and over the word that as good as became my name. *Medic*.

Anything but this, I had thought. *Any time but this. Any world.* Here is my wish.

Like the wagon, the grubhawker has been looted. Their eyes and teeth are gone, the torso left open to reveal plundered insides. I don't need to look closely to know what has been taken. Liver, kidneys, heart and lungs. Pancreas, if the particular band of Seekers had the time and skill to take it. They left the guts, tended to. Too messy and not enough call for them, out here.

'Was it them?' the General asks. 'The Seekers?'

She stares down at the corpse, her face blank.

'Must have been.'

'I thought you said they left nothing behind.' She squints at the wagon. 'There is salvage here yet.'

'Organs need to be transported quickly. Can't risk them spoiling.' I glance at the sky. 'They'll be back for the rest.'

The General frowns at the corpse. I wonder if she is thinking of LaSalle, whether he was similarly plundered. 'What do they want it all for?'

'Black-market organ trade.'

'We have synthesised flesh for that.'

'Not out here we don't. Which means there are always a few people desperate or stupid enough to make a deal with them. Anyway, some say they don't even sell the organs, they take them as tribute, to Hel.'

The General looks at me sharply. 'Who?'

'Hel. The Converter. Leader of Seekers. They say Hel was among the first settlers on this moon, the first to go into the Edge.'

'And the Accord let this person live?'

I laugh humourlessly. 'The Accord claim to have captured and executed Hel. Twice.'

'Moon full of lunatics,' the General mutters.

I leave her poking through debris while I kneel beside the body. I can at least find out the man's name. Most people carry their name out here, usually on something that can be easily dropped, a coin or a necklace or a bracelet. Sure enough, around the grubhawker's neck, I find a chain.

It's a dog tag, prison issued, stamped with a name and number. I scrape the dried blood from it with my nail.

FOUR BRINKMANN, it reads on one side. #4570263, AFP NORDSTROM.

On the other side, words have been scratched into the metal.

Should I be taken, this is where I stood. May those who loved me remember Jeddes Brinkmann.

My lips form the name. Nothing more I can do for him now. I dig a hole with my hands in the blood-soaked dust, so that I can bury the tag, so there is at least one thing the Seekers can't take.

Dirt catches beneath my nails, thicker and cooler beneath the hot surface. Something sharp catches my hand and I snatch it back in pain. A shallow cut runs across my fingertips. As blood wells and drips into the hole, I look down. Metal pokes through the dirt. Did the Seekers bury something first? I scrape away the sand and pull the thing free.

It's a prison collar.

I let go immediately, shaking hard. *Leave it*, I tell myself savagely, *leave it buried*. But my hands don't obey; they reach out to brush sand from the collar, to read the name engraved there.

A cry of horror dies in my throat. The name is my own.

I kick it back into the hole. Has the General seen? I look around and find her gone.

Not just her. It's all gone; the wrecked wagon, the dead grubhawker, the mule, even the sky. There's nothing, only endless stretching desert and a terrible flat yellow light.

I scream. Dark sand spills from my mouth.

A blow to the head sends me reeling to the dirt. I scrabble up. The General stands above me, the sun at her back.

'What the hell's wrong with you?' she demands.

Trembling, I look around. There's the wagon, the mule, the corpse. My hands are filthy, the ground around me spattered with vomit.

I begin to answer but stop, terrified that sand will come pouring past my tongue.

'I don't know,' I croak eventually. 'I thought I saw…' The hole I dug is empty, the grubhawker's tag still in my hand. I throw it down. Where the cut had been there is only a thin, pale line, like a scar, long-healed.

'Low?' the General barks.

'I am fine.' I force the words out and wipe my mouth. 'Just tiredness. Too much sun.'

The General sighs. 'If you're going to go mad, do it on your own time. We have a deal to—'

She stops. Our eyes meet. From somewhere close by, too close, comes the sound of engines.

•

We haven't taken six steps before a red light scores the dust before us. I grab the General, hauling her back by the shoulder.

'What the hell are you doing?' She throws me off. 'We have to run!'

'Tracking beam. Don't move.'

Cold sweat breaks out beneath my clothes, slicking the skin of my neck. 'Cover your head,' I tell her.

'What?'

'Do it. Now. If they see you're hurt…'

She must hear the fear in my voice, because she drags the scarf over the head wound without another word. I don't move an inch, not even when the shadow of the ship slides over us, blocking out the sun. The belly of the craft is scarred and battered, bearing signs of being made and remade a dozen times over.

'Can they be bargained with?' The General's voice is tight.

'I don't know.' *Few have lived to find out.*

'Weapon?'

'On the mule.'

She swears. 'I'm not going to die in the middle of goddam nowhere thanks to your stupidity.'

Her voice is lost in a roar as the ship blasts its stabilisers, whipping the dust into a choking cloud. My body screams for me to run, even though I know that would be suicide. They would pick me off in an instant.

A hatch slides open, and cables unravel. Through eyes stinging with terror I see figures emerge. Effortlessly, they slide down to the dirt. No faces, just goggles, masks, clothes like tattered wings. Silver glinting at their belts. Scalpels, the blades nicking the light.

Slowly, I raise my hands and force out the words that have saved my life more times than I can count.

'No harm. Medic.'

One figure makes a gesture. I keep my head down, too afraid to meet the dark glass of those eyes. For a fleeting instant, I find myself wishing *they* would sweep upon us, roaring and hungry, as they had at the ranch.

A Seeker steps forwards. 'Medic?' they repeat, voice rasping as if with thirst. 'Alive?'

I swallow. 'Yes.'

The Seeker shakes their head. 'No.' They turn towards the General, one hand straying to the scalpels at their belt. 'Seen you both. Walking with the dead.'

I force one trembling arm in front of the General and look into the Seeker's face.

'She is a child. She will live.'

The Seeker stops, as if surprised. I can see nothing through their goggles, only my own reflection, wavering in the dust. Mine? For a moment, another face looks back...

A roar makes my skin leap as another Seeker craft appears, banking low above us. For an instant, the tracking beam disappears.

'Go!' the General shrieks.

The Seeker's head snaps back towards us too late. I dive after the General, running headlong towards the mule. The second craft's engines have kicked up the dust and for one breath, two, we are lost from sight.

I scramble onto the mule's seat as the first charge explodes against the side. I stamp the accelerator, and we take off, skidding in the dirt.

'Can you see anything?' I yell.

The mule's engine roars, complaining that it is too hot, that we are riding too hard.

'The second craft's changing course.' The General beats on the seat. 'Faster, goddam it!'

'We're going to burn out!'

A charge sears the air red, smashing into the back of the mule. It lurches up and crashes to the ground with a sickening, grating noise. Another charge whistles past. Up ahead through the dust, I see something approaching: the edge of a gulley.

'We have to ditch the mule,' I yell.

'Are you crazy?'

'It's our only chance. Might be enough to lure them off.' I grab at her. 'Can you drive it?'

'What? Yes—'

'Then drive!'

I let go. The mule swerves and sways as the General scrambles into the driver's seat and takes the wheel. I throw myself into the back. In the chaos my hands are too slow, the mule too unsteady, but I grab what I can, slinging the medkit around my neck, stuffing my hat under my arm and a water canister into the layers of my clothes. Behind us, the blades of the Seekers' engines whip the air into a frenzy, until I can barely see. The shadow of the ship falls over us and I look up into the open panel in the belly, into the smoked glass goggles of the Seeker.

I don't wait, just seize the General by the arm and throw us both from the mule into the dust.

●

We run. Although you can hardly call it running, the way we stagger and lurch, boots filled with grit, lungs burning in the thin, hostile air, blood beating until I can't tell the sound of engines from my own heart. We run until we reach the incline at the edge of the trail and then we leap, tearing skin as we roll into a narrow gulley. Only when we reach the bottom, plunging into shadows, do I stop. My head pounds, my hands feel like raw meat as I paw at my clothes, praying that the canister is still there, that the medkit is intact.

It is. And I see we'll need it: beside me, the General is in a bad way, her face haggard, the sleeve of her flight suit torn, the flesh below grazed and bleeding. While she heaves at the thin air, I listen. I can still hear the engines, but more distantly.

My voice emerges as a croak. 'Sounds like they've taken the bait, gone after the mule. Should keep them busy for a few minutes.' I look down at her. 'Can you walk?'

She coughs. 'Where to? Without the mule we're carrion.'

I look ahead. The gulley splits into two paths, and I nod to the narrower of the two. 'Their ships won't be able to follow us in there. It should lead to the plateau. And if we reach the plateau, we can try and intercept the Air Line Road. That runs all the way to Landfall.'

The General glares at me in disbelief. 'You almost get us killed out in the goddam wastes, when there's an Air Line?'

'There's no way through these gulley by mule. It would have taken us another four days to ride around. And going on foot would not have been my choice. As it is, you owe me a new vehicle.'

I knock the hat back into shape, and jam it on my head, listening to the distant thrum of engines. Have they truly let us go? By rights, we shouldn't be alive. Luck, that's all it is. Luck. Not *them*. I swill my mouth with a few drops of water and spit out the taste of bile, the memory of the sand.

'Come on,' I say. 'We have to move.'

It's hard going. The gulley becomes a steep ravine full of boulders that shift and tumble underfoot. Rock walls tower, turning the sky into a ragged strip of white, a layer of skin torn from the world. There's no sound but that of sliding stones, their echoes magnified again and again until I'm half-convinced we're being followed.

For all my confident words to the General, I have only the vaguest idea of where we are heading. I try to bring to mind the map I once saw of Factus, laid out on the screen of the lifecraft as I fell hurtling towards the moon, but those memories seem to belong to another woman.

If we die here, we might never be found.

Once, that thought seemed appealing, as I lay wretched in my cell surrounded by the screaming metal of the hulks. The idea that I could close my eyes and be forgotten by the world in an instant… But that was before I made the choice to live, and to live by the tally. Now, all I can do is set one foot in front of the other.

The General starts to stagger. When I call a halt I find that her skin is burning, her eyes narrow and bright.

'Why are we stopping?' she demands.

'Because you are sick. We cannot keep this pace without resting.' I glance at the sky. 'If the night is clear we can travel by dark.'

'I'm not sick,' she rasps. 'Or if I am, it's from this damn moon.' Nevertheless, she sinks to her haunches beside me, and accepts a bead when I offer one.

'What are these things?' she says, turning it in her fingers.

'Mostly dex-amphetamine. People call them breath.'

Suspiciously, she puts it in her mouth and bites down. A few moments later her eyes open in surprise and she grunts appreciatively.

'I have been in far worse states than this, you know,' she says. 'I caught the virus, when I was sent to Tamane.'

Every nerve within me freezes. That name.

Tamane.

'It nearly killed me,' she is saying, 'but I never left the field. Fought through it all. The infantry were not so lucky. We lost two thousand in my training camp alone, before we were able to contain it. So much promise wasted.' She turns burning eyes on me. 'What do you say to that, traitor?'

Swallowing hard, I shove the name away, and all the darkness it drags with it.

'I say you should stop talking.'

'I could cut your throat,' she says lazily.

My skin prickles, but she just sighs and leans back, her eyes drooping closed. I put the medkit away, hunkering down to watch the coming dusk.

I must have slept, because when I wake the voices have started up. It's the night wind – part of me knows that – the first gusts racing down from the sky to sweep Factus clean. But in my exhausted state, the canyon seems like a throat from which voices emerge. Eight thousand cadets, all of them young, begging, crying, choking to death.

Tamane.

Then, above the voices, I sense *them*. They watch with lazy interest, as if satiated and satisfied, but still curious. I glance down at the General, her lips twitching in sleep.

'Get up,' I say.

She groans, rolling onto her side. 'Give me one of those beads.'

I do, and take one myself to stave off my hunger pangs. It works, but it also makes the voices on the wind worse. I try to ignore them and focus on the trail.

As the hours pass, Brovos crosses the sky above us, like a huge eye rolled to the bloodshot white. I realise the muttering I hear is not the wind, but the General. She's talking to herself, giving orders as if sat at some command station. I listen for a time, before touching her shoulder.

Her fist strikes out, but she overbalances. If not, I would have gone down like the man at the snake ranch. In the pallid moonlight her eyes are unfocused, her pupils huge.

'General?'

She blinks. 'LaSalle?'

I take a breath. 'Yes.'

'LaSalle. Get me General Thackeray of the Northern Air Unit. The FL have targeted Tamane. We must strike.'

'Yes, General.'

'Make the order.'

'Of course.' This time, when I touch her shoulder she does not lash out. 'The army medic wishes to examine you, General Ortiz.'

'Again?' Automatically she holds out an arm, veins up, her eyes roaming some unseen battlefield. 'Well? Be quick about it.'

Opening the medkit, I wind up the monitor, giving it just enough power to show me her basic stats. Cautiously, I push aside the collar of the stained and torn flight suit to set it against her neck.

When I see the skin beneath, I almost recoil. The moonlight picks out the angry ridges of surgical scars: one thick line from clavicle downwards, four more on either side of her neck that suggest implants. I force myself to stare at the monitor's grey screen.

Her vitals are haywire; her heart thundering, lungs heaving

to keep up. She's ill, that much is certain, and whatever it is, it's serious. I take out a couple of ampules and a syringe. *Make it to Landfall. Take your payment. Then she's their problem, not yours.*

A moment after the drugs enter her bloodstream, the General's eyes regain focus.

'What the hell are you doing?' she cries, snatching her arm away.

'You are ill,' I say. 'It is just a saline solution. And a cognitive booster.'

She stares at me. 'Was I asleep? I thought…' Her face changes, turning hard, and I know she is pushing fear away. 'How do I know you aren't poisoning me, traitor?'

'You are worth more to me alive than dead.' I shoulder the medkit. 'And you can stop calling me traitor.'

The cocktail of drugs does its work, because she starts to walk again, firm on her feet. We carry on that way, picking our way across rocks, the wind pushing us along. On either side, the canyon walls fray and crumble away until, as false dawn creeps across the sky, we crest the plateau.

In the dim light, the General's face is drawn, but her eyes are clear, taking in the view. Below, in the distance, the Air Line Road gleams, two lines of silver, running into the distance.

'It reminds me of the front, on Delos,' she murmurs, before handing me the water canteen. 'Just a dumping ground of old terraform rigs, before the Accord took charge, made it what it is today. Never did understand why those junk-merchants sided with you traitors.'

'They were proud of what they'd built on their own,' I say, raising the canteen. 'They didn't want Delos to become just another company asset.'

When I lower it, I find her watching me curiously.

'You must have fought? Before you were sentenced?'

'I doubt you would call it fighting.'

Her eyes narrow. 'But you *were* in the FL?'

'For a time.'

'Which cell? Where? Perhaps we faced each other in battle.'

I can't fathom her tone of voice.

'The Cats, at first. And I don't think so.' I screw the lid on the canteen, hard. 'I wasn't a soldier.'

'No,' she says derisively. 'None of you were. If you had been, you would have seen how stupid your little social experiment was. Did you truly believe people would give up what they worked for? Just hand it out to strangers?' She stares at me, her gaze searching. 'You would have led them into poverty and ruin. Do you see that now?'

I walk on without a word.

•

By the time we reach the Air Line Road station, it's after noon. I go first, approaching with caution. This is civilisation of a sort, controlled by the Accord, or at least by the freelance Peacekeepers in their pay. Not a good place for a convict, ex or no.

Felicity, the sign reads. Someone has scratched *is dead* beneath.

To my relief, the station yard is empty of mules and vehicles. It is evidently hours yet before the Air Line is due, and the whole place is silent, the sun smacking down upon the rails with such ferocity that the air seems to ring.

Even the station building is near deserted. The only person there is the stationmaster, reeking of bad benzene. He barely blinks at my filthy, dust-covered state, seemingly interested in only two things: overcharging me, and continuing his nap. Eventually, I manage to barter a pair of dry-looking steaks, half a bucket of water, and an ancient waterproof poncho to cover the General's flight suit. By the time I push the door open to leave, he's already half-asleep and so doesn't see me freeze at the sight of the wanted poster tacked to the wall.

It's crudely done, a bad sketch on carbon paper, no doubt copied down from the wire bulletin, but the words are undeniable:

WANTED

THE WOMAN "LOW"

FOR THEFT, ATTEMPTED MURDER, KIDNAPPING AND THE SUMMONING OF MALIGN FORCES. LAST SEEN HEADING FOR LANDFALL FIVE.

THE BROTHERS KWALKAVICH OFFER
A REWARD OF
100 CREDITS

(OR THEIR OFF-WORLD EQUIVALENT)

I rip the poster from the wall and ball it in my fist. Thoughts race ahead of me as I shove my way outside. Perhaps the news has not spread far yet. Perhaps without the poster to remind them, no one here will think to look.

Keep your head down. One more day and it will not matter. You'll be rid of her and you can go back to the Barrens where no one cares about a name if you can give them what they need.

I dump the food and water in front of the General without speaking. She doesn't seem to notice my apprehension in her eagerness to eat and drink. The steaks are nothing but protein mulch fried in old fat. They turn to paste in my mouth and taste of nothing much, but they work to quiet the ache in my belly. Even the General doesn't protest. I suspect she is in pain once again; her eyes look glazed and there are lines of strain about her mouth.

And what of me? My reflection looms in the bucket, almost a silhouette against the whitening sky. It shows a woman with a stubbled scalp, a grubby, sunburned face, framed by those two puckered scars. Something flashes across the light and, for an instant, I think I see the woman I once was: clear skin, sleek brown hair, a crisp twin-triangle tattoo upon my temple beneath a nurse's cap. How I looked the day I made the decision that severed my life in two.

I plunge my hand into the water, shattering the image, and scrub hard at my face, careful not to disturb the scarves around my neck, even when the water runs down my back in rivulets. When

I look up, I find the General holding the crumpled wanted poster.

'What is this?'

'Nothing to worry about.'

'"Kidnapping",' she reads, and looks me over, amused. 'They give you too much credit. Why would they say that, anyway?'

'I told you, children are rare on Factus. If they can keep you for themselves, they will try.'

She strokes the poster. 'Perhaps it would be better,' she murmurs. 'Perhaps I could have a life here, a real family, with parents who love me and would never make me fight.' She meets my eyes, her own wide and brimming with tears. 'Low, do you think I could? Is it too late?'

I stare at her, unnerved. Is her mind wandering again? 'I am not sure…' I start, only to realise that the General's mouth is trembling with suppressed mirth. I sag.

'You believed it.' She laughs, wiping her eyes. 'You *actually* believed it.'

A wagon comes into view around the station house, a charabanc, filled with passengers.

'Cover up,' I snap, shoving the poncho at her and cramming the hat back onto my head.

She grimaces at the garment. 'It stinks.'

'You want to be caught by Peacekeepers? Then go ahead and ignore me.'

Huffing, she pulls the thing over her head. 'When I get to Landfall, I demand a bath, no matter what.'

The passengers on the wagon are the first of many. Soon, other vehicles arrive. There are mules bearing whole families, towing goods behind, other folk on foot with nothing but a bag on their backs. Before long, the Peacekeepers show up, with their ex-army vests and Accord-issue rifles. I watch them pass from beneath the brim of my hat as they head straight for the board where the wanted bills are posted. I shuffle down a little further in my patch of shade.

Talk and noise fill the station, and the smell of food: fresh protein and frying fat, even coffee. My stomach groans for it, but I can't take the risk. The Air Line is due within the hour, some say, others insist it won't arrive until dusk. There is little anyone can do but wait. Once again, we're at the mercy of the First Accord and their failed promises: of land, of space, of faster travel than we could imagine. Of freedom. I slide a glance at the General. She is staring darkly at a pair of children who stand, pointing at something and laughing.

Abruptly, she's on her feet. I catch the edge of the poncho.

'Where are you going?'

She jerks free without a word. Swearing, I follow. The children are part of a cluster of people, all staring down at the same thing.

A sideshow. For a second my stomach reels, remembering Valdosta, the snakes, the clatter of bone dice on wood and the chaos I left behind in Redcrop. But this is nothing so grand. A showman – if anyone would call him that – crouches in the dust, theatrically cracking a miniature whip. Before him two warrior ants are doing battle. They've been allowed to work themselves into a fury, and now the tiny hairs that cover their carapaces glitter in the afternoon light.

'See them now, see them, gentle folk, they are in their red rage,' the showman patters, cracking the whip. 'See how they wish to fight and die, beautiful and fierce.' He points to the larger ant. 'This here is Roseinvale, named for the great conflagration of that moon, and the other is the Tragedy of Tamane. Two great battles between the First Accord and Free Limits and now, which will win? Now will history be rewritten? Do I have a bet from you, madam? Roseinvale or Tamane? Choose now for there shall be no other chance!'

Some people shake their heads and hurry away as fast as possible. The showman's game is too much like chance, enough to tempt the Ifs. But others stay, their fear dulled by life in the Barrens, by their hunger to see anything new. There's always money to be had from those who can stand a little danger.

I know I should turn away, but the man's words ring in my head, *the Tragedy of Tamane*. I watch as the two ants snap at each other, shimmering in fury. The General watches too, her eyes – like mine – fixed on the ant the man has named for Tamane. It struggles until finally, the larger ant strikes, opening a seeping wound in its abdomen. As it falls, my skin turns cold, despite the sun.

'Roseinvale! Roseinvale has taken it! The champion, and a victory for the Free Limits at last! Come folk and collect your winnings…'

People move away, muttering or grinning and shoving pieces of metal into their pockets. I tug on the General's arm but she does not move, not even when she is the last one left and the showman starts to pack up the ring. The defeated ant is still alive, still trying to fight, dragging itself towards the other, now safely stowed inside a tiny cage.

'Don't be sad, little lady,' the showman leers, revealing scratched fibreglass teeth. 'Old Tamane here had a good life while it lasted, full board, all the leaf litter he could eat.'

'How dare you.'

The General's tone does not belong to a child. Before I can move, the man is in the dirt, the General's knee pressing down on his windpipe.

'Stinking maggot,' she spits into his face. 'How dare you? Those who fell at Tamane were heroes; they were beaten not through strength but through cowardice! And you mock them!'

The man is turning purple, his eyes wild. Using all my strength, I grab the General and haul her back, digging an elbow into her sternum. The air goes out of her and she lets go.

'I am so sorry, sir,' I babble to the man, 'so sorry for my daughter. We lost my wife, you see, to the germ warfare on Tamane, the girl saw some terrible things.'

'She's crazy!' the man chokes, rubbing at his throat. 'Keep her away from me, I should call the Peacekeepers.'

People are starting to look. Swiftly, I drag the pouch of breath beads from beneath my clothes and throw it at him.

'Here, sir, for your trouble.'

He opens his mouth to yell, until he sees what's inside. 'Well,' he croaks, hauling himself up from the ground. 'We all saw terrible things.' He shoots a glance at the General, still wheezing in my arms, and for a moment, his face drops into the lines of grief it must wear when he is alone. 'Think yourself lucky you still have her,' he says. 'My family were on one of the ships heading for Brovos. Got caught in the strikes. I only escaped 'cos I was on the hulks.'

I bow my head. 'May your thoughts be clear.'

His hollow laugh follows me across the yard as I haul the General away. 'Best that they are not.'

•

The General sits in the corner of the Air Line car staring at the gritty metal floor. I had been so concerned with boarding, with avoiding further scrutiny, that I had taken no notice of what she did, so long as she kept quiet and walked when pushed. Now that we are underway, the Air Line hurtling along the tracks and the air growing thick with the smell of sweat and breath of many passengers, I look at her.

At her feet, a tiny creature crawls: the wounded warrior ant. It pulls itself around in circles, one of its pincers waving, seeking to fight even as it dies.

'Why did you take it?' I ask.

She shrugs and pokes the ant. It swipes at her, attacking blindly.

'Don't taunt it,' I say. 'It will fight until the end. That's what they're bred for.'

She ignores me and continues to goad the ant, letting it roam in wretched circles.

'Were you ever a child?' I hear myself ask, over the rushing of the rails.

She doesn't look at me. 'I was conscripted at seven. Childhood as a concept was deemed unnecessary.'

'Unnecessary.' I repeat the word, to test its reality. No doubt the Army of the First Accord have used that word on their paperwork, stamped it with approval and sent it out to families across the settled planets.

'What would *you* have had us do?' The expression on the General's face is almost like grief. 'Should I have waited out the war, weak and unprepared, like *your* children? Sitting huddled, silenced, kept away from every possibility of action?' Her lips shake. 'You would have had others fight and die for me. You would have left me to grow up drenched in the blood of my elders. It was *right* we took part. It was our fight. Our future. And the Accord let us shape it.'

Deep within me, something trembles at her words. 'What they did to you was barbaric. I am not going to argue about that.'

'Worse than what your forces did? Worse than killing thousands of innocents?' She smiles, cruelly. 'They gave me a gift. They gave me tactical skills that people like you couldn't dream of. They made me unassailable. They knew that even the enemy would stop short of attacking a child, or risk being forever shunned by their own. It's why we're so valuable. You find it too hard to fight us.'

As if in triumph, she shoves the ant and it falls on its side, its legs twitching, trying to reach her.

'Pathetic,' she murmurs.

We are silent after that. What more can we say?

I think the General might have been asleep, but when I glance down her eyes are open, staring blindly at the strips of light that come through the scratched windows. She looks a thousand miles away. But where? On the command bridge of a ship, watching in grim satisfaction as the Free Limiter field hospitals on Roseinvale are bombed, one after another? Behind a desk in a glass-and-chrome office, ready to give a killing order? On an operating table, smiling as the Accord surgeons cut into her body to make it stronger and faster?

And where was I? I close my eyes. I was a young woman again, dreaming of life beyond a small cluster of satellites, hearing discussions of liberty and autonomy and new ways of living that made my heart beat faster. I was on Prosper, in the hospital vault, about to become a murderer. I was on Tamane, surrounded by the fallen, by the evidence of my sin. I was in the cell on the hulks. I was staggering, wounded from a lifecraft. I was here. I was nowhere. Is that why *they* follow me?

The hours pass with neither of us speaking. I twitch, sorely regretting giving the showman my remaining beads. The sun slides across the carriage, people barter and laugh and sob and argue with each other, and on the walls above us the Accord posters speak of loans to repay our war debts, advertising seed banks and land grants, emblazoned with slogans like *Time to Heal*, and *For the Future*. I turn my head away.

Beside me, the General sleeps, the dead ant crushed at her feet.

•

I've not been to Landfall Five in many months, and sure enough it's already changed. Here is the new-found prosperity brought by restitution payments; here are real blacktop roads and buildings made from girders and concrete. There are mules and crafts that aren't a decade old and clogged with dust. Here there's trade, official and bootleg, pumping life onto this dry moon. Here are people from across the now-Accorded Nations, more than I have seen in a long time, all scrambling to make a home, to remember themselves and their ways however they can.

At the edges, the original stinking, hardscrabble town of Landfall remains; evidence of those who first arrived here as convict work parties, huddling against the army for food and warmth. Had I been on my own, I would have run for those shadows. As it is, I have no choice but to keep my head down and walk the new, sticky roads towards the centre of the town: the army base where the ships had first touched down, thirty years ago.

It's almost night. Out in the Barrens the sands sigh, the air is cold blue and voices from between the stars ride down on the winds. None of that here. The smell of cook-smoke and pepper and unnamed meats from the Chuan stands mixes with the hot oil and frying protein-maize from the arepa sellers to remind my stomach it once knew real food. The air fizzes with sparks from engine repair shops, competing with the lights of the snake-soup canteens, the wire-and-picture sellers, liquor stores hawking scorpion whiskey and snake wine and distilled venom "for medicinal purposes only". At a metered water fountain, people queue with their drums and buckets, gossiping, coughing, glancing at the sky. Folk aren't so afraid of the Ifs, here. With enough activity, the implausible is just that: happenstance, coincidence, bad luck.

I'm glad of it. I don't want *them* here, not now, when this business is almost done. Perhaps they will transfer their interest to the General. Perhaps they will follow her to whatever planet she is posted to next and leave me be. Did they venture beyond Factus? I have never heard reports of them anywhere else.

I sigh. 'We are almost there.'

The General nods. Though she looks around with narrow, searching eyes, I can tell she is struggling. Her jaw is tight, beads of perspiration on her forehead. Not my problem. Her people can heal her, with the seemingly unlimited resources they so rarely share with the rest of us.

Soon, the base comes into view, high metal and wire fences surrounding clean-edged, utilitarian buildings. A flag flutters in the faint wind that finds its way here from the desert.

'About goddam time.' She strides forwards. When I don't follow she turns, impatient. 'Well?'

'I am not going in there.'

She rolls her eyes. 'Tiresome. What of your payment?'

'I will wait.'

'It'll take time to make an inventory of supplies, to see what can be spared.' When I don't move, she sighs. 'Alright. I'll order it to be delivered to you. Where will you be?'

She has become a military official before my eyes; that flag, with its golden triangles, has swallowed up any part of her that seemed lost or in pain.

I jerk my chin. 'There's a benzenery, in Tiger Town. Malady Falco's. They will know of it at the camp.'

'Just the sort of place for you. Fine. Expect delivery there by 2230.'

'And if it does not arrive?'

'I made you a promise by the First and Last Accords. Or have you forgotten what honour looks like?'

I half smile and shake my head.

She frowns at me for a moment longer. 'I won't say it has been a pleasure, knowing you. But even if you are a traitor, you kept your word. Perhaps the times are changing, after all.'

With that, she turns smartly and walks towards the gates, her head held high. No thanks, no emotion. I watch as the soldiers level their guns at her, as she makes a dismissive gesture, flicking her head to show the tattoos. They snap to attention. I watch as the huge, riveted gate slides open and she walks through, her small figure swallowed by the dark.

There is a pain in my chest and noise in my head. I don't want it there, and so I go to find myself a drink.

•

Landfall might have changed, but Falco's is the same.

The bar had once been a container used to ship arms for the Accord. Falco has decorated every inch of the walls with bright, brash, obscene graffiti, at odds with the drabness of the Accord base. *They might have built this moon*, she once said with a laugh, *but that doesn't make it theirs*.

Unlike Sorry Damovitch, or most people, the prison hulks didn't hold Falco back for long. The story went that she had been born to a wealthy merchant family, but her parents had lost everything in a trade deal gone bad. Other people said she had been born on one of the original supply haulers, during their first long trip to Brovos and the border moons.

Whatever the truth, it's a generally accepted fact that, when the war came, she enlisted with the Accord for the sole purpose of robbing them blind. After years of racketeering, profiteering, fencing and blackmail, she was finally caught and sentenced as a Nine. But facility after facility found themselves compromised by her activities; prison walls seemed to turn into sieves around her. Finally, after eighteen months a warden gave up, commuted her sentence to time-served and issued her the name *Malady* as an insult. It didn't land. In fact, they say, she was delighted.

Now, Falco's is the number one place in Landfall Five to do business. I step through the first door of the airlock and wait for the second to open. As soon as it does, my chest loosens. Despite the crowded bar, the air within is cool, clean. I breathe deep, feeling the rush of oxygen to my head. Few people on Factus are powerful or well-connected enough to have their own augmented air supply.

Music plays, a bouncy, jittery pop song I've never heard. I pause beside the bar to listen as the song ends and the announcer takes over.

… another icy hit from the steel-eyed sirens. I'm Lester Sixofus and we're coming at you from – where are we? – somewhere near Ithmid XBI and rollin' on. News from the cruise: cow-quarantines on Brovos, tech warehouse strikes on Jericho and nickel tycoon Lutho Xoon has been appointed First Premier of oh-so-glamorous Delos. Well done, sir. Now…

'Taplicker!'

I'm shoved back as two leathernecks square up to each other. Their fight lasts all of three seconds before one of Falco's G'hals stands up, hand on the weapon at her hip. The men, belligerent as they are, immediately take their quarrel outside.

My neck prickles with the knowledge of someone watching. Falco sits at her usual table in the corner, one brown eye narrowed, the other a mass of scar tissue. Pulling off my hat, I make my way towards her. There's a G'hal at her side, tall and lean with shaggy, grey-blonde hair and skin tanned the same fawn colour of the Barrens. Their gun-belt and holster is graffitied, studded with bright bits of metal. They stare at me with a steely expression, evidently wondering why the boss would waste time with an outcast like me. But Falco smiles.

'Pegeen,' she says, kicking out a chair for me to sit down. 'This is Doc Low. She's the one who pulled that bullet outta my head.'

The G'hal looks at me with renewed interest, though still a little distaste at my ragged state. Falco reaches out and pats their hand.

'Bring us a bottle, Peg, and couple of airtights. Looks like the Doc needs it.'

I slide the medkit from my shoulder. 'How can you tell?'

'Call it intuition. It *was* you seen not long ago getting off the Air Line with a child?'

Her informers work fast. 'Long story, Mala. And I don't think you will believe the half of it.'

'Oh, I've got some notion. You know you're wanted by some snakers, named Kwalkavich?'

I roll my eyes. Pegeen returns with a bottle of benzene, and two tin cans, already open. 'Cherries?' I ask, my mouth already watering. 'And peaches? Where do you get these things? Business must be good.'

'It is,' Falco says, pouring the liquor. 'And I don't need any trouble.'

'Neither do I.'

'Well,' she pushes a cup across the table, 'let's drink to that.'

The benzene is actually whiskey, cut with Falco's secret cocktail of chemicals. It gives you an almighty headache the next day, but before that it makes your heart sing. I down the first cup like water.

Falco smiles. She looks well, far better than when I saw her last, after a bullet from a shoot-out with a rival gang went straight through her eye to brush her brain. I pulled it out, no choice but to take the ruined eye with it. When she finally came around, I was worried she would blame me for not having the skill to save her eye. But she'd only grimaced, her face racked with pain, and told me that she'd get on with one.

She dismissed the idea of wearing a patch from the start, and now I see that she has toughened the pinkish-brown mass of scar tissue with alcohol. Her other eye is bright, her ochre-brown skin clear, the dull undertone gone. Her scalp is shaved clean, and she wears her usual mockingly customised military jacket, dyed bright blue and yellow, and iridescent paint on her lips.

'So,' she asks, spooning a cherry into her glass. 'Are you going to talk?'

I help myself to the fruit first. When the sweetness bursts on my tongue, it's all I can do not to close my eyes with pleasure. I chase the berry down with a drink. So much has happened that I can't easily explain. The General, *their* presence, the fact the Seekers let us go… I drink again. Simple words, I tell myself, simple thoughts. Best to forget.

'I was out in the Barrens, north of Redcrop,' I say, my head turning warm and sparkly from the benzene and the extra oxygen. 'Minding my own business when—'

'You discovered a wreck.'

'I saw it,' I admit. 'Or what was left.'

Falco spins her glass. 'Word is it was an Accord State ship, carrying a General, who died in the wreck like everyone else. You can bet the brass aren't pleased about it.'

I stop, the cup halfway to my mouth. 'What do you mean, died?'

Falco raises an eyebrow. 'It was in the bulletin. A scouting party found her body before the Seekers got to it. It's being shipped back as we speak for a state funeral.'

I stare at her. The benzene is no longer welcome in my head, it is too hot, curdling with the ice that chases down my spine. *Forget it*, I tell myself viciously, *forget it and drink*.

'Where's the wire bulletin?' I ask instead.

Falco signals one of the other G'hals to bring it over, before staring at me, intent. 'What's wrong? You've gone the colour of dry cheese.'

'Just… let me read it.'

She says no more, just places a much-handled bulletin board in front of me. I jab at the surface until it wakes up, the ink flashing into life. I flick through the latest issue, past news of trials and factory openings and settlement elections, until I see it:

General of the western forces killed in wreck

Captain-General Gabriella Ortiz, Former Commander of the Western Air Fleet of the Accorded Nations was today officially declared dead after her body was recovered from the wreckage of her ship, the **FAS Tramontana**, which was destroyed upon impact on Brovos's outer moon of Factus. The General was on her way to oversee training and further peace measures on the moon of Prodor. While investigations are ongoing as to the cause of the crash, experts believe that a fault in the ship's gravitational systems may be to blame. Accord Scouts were able to recover the body of the General by 0900 on the day of the crash. There were no other reported survivors.

The words blur across my eyes as the bulletin automatically skips to the next page. There's a photograph – it shows a girl, unsmiling, looking older than her years. Her black hair is pulled back to show her tattoos of rank, her chin raised above the collar of a uniform thick with ribbons and medals. It's her. It's undoubtedly her.

'What the hell is this?'

Falco's head whips up. I follow her gaze to see four Accord soldiers step through the airlock.

'You tell me,' she says.

•

The place falls silent. Slowly, Falco's G'hals rise from where they are sitting, their hands creeping towards belts or sleeves. Pegeen shifts, ready to step in front of Falco.

The soldiers look about the place, seemingly unbothered by hostility in the air as thick as burning tar.

'Looking for a medic named Low,' one of them demands.

Every fibre of my being wants to hide, to lower my head and cower until they are gone. But I can't. They have my payment, the supplies I need to do the work the tally demands.

I stand. For a second, my vision clouds and I swear I feel *them*, the empty rushing feeling that heralds their approach. But as my eyes clear, the sensation fades.

'I'm Low.'

Every person in the place watches as the lead soldier inclines her head and gestures outside. 'We got your goods.'

The cherry and benzene stick to the sides of my throat as I try to swallow. I wish I hadn't drunk it.

'Fine.'

Three of the soldiers turn and leave, but the lead one remains in the doorway, her eyes locked on mine. Sweat breaks out on my neck beneath the tightly wrapped scarves as I turn back to the table. Falco is staring at me hard.

'Let me pay you for the drink,' I say loudly, nodding to the bottle of benzene, and the half-empty tins. 'Though I will need change.'

'Of course,' she says. 'I'll see to it myself.' She strides towards the bar, throwing a smirk at the soldier as she passes.

I try to breathe. The delivery is here, just as the General promised. But if the General is dead, who the hell had made me that promise? Who the hell have I escorted across the plains?

Something laughs inside my head. *You brought one version of her. But what of all the others? The General Ortiz who died in the wreck, the one you murdered in the desert? The one you left for the Seekers...*

'Here.' Falco is back, tossing a handful of metal pieces down onto the table. I stare at them. I thought she'd understood that I was asking for more than money. 'Next time, Doc, don't bring the filth to my bar. If you were anyone else, I'd kill you for it.'

'Falco—' I begin, but the other woman seizes me around the neck in a tight embrace. As she does, I feel something slide down the front of my shirt, landing hard and heavy against my belt. A weapon.

'Whatever you're into, be careful,' she hisses.

I squeeze her back, before letting go. Then, I have no choice but to pick up my hat and my kit and follow the soldier out of the airlock, the gun cold against my belly.

•

'Where are we going?'

I know it's useless to ask, but at the same time, I can't just passively follow a quartet of Accord soldiers through the streets of Tiger Town; not when every third person spits in our wake.

'The goods are being held up ahead,' the lead soldier says evenly. 'We did not deem the bar a suitable place for the transaction.'

I glance at her, looking for any trace of deception. For all her stiff words, the soldier is young; she can't be a day over sixteen. Had she once been a Minority Force candidate? Had she been weeded out from the ranks of children for being too weak, for having too much of a conscience, for being unable to bear the mental pressure of enhancements? Her black hair is neatly clipped at the neck and ears and shaped flat on the top, her uniform correct to the last button. I feel like a desert toad next to her, dusty and croaking, my breath hot with benzene. And all the while, beneath my vest, the gun thuds against my belly…

'How many boxes did you bring?' I ask.

'Four,' the answer is immediate. 'Corporal Toulio has the details.'

'Eight packs of immune boosters,' one of the other soldiers reels off. 'Sixteen of antibiotic compounds. One crate of bandages. Five hundred analgesic ampules. Thirty packs of assorted sterile dressings…'

The list goes on. If what they are saying is true, I wouldn't need to scramble for supplies for a year or more. And the drugs would be army-grade; I could water them down and still they'd be more effective than anything I could buy on the black market. I walk faster, keeping up with the lead soldier.

'The General sent these herself?'

'We were ordered to deliver them without delay.'

'By the General?'

'By our commanding officer.'

'And that is who?'

The soldier stops. I think she's going to reprimand me, but instead, she points.

We've reached the edge of Tiger Town, where the ramshackle houses made from shipping crates and old vehicles fall away into a wasteland of century-leaf fields that adjoin the base. There, guarded by an Accord soldier, sits a pristine mule with a neat stack of tarpaulin-covered crates upon its back. Hardly able to believe it, I take a step forwards.

Before my foot touches the dirt *they* are with me, showing me my own back as I am shot a dozen times, showing me Falco's face as she watches my body being dumped into the municipal boneyard, showing me the General, a corpse in a cellulose coffin…

The instant my foot lands I drop, rip the weapon from beneath my shirt and fire.

•

The mule might be real, army-issue and clean, but the crates upon its back are fake. Every one of them is empty. I swear.

If not for *them* I would have fallen for it.

My blood is hot with liquor and adrenalin, head filled with *their* presence. The stun pistol is still in my hand, buzzing as it charges up. On the ground, one of the soldiers groans and rolls onto their side, blood dripping from their nose. When they reach for their weapon, I kick it away.

'Talk,' I order.

The soldier's grey eyes are wide, roaming over their downed comrades.

'I don't… I don't know anything, I swear. Garnet was in charge.'

I swing the medkit from my shoulder. For a second, the soldier looks relieved, until they see the syringe in my hand.

'Talk,' I tell them again.

'We were given orders to terminate a medic known as Ten Low.'

'Who gave the orders?' For the first time in what feels like years, my head is clear. There's no doubt, no hesitation. 'Was it General Ortiz?'

'General Ortiz is dead.'

'Then who did I escort here? Who did I leave at your base not two hours ago?'

'Commander said— Commander said she's a decoy. The General's decoy.'

I grip the syringe.

'Please,' the soldier's voice trembles, 'please, don't kill me, you already have three deaths on your hands.'

'You are out by thousands,' I say, and plunge the needle into their neck.

I check their pulse, before pushing myself away. What if it's true? That the General, *my* General, is nothing but a decoy? But she spoke of Tamane as if she had been there... I saw again the savage grief on her face as she stared at the dying ant, dragging the memory of thousands of souls behind it.

I could take the mule now and flee for the Barrens, supplies or no. I could leave her to her fate. Possibilities course through me, making my muscles twitch, my palm slick with sweat around the gun. I smile bitterly.

They know what I'm going to do. They know the tally demands it.

•

'Halt!'

I bring the mule to a stop. The metal walls of the army base loom, gates firmly closed. I keep my face lowered, staring at the inches of wrist exposed by the too-small army jacket.

'Sergeant Garnet?' someone calls from the sentry box beside the gate. From the corner of my eye, I see a soldier emerge and move towards me, staring at the thick bandages wrapped about my neck. 'What the hell happened? Shall I call the medic?'

'No need.'

I fire the stun pistol.

The soldier falls back, straight into a second sentry who has come running. It's the work of seconds to stun him too.

The gate – intimidating though it looks – is a cheap thing, card-operated. Either the base doesn't have much to protect, or the Accord doesn't think it worthwhile to invest in an outlying moon like this. More fools them. Within moments, I'm through the gate and into the compound.

As I ride I see a brightly lit parade ground, ringed by dust-battered buildings, the flag of the Accord flapping over it all. I swerve into the shadows.

Is the General still alive?

You are risking everything to find out.

A life is a life. And she is a child.

She is a murderer. At any other time, in any other place, she would kill you without remorse.

But we're not in another place. We're here.

You'll die for a sick brat?

Who says anything about dying?

The clouds scud across the dark sky like oil on water. *They* want this, I tell the voice at the back of my mind, the woman from the past with no mercy. *They* will help me.

In the darkness, I listen. No alarms, no sounds of panic. That makes two things obvious: one, the base is understaffed and underequipped; and two, somewhere, something important is happening.

Where would she be? Bases like this come pre-fabricated, dropped from ships in the correct layout. The General is ill. That means the infirmary. I think back to the early days of FL training, though I don't like to. Too many other things, down there in my memories: awful, clinging things that should never be dredged up.

A door slams, reverberating across the night, and I pull my mind from the sludge, opening my eyes in time to see a figure hurrying across the parade ground towards the gate I left open.

Time to move. I steal around the edge of the buildings, the stun pistol at my belt. I sense *them* at my heels, eager as dogs. Hungry for what's to come.

A stretcher in the corridor confirms that the infirmary is where I expect it to be. The walls are pasted with faded posters warning of soil contaminants and parasites in edible insects and signs of yellowrot. The air is thick with the smell of sanitiser.

I'm halfway along the corridor, too far to turn back, when a pair of soldiers appear, hurrying towards me. For a second I freeze, expecting them to shout, but they're absorbed in speaking to each other in low voices. I remember the uniform I'm wearing, the bandages that wrap my neck like a patient. I keep my head down as they pass, sneaking a glance at their insignia.

They're members of the Air Fleet. What are the Accord's finest doing, dirtying their boots on a moon like this? Quietly, I run down the corridor.

First, the wards. The FL trained me well; I could map this place with my eyes closed. Next, the surgery. The scanner. The storeroom. I stop, one hand on the wall, staring ahead. Voices echo from the examination room. One soft and anxious, the other unmistakable…

Pulling the stun pistol, I stride forwards and shove open the door.

Three people turn to stare: a medic in green uniform, syringe in hand, a heavy-set man in the uniform of a captain, and her.

Alive, clean and in full battle-dress with the sleeve of her shirt rolled up, there sits General Gabriella Ortiz. Her face drops into shock at the sight of me, at the Accord uniform I wear.

'What the hell are you doing?' she demands.

I don't answer. Instead, I fire and the captain crumples to the ground. The medic cowers, gripping the syringe. The General doesn't move.

'I see,' she says. 'You have come to kill me after all.'

'The opposite.'

She frowns. A second later the medic lunges towards me with the needle. I duck, driving my shoulder into their sternum. The needle clatters across the floor as I press the mouth of the gun to the back of the medic's neck.

'I'm not trying to kill you,' I say. 'They are.'

'What?'

Before I can answer, the medic jerks their head, watering eyes fixed on the blank screen that takes up the entirety of one wall, their lips moving, mouthing silent words.

'What's in that syringe?' I demand, digging the gun into their neck.

'Go to hell.'

Slowly, the General slides from the examining bed and picks up the syringe, filled with a blueish serum.

'It's supposed to be an immune booster,' she says thoughtfully, before stepping in front of the medic. 'You. Speak. What is this?'

'J-just an immune compound,' the medic wheezes. 'Like you say. What else could it be?'

I can see the sweat on the nape of their neck as they look again at the screen.

'That uniform belongs to Sergeant Garnet,' the General says suddenly.

'Sergeant Garnet tried to kill me.'

'The delivery?'

'There was no delivery. Only an ambush.' I look at her. 'They've declared you dead. I read it in a bulletin. This isn't an examination. It's an execution.'

The General's face goes still. When she speaks, her voice is soft. 'You're mad, traitor. Like I thought.'

I nod at the syringe. 'See for yourself.'

The General holds my gaze, before abruptly leaning forwards and stabbing the needle into the medic's thigh.

The medic shrieks and struggles madly, flailing at the syringe. The General holds it firm, her thumb on the plunger.

'What's wrong, if it's only an immune booster?' she says viciously.

'Help!' the medic screams. 'Help me!'

A flash of light and the screen flickers into life. It shows a viewing room filled with people in uniform. Sitting in the centre is an older woman with grey curly hair, closely cropped to show the tattoos of command; two faded triangles underscored by four thicker lines. Medals and ribbons drip from her chest.

'General Ortiz,' her voice booms. 'Stand down.'

The General gapes. 'Commander?'

The older woman's face is like stone. 'By the ordinances of the Army of the First Accord, I, Commander Beatrice Aline, have issued an order for your compassionate termination, with immediate effect.' A moment later her face changes, softening into pity. 'Stand down, Gabi.'

'Compassionate termination?' The General's voice trembles.

The woman nods, glancing at the medic, who sits hunched

against the wall, gripping their thigh. 'You are dying. In a few months, perhaps less, your body will fail you completely.'

'Is it true?'

She's talking to me. I tear my eyes from the Commander's face and look down.

'You treated me,' the General continues. 'Is it true? That my body is failing?'

She is ill in some way, of that I am certain. But dying? I meet her eyes. 'I don't know.'

'Enough,' the Commander barks. 'We are the experts in this matter. We do not need the opinion of a convict.' She leans forwards. 'We have seen this process before, Ortiz. It began two years ago, with the A-series. As they aged, they simply broke down. We have tried to counteract it, but there was nothing we could do. It is a painful, wretched end.'

The General looks dazed. 'The wreck?' she asks distantly.

Aline takes a breath. 'Unfortunate. You were the only intended casualty. An error evidently occurred.' She shakes her head. 'The termination order was issued to prevent this kind of suffering, Gabi, to allow you to die with honour. As befits someone of your rank.'

The General makes a noise and drops her head to the floor. She sat in the same attitude in the train car, staring at the dying ant. Had she known, even then, that she was doomed?

'What happens to the traitor?' she asks, her voice a husk. 'When I die, what will be done with her?'

I keep my eyes averted, clenching my hand to stop myself from touching the bandages about my neck. *They* cannot have sent me here for this.

The Commander seems surprised. 'She is obviously of unsound mind. But if you wish it, we'll make special dispensation and send her to be cared for in a secure facility.' She does even glance my way. 'We will do that much, in recognition of your great service, General. In recognition of your legacy.'

'My legacy,' the General murmurs, and raises her head. Her eyes are red-rimmed but dry. 'Yes. I see.'

'General.' I reach for her.

'Stand aside, traitor. This is not your choice.' For an instant, a tiny smile twists her lips. 'Strange, but I'm pleased you're here.' She holds out a hand. 'I thank you for your efforts.'

I force myself to return the gesture. Her fingers are small and callused in mine.

'Alright,' she says, letting go, locking her hands behind her back. 'I'm ready.'

The Commander nods. 'Medic?'

'What about her?' the medic asks, eyeing me with hatred as they climb to their feet.

'She will remain silent, if she wishes to live. An escort is already on its way.'

Swallowing hard, the medic goes to the workbench and fills a fresh syringe from a vial that waits there.

'On my word,' the Commander says.

The medic sets the point of the needle against the General's arm.

I cannot watch. Instead, I lower my head to stare at the unconscious captain, blood beating in my ears, so certain that this is wrong… Then, something catches my gaze: the holster at the captain's belt hangs empty, where before it contained a pistol. I look up at the General in alarm.

She and the Commander stare at each other, their pupils like the dots on two sets of dice. The air shudders around me.

'N—' I begin.

An explosion like thunder and the medic is thrown back against the wall, their chest burst open by a plasma bullet. The General spins and fires directly into the camera. It shatters and the screen goes blank.

She turns and smiles, her face coated in blood, the pistol glowing in her hand.

'Run,' she says.

TWO

THE
BOOK
OF
MALADY

COLD METAL. PAIN *on the wings of black birds. A figure gloved in blood…*

There are cries, alarms, the smell of burning plastic and gore. It's all over me, I realise, spattered from the medic's chest. I hear footsteps and turn, expecting to see soldiers. But it's the General, her face a mask of blood.

'Move!' she orders.

Are *they* with us? Is it *their* intervention, somewhere in the web of time, that ensures the security systems of the base are activated two seconds too late, that the tracking beams of the automatic guns are only able to spray the dust at our heels as we plunge across the parade ground? Are *they* showing the General the path to take through all those potential futures, as they have shown me?

By the time we reach the mule, the camp is on full alert, the air thick with gunfire and roaring engines and thudding boots.

'They have a shock cannon at the gate,' the General says, 'and I am damn near out of charges. If we distract them, and try to ram it—'

My head is ringing with the noise and the chaos. I squeeze my eyes shut. Had I known it would come to this? The General swears and shoves at me as more beams blink into life and sweep the ground.

'We need to move.'

'I know.' Neither of us will die here. 'Follow me.'

'Low!'

I count the seconds between each beam and run for a few inches of shadow cast by a wall.

'Low,' the General hisses, stumbling close behind me. 'What the hell are you doing?'

'On the western side of the base,' I say, buttoning the medkit into my jacket, where my heart thuds madly. 'There should be a waste pipe. If they haven't buried it, we can use it to get out.'

'And if they've buried it?'

I don't answer. We have thirty seconds grace, perhaps, to make it out alive before the base marshals its scattered forces.

Whose grace? I look into the sky, as I once did every night as a child during prayers, but dust-filled clouds drown the stars.

I grab the General and run. Above, there's a terrible whine, the screech of an alarm, and one of the automatic guns opens fire, charges searing into the metal fence behind us. No time to stop. We round a corner and there – I choke with relief – there is the waste pipe, large enough to transport the leavings of the entire base.

'You're crazy,' the General yells, ducking charges. 'I'm not getting in there.'

I grab the pistol from her and empty the remaining charges into the pipe's join until the plastic melts and it begins to leak foul-smelling water.

'Help!' I kick at it.

With a curse, she puts her boot to work with mine. Within seconds, the pipe breaks open. It plunges into darkness, through the fence and down the hill on the other side. A nauseating stench rises from it, but I shove the General forwards.

She scrambles in and I hear her retch. I follow, charges from the automatic guns thudding and burning through the plastic above.

'Go!' I scream.

I push myself along desperately on my elbows until the pipe drops away, sending me scrabbling head first down an incline that ends in darkness. There isn't even time to gasp before I hit the water.

Even expecting it as I am, when I surface the stench almost makes me vomit. Excrement mixed with powerful chemicals, all trapped in a space not much larger than my outstretched arms. I cough sewage from my mouth and nose, kicking madly in the total darkness, the uniform and boots threatening to drag me down.

A fist connects with my face; the General flailing to stay afloat.

'—hell?' she half shrieks.

'One of the treatment tanks.' I fight down a retch. 'Don't swallow.'

Beyond the tank, I can hear the sirens of the base. The General's fists hammer at the smooth plastic.

'We're trapped. I'm going to die in a fucking shit tank.'

'Quiet.' With a burst of effort I reach upwards. The liquid level in the tank is too low, the roof somewhere above out of reach. 'I'm going to lift you,' I wheeze.

Before she can protest, I reach down into the muck and take hold of her about the waist, boosting her out of the water. It rains down onto my face, and I close my eyes tight. Her fingernails scrape at the plastic.

'There's nothing—'

My arms burn, legs kicking desperately as I move us forwards. Then, I hear a grunt of effort and the sound of plastic cracking.

Air spills over us, air like clean water, like drenching rain. Through the hatch I see the dark sky, the sickly glow of searchlights. With a last heave, I push the General up and she scrambles free.

A moment later, her face appears. In the semi-darkness, I can't quite make out her eyes.

'General!' I reach up.

She doesn't move.

'Help me,' I gasp, my lungs burning.

Where are *they*? I strain my awareness, but there's nothing. Only sirens and the face of a girl, deciding whether I should live. Is she seeing my death, the possibilities of a world without me?

'Help!'

She shoots out an arm. I grasp it hard, my fingers like claws, but she doesn't complain. She hauls me out of the tank, with more strength than any child should possess.

We stagger away from the treatment plant, crawling past its perimeter into a dusty agave field, keeping to the shadows.

Finally, beyond a broken wire fence, I see the flickering lights of Tiger Town. Our one chance of safety.

'We have to get to Falco's.'

'The benzenery?' the General spits. 'They will tear this town to pieces looking for us. We have to get out of Landfall.'

'How do you propose to do that? We have nothing. Falco will help.'

'You think I'm going to trust another criminal?'

'You don't have a choice, *ma'am*.'

I drag her into the shadows as a scout drones overhead, its motor whining as it clogs with dust.

She wrenches herself from my grip. 'I know how to look after myself.'

In taut silence, we creep into Tiger Town. Luckily, at this time of night, many of its citizens are distracted; lulled by century smoke, or knocking back benzene, or clacking their teeth on beads.

When I see the lights of Falco's, hear the din coming from inside, I almost sob with relief. I make my way around the back, muscles trembling with ebbing adrenalin. But before I can raise a fist to knock, the door flies open and the muzzle of a gun is jammed between my eyes.

'It's me,' I croak, hands raised, 'it's Low.'

Beyond the gun is a familiar face. It's the G'hal from earlier,

Pegeen. They make a noise of disgust at the smell, before looking beyond my shoulder to the General. Their eyes go wide.

'Guess you gutspills better come in.'

•

The General slumps on the threadbare mattress, allowing me to swab a graze on her arm.

The light from the single bulb in the ceiling illuminates the surgery scars that criss-cross her neck and shoulders, exposed by the bright pink dyed vest.

She shifts in the borrowed clothes and I wonder if Falco chose the garish colours as a deliberate taunt. They obviously make the General uncomfortable, and I can tell she wants her uniform back.

Falco refused to let us into her bar, filthy as we were, and demanded that we shed the sodden, stinking clothes before being hosed down in the vapour shower. I hadn't been able to hide the shudders as the blasts stung my skin. It was too much like the hulks. All through the weeks in the prisoner camps, the holding cells, even the military trial, nothing had prepared me for the finality of that first day as a convict, standing beneath the sterile shower, as everything was stripped and scraped from me: the girl from the far-flung Congregations, the medic, even my name until only a body was left to be labelled and collared and stored – the embodiment of my crime – nothing more.

I drag my thoughts back to the present, to the child before me who needs healing.

'It should mend well,' I say.

'What do you care if it does?' She looks up at me in the artificial light. 'Why did you even come back?'

Because I had to. Because it is what they want. I pack away the swabs.

'I couldn't just let them kill you. I told you before. I have my own reasons for wanting you to live.'

'You shouldn't have bothered. Didn't you hear? I'm dead walking.' Beneath the ferocity, I hear fear. 'Do you believe it?'

I shrug helplessly. 'Without the equipment to run tests...'

She swears and sits back. 'I need to talk to the others.'

'Others?'

'Other Generals. Like me.'

She falls silent. I wonder if she's feeling what I feel: the sickly grey emptiness left behind by *their* presence. I wish I had some breath beads to sharpen my mind, but Falco doesn't believe in them, says they make you too dependent.

'I'll bandage your arm later.' I sigh and let my head fall back against the wall. 'Pegeen is bringing fresh supplies.'

When she doesn't answer I wonder if she's fallen asleep. But I open my eyes to find her staring at me, her gaze fixed upon my neck, upon the livid scar that runs from ear to ear, badly healed, puckered pink. I move out of the light.

'What's that?' she demands.

'A scar. You have plenty of your own.'

'None like that.' She looks almost impressed. 'What happened?'

I swallow, feeling it again, the terrifying rush of my own blood over my hands as I tried to hold my skin closed.

'My throat was cut,' I murmur.

'Why didn't it kill you?'

'Luck, I guess.'

Luck. That's what I always thought, before I came to Factus. Now I wonder: had *they* been there with me, watching the blood run, making sure my hand found the cauterising iron in time? Were *they* here even now?

'Well,' the General smirks, 'at least it covers up the prison collar scars.'

The trap door above slams open and boots appear, clattering down the stairs. I push myself up as Falco storms into the cellar.

'If I had known what you intended to do with that stun pistol, I never would have given it to you,' she snaps. 'All your talk of saving lives and not killing—'

'I killed no one!'

'No? Then explain to me why the camp is in uproar and why my informer is blathering about a dead medic and six wounded soldiers.'

'Seven. And I didn't kill the medic, she did.'

Falco regards the General, face inscrutable. 'General Ortiz. Aren't you supposed to be dead?'

The General hunches her shoulders, making herself seem tiny on the thin mattress. 'They said I'm dying. I'm so scared. Please – will you help me?'

'Poor little one.' Falco kneels before her. 'Of course I'll help.' She smiles. 'I'll take you straight to the nearest orphanage, where you can laugh and play with the other flea-ridden children.'

The General's innocent expression drops. 'Very funny.'

'Serves you right for trying on that terrible act,' Falco retorts. 'Now, both of you. Explain.'

'It was an ambush,' I say. 'Those soldiers had orders for my termination. I knew the General was likely in danger.'

'So you went in?' Falco is incredulous. 'You just… drove into the base? For *her*?'

The General makes an affronted noise.

'A life is a life.'

Falco shakes her head, hostility turning into pity and disbelief. 'Look, you can't stay here, Doc. I can keep them off for a time, but not forever.'

'I know, Mala.' I rub at my scalp. 'We need to get out of Landfall.'

'And go where?'

My brain feels scrambled. In the past, I would have run for the Barrens. A person alone can get by alright there. But going with the General would be like painting a target upon my back.

'What about Otroville?' I say, trying to think.

Falco scoffs. 'The capital is crawling with snitches. I should know, half of them are mine.'

'The Dhu Tran rest stop, then.'

'Seekers took it. On orders from Hel, people are saying. Nothing left.'

'If we could make it to the U Zone, if you had some contacts there—'

'No,' she dismisses, fast. 'Too many Peacekeepers. You wouldn't last a day.'

'Where then?'

The General watches the exchange between us, her eyes narrowed.

'Even if the Accord try to keep this quiet, once they give an order for her apprehension every bounty hunter from here to Prosper is going to be down on this moon.' Falco pauses, worrying the paint from her lips. 'Reckon your only choice is the Pit.'

I laugh. 'You may as well shoot us here.'

She shrugs. 'Word is power changed hands recently. Whoever's running the place has it cleaned up. Course it might just be hearsay. But a fact's a fact, it's the one place on this rock where the Accord won't follow. Except for the Edge, which I hear is lovely at this time of year.'

'What the hell are you talking about?' the General demands.

I hesitate, wondering just how far we can trust Falco. 'The Pit's a crater, a few days north of here. Deep enough to hide lights, signals. The land around it is mined and trapped for miles so the Accord won't go near, without proper support.'

The General's jaw twitches as she looks at Falco. 'I need to get off this stinking moon and make contact with my peers. I could buy passage in this… Pit?'

'You can buy anything in the Pit.'

'And how would I get there? On one of those godforsaken mules, I suppose.'

'A mule? You'd never make it alive. You'd need a better vehicle than that. And an escort. And they don't come cheap.'

'I can pay.'

'With what, ma'am? Don't the Accord seize the assets of their dead?'

The General shoots her a withering look. 'I have an anonymous account, out of reach of the Accord. How much would you charge, since you know so much about this place?'

'Me?' Falco smirks. 'More than you could afford.'

'I'm not in the mood to barter with criminals. Name your price.'

Falco does. A figure so absurdly high it's laughable. But the General only grunts.

'For that amount of money, I'd expect a guarantee of safe passage. And your word that you won't sell me out to the Accord.'

'I'll guarantee passage, and if I receive a better offer for your head, I'll do the courtesy of letting you know.'

The General stares up at Falco, her lined face stony. Abruptly, she turns to me. 'You, traitor. Do you trust her?'

She has nothing, I realise. Without the Accord she is totally alone, and she knows it. 'Slightly more than anyone else on this moon.'

Falco smiles. 'Then you're going soft.'

The General nods briskly. 'Very well. It's a deal. You'll take me to this Pit.'

'And what about the Doc?' Falco demands. 'She risked her neck to save yours.'

'Her conscience has repaid her, no doubt. I'll send some money to settle our debt when I'm safely off-world.' The General raises an eyebrow at me. 'Agreed, traitor?'

Looking at her, something squirms in my chest, like a grub held to a flame. There would always be a debt.

'No,' I say softly.

They want me to go with her, I'm certain of it.

'*Here's* the deal,' Falco interrupts. 'I take both of you to the Pit. You pay half upfront, half there, and you guarantee to give the Doc whatever she's owed. If you cheat me, my people will find you, and the fact you're a kid won't mean shit to them.' She bends down. 'Agreed, sweetie?'

The General's smile is like steel. 'Agreed.'

•

'Taking a holiday, Mala?'

The wagon lurches to a halt. I lie as still as I can, trying to breathe evenly through the mask. Despite Falco's promises, the stench is almost worse than the waste tank. It makes my eyes flood and my throat close. For the second time in less than a day I fight down nausea.

The General lies next to me, tense with rage. She's furious, has been ever since Falco insisted she cut her hair, saying it marked her as Accord a mile-off.

They argued about it and, of course, Falco won. The General snatched the scissors from Pegeen and spitefully hacked at the thick, black bob until it stuck out in an uneven crop. Coupled with the baggy, colourful clothes it makes her look all the younger – like the child she truly is. Her anger hadn't abated when she saw Falco's foolproof method for sneaking us out of Landfall past the sentries.

Now, I hear Falco's muffled laugh from the front of the wagon.

'Holiday?' she calls down to the soldier. 'This is business. Some things you can't trust to anyone else.'

Behind us, a squeal of brakes: the G'hals pulling up on their mares.

'Riding with a crew, huh?' There's an edge of humour in the guard's voice. 'Must be something good under there. You're not running arms again?'

'Me, Segun? That would be illegal. No, I'm diversifying. Agriculturally speaking.'

'Didn't have you down as a muck-pedlar.'

'Business is business. And since the bovine flu killed off half the cattle on Brovos, fertiliser is *big* business.'

Another snort. 'Alright, Mala. Ride safe. I hear there's dangerous folk out there.'

'Don't I know it. May your thoughts be clear, Seg.'

A slap on the side of the wagon, and we're rolling again. Another few metres, and we'll be free…

'Stop!'

The wagon lurches and I roll against the General. I feel her rapid breathing, but don't dare move, not when I hear the whine of guns charging, boots in the dust and angry voices.

'Private,' someone barks. 'The order is to search and verify all cargo leaving the settlement. Has this wagon been searched?'

'Well no, sir, but…'

I tense as a corner of the tarpaulin is thrown back. There's a silence.

'What the hell is this?' a choked voice demands.

'Snake guts,' Falco calls down from her seat, voice dripping scorn. 'Prime trimmings and gristle, combined with waste from the kitchens, all rich in nitrates, *sir*. Care for a sample?'

'Don't push me. Where are you taking it?'

'Out to New Despair. Word is the ranches are in dire need of organic matter. They're paying double.'

'You're a goddam vulture, Falco.'

'If you're done with my goods?'

There's another silence, before finally, the tarp is dropped. 'We'll be watching. Those G'hals of yours better not get any ideas while you're gone.'

'Ideas? Never. Though they might have a notion or two.' She stomps the wagon's pedal, sending us shooting forwards in a cloud of choking dust.

Half an hour later, in the wilds beyond the Air Line tracks, we're finally able to slide free from our fetid hiding place. As soon as she gets the respirator off her face, the General starts to heave and retch.

'You bitch,' she croaks at Falco.

Falco just laughs at her, though she'd have anyone else who called her that beaten to a pulp. She hands me a canteen of water. 'You alright, Doc?'

I suck in a breath, pulling the thin desert air into my lungs. 'No worse than swimming in a waste tank.' I look around. 'What's the plan?'

'We're losing the muck, you'll be pleased to know.' Pegeen unhooks the trailer from Falco's wagon, and reattaches it to two of the mares. They're beautiful vehicles, up close; sleeker and faster than mules, painted in blue and gold dazzle, to blend with the desert shadows, I realise.

'Take it to the nearest ranch,' Falco is telling the G'hals who wait, 'we might as well make some cash from it. Peg, you're with us. And Boots.' She nods to another of the G'hals with half-shaved short blue hair and thick-lensed glasses.

I climb onto the wagon, thankfully behind the driver's seat this time, and settle the new hat onto my head. Falco's clothes, I have to admit, are far better quality than my old ones, including as they do an armoured vest. At the last minute, without a word, Falco handed me a patterned scarf to hide my neck. Sometimes I wonder how much she suspects.

The General is already hunkered down in a seat, looking smaller than ever in a huge yellow canvas jacket, a bandana tied over her head to hide the tattoos. Although she has stopped heaving, the fabric over her forehead is wet with perspiration, and her lips pale and compressed.

In a few months, perhaps less, your body will fail you completely.

Is she truly dying? Or was that a lie, to trick her into submitting to her own termination?

Either way, there are no answers in Landfall. Falco kicks the engine into life, the G'hals whoop, and the wagon takes off, towards the hard white line of the horizon.

•

It will take almost two days' riding to reach the Pit. We push the wagon hard, stopping only to relieve ourselves, or when the engines threaten to overheat beneath the beating sun. Falco – ever restless – passes the time by telling stories of her many adventures across the settled planets, from running an illegal poker den on a mining ship, to hawking stolen tinned peaches, to swindling a pair of bounty hunters in the Golden Web.

'Doc, I ever tell you about the first scam I ran, in the AC?'

The General's head jerks up.

'*You* were in the Accord?' she asks.

'How can you ask me that?' Falco replies in mock-outrage. 'I joined up first chance I got to do my duty as a star-born daughter. To fight for law and order across our brave, new system and defeat the anarchists who threatened to tear us apart.'

I catch her grin in the wing mirror and fight back a smile of my own. There aren't many who can make me laugh about the FL, these days.

'If you were in the Accord,' the General says suspiciously, 'what happened to your tattoo?'

'Had it removed. Properly, not by some drunk with a soldering iron.'

'That's illegal.'

'Oh, I'll tell the beautician who did it. I'm sure he'll hand himself in.'

The General huffs and turns away, but I can tell she's curious. 'What division were you?' she asks at last.

'Thirty-fourth Security, the Pangolins.'

'Security,' the General scoffs. 'Should've known.'

'We had a very important job, *ma'am*, escorting all those necessities to the front, stopping the FL from hijacking such fine, top-class, Prosper-made goods…'

I listen, eyes half-closed against the sunset. All of us fought different wars. Falco's seemed full of opportunity and near misses and daring deals. But – I know – these stories of hers are a kind of armour, a coating of words around pain to make it safe, to stop it bleeding into the everyday.

Finally, after hours, I must have slept, for I wake to find the wagon slowing in the emptiness beneath a brilliant, star-strewn sky.

Falco cuts the engine, the G'hals stop their mares. My ears ring in the sudden silence. There's no wind, no voices; the sands are dead still, the stars throbbing strangely through the terraform. For a moment, in that haze of waking, I imagine I am back on Ty-Hala, that my best friend Adán and I have snuck out of the dormitory onto the flat roof of the Children's Domicile to lie and look at the stars.

In those days, the central planets were nothing to us but lights in the sky. We would pick them out and recite what we knew, gleaned from bulletins and the occasional advertisement. The faint shimmering blue light was Prosper, Adán would say, where no one touched the ground or knew anyone else's name. I would reply by pointing to the darkness and telling him of far-distant Brovos at the very edge of the known system, where strange fungi covered the ground and there were twenty animals to every person and the cows were bred as big as elephants. We would thrill each other with talk of seedy, bustling Jericho, where whole cities existed between warehouse walls, even the distant whispers of the border moons, promising land and freedom.

Lying there, we felt we were special, star-born, one of the first generations conceived and raised away from Earth, and all those worlds were waiting for us to make our marks upon them.

Well, I had achieved that.

I look down. The General sleeps, curled in a tight ball. Dust has settled on her face, in the wrinkles at the edges of her eyes that should not be there. Which planet or moon did she come from? Does she even know? Gently, I slip the coat from my shoulders and cover her with it.

'She looks so small, don't she?' Pegeen whispers, as I climb down. 'Like a real kid.'

I try to smile. A *real kid*. Were any of us real, anymore?

'I keep thinking,' Peg continues, as we start to make a fire and

Falco and Boots see to the wagon, 'I could've been like that. If I'd been a few years younger.'

'How so?'

Peg sighs, balling up leaf fibres. 'Minority Force are mostly orphans, right? Pulled outta the camps and shelters. Like me.'

'Was it the war took your parents?' I ask carefully.

'Nah. Folks didn't have politics. They were scrappers on Delos for years, finally saved enough to buy a farm, near Renown. It's what Ravage used to be called.'

I wince. 'Yellowrot?'

'Accord always said it spread from black-market fertiliser, but everyone knew it came up out of the ground.' Peg bends, squinting at the dry matter as a flame takes hold. The flickers of light catch upon the deep pockmarks that scatter their face and neck. 'Folks died quick and that were a blessing. My sister fought it for months...' Peg trails off. 'They put me and my brother Joby in a quarantine unit for a year before we shook it. Took the ranch as payment for the medical bill.'

I throw a ball of fibre onto the crackling flames. I've heard the same thing many times over, on Factus and on other neglected moons. The FL made a point of collecting stories like these.

'What happened to you both?'

Peg shrugs. 'Put in the Institute, in Otroville. Cracked out of there when I was sixteen and hooked up with a raiding party. Joby joined the Accord when he was old enough and got posted to some satellite at the other ass-end of the system so I was on my own. Until I tried to rob one of Falco's couriers.' Peg's eyes light up with a smile. 'She offered me to join, and now—'

'Now I got the best damn shot from here to Delos at my side,' Falco says, dropping down beside the fire, planting a loud kiss on Peg's face.

Peg laughs, pulling the goggles from Falco's head. 'Look at these. Filthy again.'

'Why bother cleaning both lenses?'

'What about you, Doc?' Boots asks, dumping down an armful of blankets. 'You got family?'

I hesitate, unsure of what to say.

'Enough chat.' Falco reaches for the supplies. 'I want my dinner.'

I catch her eye, grateful, and she gives me a small nod.

Together, we prepare the food – or rather, I get in the way while Falco, Peg and Boots work in well-practised unison. Boots is the best cook, having laboured for a time with a prison detail on a mining satellite. 'Damn machines ate better than we did,' she says as she stirs pseudosalt and cricket powder and dried protein into a thick porridge. 'Fine oils, fancy lubricants, all we got was dehydrated nutrient paste. Got so sick of it, we boiled it up with whatever we could find.' She sticks her foot out. 'And since prison-issue shoes are made from bovine collagen…'

'Boots?' I laugh.

'Boots,' she agrees. 'Was probably half out of my mind but I swear it tasted better.' She doles out the food. 'At least this is salty.'

'Close your eyes and it could be grits,' Falco says, looking doubtfully at her bowl. 'Almost.'

'Gabi told me leave her alone. Says she'd rather sleep than eat whatever muck we're cooking,' Peg says, coming back from the wagon, where the General is curled on the seats.

'Kids these days got no manners.' Nevertheless, Boots spoons out a portion to set aside.

We eat, Boots telling funny stories about her time in the mines, Falco and I laughing around mouthfuls of food, Peg rolling their eyes, and for a few minutes, we could be any group of travellers sat in the night, filling our stomachs. But then the food is finished, the plates and pots scraped clean with sand. Falco and Peg go off for a few moments together, Boots to relieve herself, and I am left alone. I should go and check on the General. There's every chance her absence is due to illness rather than any lingering resentment, but in that quiet, I find myself letting go, thoughts unravelling like cotton thread.

'You won't save her.'

I look up, my eyes dry and hot from the fire, no idea how much time has passed. Beyond the light's edge, Boots already dozes on her blanket. There's no sign of Pegeen. Falco sits opposite me, her fine-boned face drawn, the shadows pooling in her empty eye socket.

'What?' I ask, as Falco takes a swig from a bottle of benzene.

'I said, you won't save her.'

I scuff my boot through the dust. 'I have to try.'

'Then try, but don't hold out hope.' Falco sighs. 'I've known kids like her. Not ones from the M-Force. Just kids who had everything taken from them, their memories, even their names, had it replaced by war and learned too soon to hate. Can't think of many who lived long enough to learn a different way to be.'

'She might.' I toy with the scarf around my neck. 'Anyway, I think *they* want her to live.'

'The Accord want her dead.'

'I don't mean the Accord.' The fire crackles between us, struggling with its own meal.

'You talking about the Ifs?' Falco says slowly.

'Something has been happening to me, Mala,' I murmur to the sand. 'I know you'll think I'm mad but I've been sensing *them*. More and more these days. Sometimes, it's like they're showing me things that haven't happened, or that might happen.'

I risk a glance at her, waiting for her to scoff or laugh, but she doesn't, just stares at me. I can't hold that piercing gaze, so I look down at my hands, trying to think of some way to explain.

'I'm from the Congregations, did you know that?' I ask eventually.

Falco shakes her head, thoughtful, as if filing everything I say away for later use. 'Always wondered why you speak the way you do. Sort of old fashioned. Didn't have you down as religious, though.'

'I'm not, not now. My faith didn't last long, once I left. But back on Ty-Hala, my fathers used to talk about God's will,

God's grace. I didn't really understand at the time, but…' I grip my arms, hard. 'What if it was never God's will? What if it has always been *theirs*?' I was raised to believe that what I am about to say is the worst kind of heresy, but I force myself on. 'Perhaps *they* have always been with us, but people were too noisy to hear them, too distant, back on Earth. Perhaps we only felt them faintly and people called what they felt God or luck or fate, but now we are out here, surrounded by so much space and silence, and some of us can feel them properly for the first time. Feel *their* will.'

Falco's expression is indecipherable as she takes a long drink of benzene. 'I don't know about God,' she says at last, passing over the bottle, 'but you're crazier than I thought.'

There's no answer I can give. I raise the bottle to my lips when out of the darkness comes a yip, and a whistle. Falco's head jerks up, her hand flying to her gun.

'What is it?' I ask.

'Peg's seen something.'

She draws the weapon. The next second Pegeen appears, breathless, holding a pair of night-vision binoculars.

'Birds, a whole flock of them. Coming from the east.'

'Seekers?'

'No. Not Accord neither. Looks like bandits.'

'How far?'

'Twenty klicks. Maybe less. They'll have seen the fire.'

Falco swears and kicks sand over the embers.

I grab up the blankets while Peg shakes Boots awake. 'There is still a warrant on me for that Kwalkavich business,' I say. 'And if they've come from Landfall…'

'It won't be that.' Falco looks over her shoulder. 'They're hunting.'

Within a minute she hauls herself into the driving seat, arming her guns. I scramble up behind her as she starts the engine.

That's when I hear it, the distant churn of engines cutting the still air, growing louder. For a moment, the stars spin in my vision. *Cold metal, hot blood, pain on the wings of black birds…*

The wagon screeches forwards.

'What's going on?' The General is awake, grabbing hold of the seat.

'Company,' I yell, snatching up a pair of binoculars that hang beside Falco, blinking hard to clear my vision.

In the pale light of the near and distant moons, I see twin clouds of dust: Pegeen's and Boots's mares racing behind us. And beyond them…

Shapes, like ragged holes punched in the stars. Eight craft, low-flying and slick-winged, a painted shimmering oil-black.

'It's the Rooks!' I yell.

The wagon picks up speed, rattling and groaning at a pace it will never be able to keep.

'Whoever they are, they're closing in,' the General calls, kneeling on the seat beside me. 'Convergence in five, four, three…'

'Hold on!' Falco bellows.

I grab for purchase as she wrenches the wheel, sending the wagon whipping out, fishtailing to one side, then the other. Pegeen and Boots do the same, kicking dust into a blinding cloud.

I can't see, can't breathe, all I can do is hold on. Nearby, someone yells. It takes me several seconds to realise it's the General. I open one eye a sliver to see her crouching low in the seat, shouting something I can't hear over the noise of the engines.

A rushing sound, and fire zips past. Too late I realise it's on Falco's blind side; I holler for her even as the explosion sends the wagon reeling onto two wheels before crashing back to the dirt. Falco swears, craning to see the damage. Something booms and splutters to our right; Boots's mare smashes into the ground, billowing black smoke. Peg breaks rank to speed towards it, pale hair streaming out behind as Falco screams in rage.

My knuckles are white on the back of the seat, but beside me the General is on the floor of the wagon, scrambling with something as she's thrown from side to side.

An almighty roar, a scream of metal and I know it is too late. The greasy belly of a craft appears above us; an automatic turret dropping down.

'Low!' the General yells. 'Keep me steady!'

She leaps onto the seats, a rifle in her arms. Falco veers again, and the General almost falls before I grab her legs tight.

She stares up at the craft, her dark eyes narrowed in concentration. Even when the turret spits charges she does not flinch, just takes aim and fires.

There's a hiss and liquid streams out behind the craft. I smell fuel and tug on her, yelling for her to get down as another round of charges smashes into the wagon, but she isn't listening. Like a machine she lowers the gun, reloads and fires once again.

And in between the flashes of bullets and charges, I feel *them*. They are not here for me, I realise in horror; they want her. Can she see them as they whirl, tasting, feasting on her, savouring every eventuality that she embodies?

I want to drag her out of sight, hide her from *them*, even though it will not help. If *they* have seen her, they will follow us, they will tug at the threads of both our lives until we walk in chaos.

I cry a warning, but it's too late. She pulls the trigger, and the Rook's fuel tank explodes in a paroxysm of flames, sending it crashing to earth.

●

We don't stop until we're certain we are not being followed.

'Is it safe, here?' I croak, in the abrupt silence.

'Don't know.' Falco pulls the scarf from her face. She looks haggard. 'But the engine is fit to bust. If we don't let it cool we won't make it another mile, let alone to the Pit.'

'You think they'll follow us?'

'Moloney might look like a bit of meat with eyes, but he's a vicious bastard. Rooks don't dare mess with us in Landfall. Out here though…'

A mare rumbles up beside us. It carries Pegeen and a second, slumped figure.

'Boots is hurt!' Peg yells.

The other G'hal is bleeding heavily from a head wound, her glasses missing, her skin grazed and torn from scalp to hip. She's conscious, but barely. When we slide her from the back of the mare, she lets out a cry of pain.

Falco's eye is bright with tears as she holds Boots's face. 'Doc?'

'Bring her up here.' I unclip the medkit. 'I can treat her as we ride.'

The General gives up her seat. All the savage energy of the fight has left her, and now her eyes are raw and red, her face strained beneath a paste of dust and fuel.

'What can I do?' she asks.

I glance at her. Had she fought in the war like that, with so little thought for her own life? Or is it the recklessness of the dying? 'You have done enough,' I say.

'We owe you our lives,' Pegeen agrees, tearfully.

Falco shakes her head. 'Never thought I'd be thanking a starred General of the Accord for anything, but Peg's right. You saved our hides back there. Though god knows how you did it.'

The General smiles at last, her dry lips cracking. 'That ship was a repurposed scout. A Peregrine 420. They have a tank in the belly for easy refuelling. Stupid design.'

'Still, must have been a thousand to one chance of hitting a target like that, let alone moving, let alone in the dark.'

The General shrugs. 'For you, maybe.'

I know what she means. For us ordinary humans. I stay quiet as Falco starts the engine and we move on, concentrating on treating Boots, and ignoring the clash of awe and pity and horror that fills me every time I look at the General.

Finally, when Boots's wounds are dressed and she lies on the seats, breathing more easily, I look down. The General hunches on the floor of the wagon in her yellow jacket, like a sick bird, her eyes closed.

'How are you feeling?' I ask awkwardly, reaching to touch her forehead.

She snatches her head away, but not before I feel that, in the already warm morning, she is far hotter than any human should be.

'Don't concern yourself,' she says, licking her cracked lips.

'General—'

'I am fine. Only sick of being in this damn box on wheels.' She lets her head fall back, her eyes close. 'I used to have my own scout ship you know. A Hawk. It was a beautiful thing. Intelligent steering, stabilisation coils, self-adjusting atmospheric pressure. Never thought I'd be stuck on the ground like this, crawling along like a beetle.'

I don't answer. *It began two years ago, with the A-series.* The Commander's words come back to me. *As they aged, they simply broke down. It's a painful, wretched end.*

'What series are you?' I ask.

The General doesn't open her eyes. 'C. There were thirteen of us. Raised at the base on Voivira, whittled down from hundreds.' Her lips twitch. 'The best class the Accord ever produced, according to reports. Late enough for the accelerated cognition process to have been ironed out, early enough that the programme had not yet been diluted to suit the bleeding hearts.' She opens one eye. 'D-series onwards are little better than figureheads. Not fit for battle. Not like us.'

I turn away.

It's genius, I think, staring at the passing desert, brilliant with morning light. Calculated, twisted genius. Not only because the children it produced are near super-human, but because they are devoted to their cause as only the young can be. Because only a sociopath would fail to feel some pity for them. Whatever the General had done, however many atrocities she had committed, I can never forget that, beneath the scars and fierce intelligence, she should have been an ordinary child. And she knows that. Uses it.

But still, I can't shake the feeling that *they* are using her too.

'The way you fired at that craft,' I say. 'Did you... feel anything?'

'What do you mean?' she snaps, but behind the insolence I hear fear and know I am right.

'You're not going mad,' I say, over the clatter of the wagon. 'It's *them*, it was the same for me in the beginning—'

But my words are cut off as the wagon bumps over something hard and metallic buried in the sand.

'That's a warning platform,' Falco calls. 'Be on your guard. We're coming up to the Pit.'

Ahead, metal glints in the sun. Strange shapes are set at regular intervals along the road, on either side of the trail. As we draw closer, my stomach contracts.

They are cages, ugly boxes half-dug into the ground. When we pass the first an arm shoots out, clawing at the air with bloodied nails. We pass another, and another. Some look empty, others seethe with flies, dried gore soaking the dust before them.

My heart beats hard in my throat. Beside me, the General has lost her usual stony expression, staring in disgust and dismay.

'We have to stop,' I say. 'There are people alive in there.'

Falco's jaw is tight, but she continues to drive, looking straight ahead.

'Much as I hate to say it, the traitor's right, why the hell haven't we turned around?' the General demands.

'We turn around, we're carrion,' Falco says. 'Told you there was a new Pit Boss. Guess this is their way of cleaning things up.'

A few minutes later we come to a watchtower, built from rusted scraps. Beyond, a huge crater yawns. The sides are lost in shadow, but deep within something glints. A thin cord dangles from the tower, disappearing beneath the dust of the road. Falco stops the wagon clear enough that I guess it is the fuse for some kind of explosive.

'Well,' a voice hoots. 'If it ain't Lady Sickness herself.'

A figure is seated high on the tower, beneath a shade of corrugated metal. I catch a glimpse of a sun-bleached yellow jacket, bright eyes in a wind-battered face.

Falco rolls her eyes, motioning Pegeen down as the G'hal snarls and reaches for their gun. 'I have a name, Carve,' she calls, squinting up from beneath the brim of her hat. 'How're the lice?'

'Hell, I'm clean as a bean now,' the man says, even as he scratches at himself. 'Who ya got with ya?' He leans down, hands on his scabbed knees. 'Hey there, Pegeen. When you gonna stop runnin' with such a bad character and come live with me? I'll take care a ya.'

'I'd take care of you first, gutspill,' Pegeen says. 'Probably in your sleep.'

'You gonna let us in?' Falco demands.

The man's leer falters. 'I ain't supposed to let no one in without the Boss saying so.'

'Heard y'all had a new boss.' Falco jerks her head back at the cages. 'Hard one too, by the looks of it.'

Carve shifts. 'Boss made a deal with the Seekers. We give them tribute, act as brokers for their offal, they leave us alone. Good deal, good for all of us.' He does not sound too certain.

'Doubt those in the cages agree.'

The man spits. 'They had a chance to turn their minds to it. Anyhow, they're going to a better place, Boss says. Boss says Seekers ain't all bad, that people got it wrong about them, that they're only part of the balance, looking for the truth…'

He lapses into silence, as if he has forgotten the reasons for the prisoners to be cheerful.

'Air-starved lunatics,' the General mutters.

Quiet as it is, Carve hears her. 'Who ya got down there?' His sharp eyes flick across me to the General. 'Who's that? And the brat?'

'This is the Doc,' Falco says coolly. 'And the kid's a new recruit.'

The man smirks. 'Ain't she a mite young to be a G'hal?'

'Ain't you a mite dumb to be a sentry?' the General shoots back.

The man hoots and slaps his knees. 'She's the type, alright.'

Falco sighs. 'Carve, let us in. We got business to see to.'

'I told you, Falco, I ain't meant to. Gotta ask the Boss.'

Falco reaches under the seat to pull out a bag. 'I was going to give you a couple of airtights for the inconvenience, but I guess if you don't want them…'

She opens the bag to reveal tins, gleaming silver in the desert light.

'What?' Carve licks his dry lips. 'What you got there?'

'Pears in syrup. Tomatoes all the way from Prosper. Beans in brine. Fish—'

'Fish?' The word falls from Carve's mouth like drool. He tears his eyes from the bag to glance behind him, an agonised look on his face.

'Alright,' he blurts out a second later. 'Throw 'em up and I'll let ya in. Quick, I'll be corpsified if they see.' Rapidly, he turns a wheel, spooling the fuse like a hissing black snake. 'Go and tie up at Melc's place, level four. It's quiet there.'

Falco wastes no time. The second the road is clear, she revs the wagon, and rolls towards a tunnel at edge of the crater, Pegeen following close behind.

'My fish!' Carve yells.

Snorting, Falco flings the sack from the side of the wagon. 'Welcome to the Pit.'

•

If my first impression of the Pit was bad, my second does nothing to improve matters. I see the gloom first, then the yawning abyss of a crater so deep that it seems to have no end. Sand and dust blow constantly over the edge, cascading like water through the metal gantries that encircle the perimeter.

The gantry we drive in on has no edge and clanks and shakes beneath the weight of the wagon. Across the Pit, I see a platform: a landing site for ships and crafts. I look away from the vast drop and close my eyes.

The General sees. 'Don't tell me you're afraid of heights,' she mocks.

I smile tightly, not opening my eyes. Sweat breaks out on my neck. It's not only the height that troubles me. It's the structure. For all it's on solid ground instead of floating through space, the Pit is the very image of a prison hulk.

It makes a horrible kind of sense, I realise. Convict labour built the hulks, and convicts were among the first to settle on Factus, and so they built what they knew. The Pit has the same metal gantries, spiralling around an empty core. No comfort, no relief, just metal constantly clanging and reverberating until the sound found its way into your head, your ears, your eyes, your very soul.

Better any of the work camps than the hulks, people always said. There, at least, there was some pretence at paying off a debt to society, some suggestion of a future where that debt is paid. On the hulks, there was only reality, hard and cold and unyielding. A place for people to be forgotten, to drift in a clanking, shuddering metal cage through space until mind or body gave in. A place for those beyond redemption.

I grip the scarf around my neck, trying to forget the terrible months before I made the decision to live, feeling again the collar bite into my neck as I lay on the hard bunk. *Remember the tally*.

I only open my eyes when darkness closes over our heads. We are in a sort of cave, carved into the rock. All around are mules and mares, wagons and charabancs, none as nice as Falco's. We slide to a stop.

'Melc?' Falco calls.

There's a scuffling and a grey-bearded man trips out from behind a threadbare curtain.

'What the—' He stares at us, eyes bulging from his head. 'What the hell are you doing? I didn't hear the alarm.'

'Carve let us in.' Falco jumps from the wagon. 'Fool will do anything for a tin of fish.'

'Including lose his damn life if the Boss finds out.' The man wipes anxiously at his face. 'Boss ain't gonna like this at all.'

Pegeen pulls up alongside us, and I climb down to help with Boots. The General follows, the rifle over her shoulder.

'Been hearing a little too much about this new boss,' Falco says. 'Can't say I like it much.'

'Falco,' Melc whines, before he looks around and sees Boots sagging in our arms. 'No.' His face turns a shade greyer. 'No, no, you can't bring her in.' His eyes find the General. 'And a *child*, here? What the hell are you thinking?'

'Melc, you asshole,' Pegeen spits. 'Boots is hurt. How long you known her? She needs to rest.'

'I'm sorry, Peg, I truly am, but you gotta understand.' He turns pleadingly to Falco. 'If the Boss finds out she's wounded, there won't *be* no discussion, she'll be out in one of them cages like a shot. Boss says we can't waste healing on the sick, when the Seekers can use them. We gotta give them to Hel as tribute.'

'Anyone so much as looks at Boots, there'll be a bullet in their skull,' Falco warns softly. 'That goes for the kid too. Now, we had a hard ride and I'm not in a chatting mood. We need rest and food and drink. And my friends here need to find a ship.'

'Can't do it.' The man backs away. 'Can't do it. No one's gonna serve you 'til you've seen the Augur.'

'The Augur?' Falco's patience is rapidly fading.

'The Boss. That's what we call them.' Melc cringes. 'Please, if you don't go declare yourselves, I'm a dead man.'

I shift my weight, and Boots let out a groan. 'Where is this Boss?' I ask.

The man jerks his head. 'Over the way, in Geremy's old bar.'

'And where's Geremy?'

Melc glances meaningfully at the crater.

'Fine,' Falco snaps. 'Take us there.' She catches his shoulder in an iron grip as he scurries past. 'And if anything happens to Boots, you die first.'

•

We follow Melc down a clanking lift and onto a lower gantry. Just as in the hulks, the gantries are half-caged, to discourage folk throwing themselves off, I suppose.

My bloody hand slips from the cable, sending me plummeting, past two gantries, three, knowing there is nothing at the bottom to break my fall, just more metal.

Pegeen nudges me, and I blink the memory clear, feeling sick. 'Look.'

Across the Pit, a strange two-storey building juts into the space over the crater, supported by rusted girders. There is even a veranda, like a mocking version of the grand, palatial villas that scatter the lagoons of Prosper. Only this one has a roof of corrugated iron, down which dust constantly trickles.

We are still some way off when there's a shriek from the building. I see a figure plummet down into the darkness.

'Thought you said this place has been cleaned up,' Peg mutters.

'It has,' Melc assures us. 'See, there ain't hardly any fights, now. Not worth it. You get injured, chances are you're gonna end up in the cages, rather than patched by the Quack.' His eyes flick to the building. 'Unless the Augur thinks you're worthy. Like me.' He shows us his scratched teeth in an attempted smile.

'Isn't this place supposed to be full of crooks?' the General retorts.

Melc chuckles nervously. 'Sure is, little lady.'

She holds his gaze. 'Then why are you all acting like bootlickers?'

'Whatever's going on,' Falco says over Melc's splutters, 'I don't like it. Never seen this place so quiet.'

We pass openings the size of cells in the crater's walls. Many are fitted out as stores, selling everything from dried snake meat and live grubs to vehicle parts and old wire-and-picture shows. Others are sleeping quarters or benzeneries. Outside one, a woman wearing battered body armour calls to Pegeen and waves, her eyes momentarily brighter, before leaning over to spit into the depths below.

But many of the cells are dark; their contents ransacked, their doors kicked in, their owners gone. Whatever has happened here, from the tension in Falco's shoulders, I know it's not good.

'Alright,' Melc says sourly, when we reach the walkway that leads out to the building. 'This is it.'

I try not to look down. There are no railings, nothing between the edge of the rickety walkway and the crater below.

'If you've double-crossed us, Melc…' Falco starts.

'No, no.' The man backs away, his eyes fixed on the top level of the building, which glints with strange flashes of light. 'Just doing as the Augur asks.'

Falco sighs and looks around at us all. 'Don't let your guard down. If things go bad, be prepared to run.' Her eye rests on

Boots, who is in no state to do anything of the sort. For the first time, I see a flicker of worry cross her face. Peg reaches out and squeezes Falco's arm hard, before renewing their grip on Boots.

Slowly, we make our way out onto the walkway. Before we are halfway across, figures step from the building, bulky-looking charge guns levelled.

'State your purpose,' one yells.

There are six of them, all wearing armoured vests. I drag my attention away, back to what Falco is saying.

'... here to rest, and do business and be on our way.'

'That one looks injured.'

'She is. And if anyone tries to injure her further, they'll be taking a dive from this platform.' Falco's hand edges towards her gun, but the guards don't move.

'That is for the Augur to decide.' A jerk of the weapon. 'This way. Leave your guns at the door.'

Our steps shake the metal walkway.

'You still got that knife in your belt?' the General murmurs.

I give a small nod. 'Not much use against a charge gun.'

'Not in *your* hands.'

Inside, traces of a saloon remain: the bar itself, a broken picture screen, a few posters for off-world pharmaceuticals and chemical fertilisers, some scratched metal tables and a sticky-looking auto-piano. But now, instead of customers, the entire place is stacked with cages. Rats, mice, snakes, birds, even bats, all rustle and squawk and scurry. The place stinks of their faeces.

'What the…' Pegeen gapes, grey eyes huge. 'What the hell is *that*?'

The General peers. 'It's a guinea pig, what does it look like?'

'How am I supposed to know? Ain't never seen one before. Looks like good eating.'

'Ugh.' The General almost laughs.

'Live contraband,' Falco murmurs, 'must be thousands of credits' worth here.'

'Drop the weapons and get moving,' the guard with the gun orders, nudging us towards a set of stairs.

A man stands behind the bar, watching us pass with dull eyes, until he notices the General.

'Here, Ona,' he says. 'Can't the kid stay with me? I'll watch her, she don't need to see that shit up there.' He smiles at the General; a sickly expression. 'Got a bottle of nice, fresh cactus syrup here, little lady.'

The General's eyes flick to the pistol that hangs at the man's hip. 'Gee, mister, that's mighty kind—'

'Save it. She ain't no kid. Anyway, Boss wants to see them all.' The guard meets my eyes. 'We've been waiting for you.'

•

At the guard's knock, the door swings open, dazzling us with light. I squint as, slowly, the room beyond takes shape. There are windows on every side. Beneath each of them a mirror bounces the desert light like a slap. At the centre of that glare sits a figure, someone with deep brown, searching eyes that look into mine.

Valdosta.

A gun in my back pushes me forwards. The more I stare, the more I feel as if my mind is slipping loose. It *is* Valdosta, I'm sure of it, and yet there are impossible differences. This person is missing the tip of one ear; they have tattoos, old and faded across their knuckles that I'm certain the charlatan Valdosta lacked. The hair is the same, black and curling, but the shimmering paint and the twirling ribbons are gone, replaced by a tight-fitting outfit of silver-shot black that must have come from a city planet. Their thickly lined eyes are almost all pupil, despite the harsh glare. I shudder, doubting my own mind, my own memories.

Not for the first time.

'They got past the gate, Boss,' the guard with the gun says. 'Melc brought them here.'

Valdosta breaks my gaze at last and looks over the others.

'Yes, Melc had that one use left.'

I squeeze my eyes closed, against the confusion, against the throbbing ache gathering in my head.

'Please,' the Augur says. 'I must finish some business before I am at leisure to talk.'

We are herded to a set of battered chairs set between two long mirrors. Pegeen immediately lowers Boots onto one, propping her up. The General throws herself into another, sprawling out a leg as she stares moodily at her own reflection. Falco raises an eyebrow at me. I catch a glimpse of my face: bewildered and pale beneath the windburn, repeated by the mirrors again and again. I swallow down nausea.

Two more guards come through the door, dragging a figure wearing a bloodied, faded blue uniform of the Free Limits.

'Hello, Four,' the Augur says lazily. 'I told you there was no use in running.'

The man in the uniform looks at us, as if we will help. One of his eyes is swollen shut. When none of us moves, he spits bloody foam at Valdosta.

'Fuck you, dogboss.'

The Augur smiles. 'In another life maybe. In this one, we seem to be pitted against each other. But I'll be fair, Four. I will give you the same chance I give everybody.' They gesture, and one of the guards places a low table before them. It holds a collection of objects; all games of chance, all banned in the townships. There are bits of straw, playing cards, even metal coins from old Earth. The shivers that run beneath my skin grow stronger when I see a set of dice, the same that clattered across Sorry Damovitch's bar.

'So,' the Augur asks, 'will you play?'

The man sniffs, wiping his bleeding nose on his sleeve. 'If I win?'

'You can be on your way.'

The man peers at the table. 'They're rigged.'

'I am a servant of fate. Why would I tamper with *their* instruments?'

I look up sharply. *Their.* My heart beats faster.

'The bones,' the man says.

Immediately, the Augur scoops up the old, yellowed dice and sends them spinning across the table.

'Fever five. Not bad.'

The man snatches the dice and holds them to his chest, before casting them.

Two twos.

He swears violently.

The Augur rolls. A four and a six.

'Ten.' Their eyes flick to mine. 'How fitting.'

Fear-sweat prickles my skin. The man's hands tremble as he snatches the dice. Deep in my chest, something lurches as he casts them a final time.

'Snake eyes.' The Augur smiles.

Guards step forwards without a word, grabbing the man by the arms.

'No!' He tries to scramble away but there's nowhere to run. One of the guards tugs a bolt from a metal door in the wall and throws it open. The wind howls in, sending playing cards flying, filling the air with dust. Below, the crater yawns.

Before I know what I'm doing, I'm on my feet, reaching for the knife hidden in my jacket. A life is a life. The tally demands it. But then, to my disbelief, the Augur holds up a hand, staring at me.

The guards stop. Three inches of floor between the man and death.

'Release him.'

Briskly, the guards back up and drop the sobbing man to the floor.

'You are lucky, Four,' the Augur says. 'Providence has spoken for you.'

The man in the uniform does not wait around to give thanks, just scrambles for the stairs. The Augur watches him go.

'He will be dead within the hour.' They sigh, before meeting my eyes once again. 'Wouldn't you say, Ten?'

•

'I would shake your hand,' the Augur says, smiling around at us. 'But you are all covered in Rook blood.'

It's true, our clothes and faces are filthy from the road, stained with dirt and streaks of fuel from the downed craft.

'They've been here? The Rooks?' Falco is rattled.

The Augur points to the mirrors. 'No. I saw it all in the glass. I saw that you would arrive here, the five of you, though I do not see you leaving together.'

'I don't like threats,' Falco says. 'And I don't like your cages.'

'It was not a threat. Merely a fact. Just as it is a fact that Moloney will seek revenge for the hurt you caused his Rooks. Just as it is a fact that the General here is being hunted by the Accord.'

I flinch, as does Pegeen. The General only narrows her eyes.

'Any fool with a wire could have found that out,' she says.

I force myself to look into Valdosta's eyes. It is like looking at a reflection of a person when the real one was standing just behind your shoulder.

'And, Low,' they say. 'So good to see you again.'

I know the others are staring at me, wondering whether I have lied.

The Augur rises from the chair. 'Remind me, where did we meet? This world? Another? Have *they* crossed the paths of realities once again?' They catch hold of my wrist with fingers that are too cold for the desert. '*They* follow you as they follow me. They have saved me, haunted me, scattered me across worlds, and they will not tell me why.' The Augur pulls me closer. 'I have been waiting so long for someone else who knows what it is to be chosen by them.'

I wrench my wrist away, terrified. And yet, part of me is desperate to know if I'm right, if *they* truly are real and not just a trick of my fraying mind. Falco hisses my name but I can't look away. The Augur drags something from a large, covered cage beneath the mirrors; a desert snake, sinewy and scarred, flailing in their grip.

They slam it down, take out a knife and plunge it into the creature's skull. While it twitches, they hack at the belly, spilling guts onto the table. Behind me, the General lets out a noise of disgust.

'Rook,' the Augur whispers, sorting through the organs, 'Longrider. Spindigo. Hell.'

The hairs of my neck stand on end as the old woman's voice comes back to me, that night at the snake ranch.

'I see it now.' The Augur's eyes are shining. 'I see. You have not made the choice yet. First you must die. You and the dead General must walk to hell.'

'I'm not dead,' the General snaps, her voice shaking. 'Why do people keep saying that? I'm not.'

'But you are. It's already too late.' The Augur grips the knife and shouts to the guards. 'Take them all to the cages. Take them for the Converter.'

In the split-second that follows, everything seems to expand, like a vast, invisible explosion. Images crash through my mind, paths shooting across realities, every outcome tangles with a thousand others. I see the General staggering beneath a flat yellow sky, blood trailing out behind her, I see the others, lying broken on the sand, I see a ship smash to earth, its pilot dead, I see my own chest, flayed open to the ribs like the Augur's snake, someone reaching in to seize my heart…

I stagger away, trying to escape the chaos only to come face to face with my own reflection. But my eyes belong to a bird of prey, and my skin is carved with tallies and as I watch, my reflection raises a bloodied hand towards my chest.

My fists fly, shattering the mirror. Distantly, as if through water, I hear cries and shouts. I see a version of Falco spinning around to seize the arm of a guard and break it with an efficient twist, while another her kicks the same guard out of the metal door into the drop below. Pegeen taking a shot to the spine, Pegeen headbutting a guard down the stairs. And the General – she is everywhere.

I stumble towards her, watching in horror the version of her that kneels upon the Augur's chest, teeth bared. Her hand scrabbles among the glass and snake guts and comes up holding the small, curved knife.

For a moment, everything hangs in the balance. Is this the path *they* want? I don't know. All I know is that, as the General sets the blade against the Augur's throat, I throw myself forwards, and choose.

•

Blood runs over my hands, but it isn't mine; it comes from the Augur's neck, from the wound the General opened half an inch from the artery.

'Rook,' Valdosta gasps, fingers gripping their throat, 'Longrider, Spindigo—'

The next thing I know I'm downstairs, among the cacophony of caged animals, all squeaking, squealing. Someone shoves a gun into my hand.

I can't, I try to say, *I can't use it. I'm a medic,* but no words come out.

'We have to make a run for it.' Falco's voice reaches me. There's a spreading bruise on her cheek. 'Before that lunatic upstairs comes to and raises the alarm. You get separated, you're on your own, Doc. I got to get Boots out safe.'

'Leave me,' Boots wheezes, eyes flickering. 'You… go.'

'You're a G'hal,' Falco says fiercely. 'We do not leave our own behind. Injuries?'

I look around the room. The remaining guards lie slumped, dead or unconscious. Peg's pale hair is matted with blood.

'I'm fine.' They grimace as Falco grabs their face in alarm. 'Honestly, Mala, most of it isn't mine.'

'Gabi?'

The General nods. She stands above the slumped bartender, arming a pistol, her knuckles swollen and grazed.

'Doc?'

Rook. Longrider. Spindigo. Hell.

'Doc? Are you hurt?'

On the back of my hand is one long, deliberate cut. I don't remember it happening. 'No.'

With a nod, Falco kicks open the door.

The minute we step outside, we realise our mistake. People emerge from the cells on the upper gantries, alerted by the gunfire, yelling to each other, trying to fathom what's going on. All of them are armed.

Falco looks at us, her eye bright.

'Run.'

We make it all of four paces before bullets rain down, clanging and ricocheting from the metal gangway. *Run*, Falco said, but we can't, not while half-carrying Boots, not while being picked off like rats in a barrel.

A hiss and Falco staggers, one hand pressed to her leg. Pegeen yells in rage and takes out three shooters at once. I see the General swear as the pistol is blown from her grip and sent spinning into the crater. Then something smacks into my chest with enough force to send me sprawling back onto the walkway.

No air, no sound. I lie, waiting for the pain that I know will come, for the bullet to do its work and end my life. From a forgotten battlefield, I hear someone call for a medic.

My vision blurs. Across time, someone bends over me. A woman, wearing my face.

I open my eyes, my lungs convulsing, heaving in a breath. The world around looks different, clearer, sharper. Simpler. I roll onto my back. People are shooting at me. I have a pistol in my hand. Well, then. I raise the gun, sight, and fire. I don't wait to see if I hit my target before moving to the second and the third, the fourth.

Six shots, six impacts. The air rings with the fizzing silence of the space between bullets.

I stand. The four people on the walkway in front of me stare in shock and disbelief. I gesture. They run.

I run with them, checking the pistol to see how many charges are left. Six down, six to go. The weapon is warm in my hand.

The moment I step onto the gantry, I hear the whine and throw myself back. The others are knocked off their feet by an energy blast. The air shakes, rock and dust raining down. I aim the pistol at the figure holding the blaster and fire twice. They fall into the crater.

The woman with the missing eye is staggering to her feet, cut and bruised and bleeding. I know her name, but I don't care. 'East gantry,' she shouts. 'We'll take west.'

Above her, guards are already taking aim.

'Go,' I say.

She does, taking the others with her. Bullets follow them, but I drop the assailant before running in the opposite direction. When I hear footsteps clanging behind me I spin, ready to fire, three charges left.

But it is the child, the one they call the General. She holds a blaster, must have caught it as the man fell.

'Go with the others.'

'We have a better chance if we split up, divide their fire.' She spits out rock dust. 'What's the target?'

'Landing platform.' There's no doubt in my mind. 'Top level, where the ships are.'

She nods. 'I'll cover the rear.'

I run, scanning for any movement. Footsteps rattle the gantry above us: I fire and hear a cry. If this place has been built to the same plan as a prison hulk, there should be lifts at four points around the perimeter. On the hulks, the lifts ended in dead metal – blank, impassable surfaces for the mind to batter itself against – but here, the former convicts have built the escape routes they only dreamed of while drifting through space: lifts that'll take us up and out to freedom.

I see one up ahead, a clumsy-looking box made from scraps of metal with a winch beside it. A figure stands guard, raising a gun. Too slow. The child fires the blaster and they tumble over the railing.

'Get on,' I tell the child, leaning over to hammer the controls.

She does, leaping onto the lift as the winch releases, sending us shooting up through the air. Gunfire follows, of course, but it can't reach us, not now, and I let out a shout of laughter. The child beside me crouches, stony-faced, watching the highest platform approach.

I'm right. The guards, the pit fiends, whoever is shooting at us from below have not yet made it up here. It's the highest point of the crater, right on the lip, and along a rusted platform, ships and birds are waiting. I kick the lift door open and see one at the far end – a cannibalised vehicle with an unwieldy cargo bay – that looks to be the smallest, the fastest. I stride towards it.

'You're going to take that heap of junk?' the General says. 'Let me choose, there's a Hawk over there.'

'Shut up.'

'What about the others?'

'You heard what she said. We get separated, we're on our own.'

'What's happened to you?' she demands. 'Where did you learn to shoot like that?' She hurries to keep up. 'You said you didn't fight, but that was military training.'

I ignore her as I reach the ship and scan it for a second. No telling what it had once been, but hopefully its controls would be simple enough. A fuel line hangs from the side. I unlatch it and thump on the button to open its hatch.

'Answer me!' the child demands. 'What were you in the war? What aren't you telling me?'

More than you can imagine.

With a rumble, the door creaks open. From the gloom inside, a shape comes stumbling forwards, a weapon in their hand.

I take aim, and see the figure clearly.

It's a young man, wearing an ancient flight jacket and torn jeans, not a gun in his hand but a pipe. A crash of images floods my mind; countless futures dying with him. At the last second, I jerk the gun sideways, sending the bullet ricocheting above his head.

In the abrupt silence, the woman who was death, who had filled my skin, vanishes. In her place comes the crashing realisation of what I have just done, the smell of blood and the feel of the warm gun in my hand. I drop it in horror.

'You?' the General barks. 'Is this your ship?'

'What?' The man seems confused. 'Err, yes?'

She arms the blaster.

'Then fly.'

•

'You can stop pointing that at me, now,' the pilot says to the General around the pipe in his mouth. 'It's not like I'm armed.'

I open my eyes. The desert blurs past fifty feet below, grey and gold in the afternoon light.

'Do you think I'm an idiot?' the General snaps. 'Where do you keep the guns?'

'What guns?'

'The guns you have hidden somewhere.'

Silence.

'You tell me, or I will start blasting this deck open.'

The man sighs. 'Under the nav panel.'

'Get them.' There's a pause. 'Low, get them.'

I raise my head. Nothing is right. The *thing* with my face took over my body. How many did I kill? Six? Eight? Wounded more, and without treatment they will die too. The fragile lines of the tally are being scored over with new deaths. It's hopeless. No matter what I do, I only take more lives.

'Low,' the General hisses. 'We do not have time for this. Get up.'

She's standing above me, her arms straining under the weight of the blaster. Numbly, I climb to my feet.

'Get the guns.'

I edge forwards and feel underneath the scratched, blinking navigation screen. The floor around the pilot's chair is a mess of pipe ash and protein wrappers and crumpled bulletins. The wiring under the nav panel is loose too, as if it has been pulled out and repaired many times over. As soon as I feel the oily metal and plastic of the guns taped to the underside I want to recoil. I use my sleeve to rip the weapons from their hiding place and send them skidding across the deck. Two army pistols and one old-fashioned thing that fires metal bullets.

'Good,' the General says. Beneath the grazes and grime, her face is bloodless. 'Now. Tell him where he's going.'

'Don't you know?' the man asks in mild surprise. 'I mean, isn't that the point of a hijacking?'

Considering he has a gun aimed at him, he seems oddly at ease. I look at him more closely, taking in the rumpled clothes, the untied boots. They're civilian garments, the shirt intricately patterned and well-made, not army surplus like most on Factus. No facial tattoos to suggest he is ex-Accord. No scars on his neck from the hulks, no dog tags to hint that he fought somewhere, with some vigilante splinter group. His black hair is unwashed and unruly, his black moustache and vague beard speak more of laziness than a particular style. Not part of a crew, then. So what was he doing in the Pit? He glances over at me, and shifts the unlit pipe from one side of his mouth to the other.

'Eyes front,' the General orders. 'And we have not hijacked you. We have commandeered this ship. It's different.'

'It's the gun, you see, it gives the wrong impression.'

'Shut up. Is there anyone else aboard?'

'Just me.'

'And what were you doing at the Pit, alone?'

The man smiles. Good teeth, real, not fibreglass or gunmetal. 'Waiting on my cargo.' He catches my eye again. 'I'm a courier. Freelance.'

Of course. I drop into the co-pilot's seat. 'He is a smuggler,' I say.

'And now I'm a hostage. Hijackee? Is that a word?'

'Well, we'll have to ditch him.' The General looks around critically. 'I suppose I could fly this… heap. What was it before you butchered it? An Orel 250?'

'Butchered?' The man sounds genuinely offended. '*Charis* is a *hybrid*. And you wouldn't be able to fly her. No one can but me. She's a complicated lady.'

The General grunts in disdain.

'What are we going to do?' she mutters to me. 'You're the expert on this goddam place, come up with something.'

I close my eyes, trying to think. 'You need to get off-world?'

'Yes, genius. And I need to use a long-range wire, to contact the others.'

'What others?'

'The other Generals. From C Class.' She licks her cracked lips. Perspiration streaks her temples and her neck. 'If Commander Aline was telling the truth about my condition, they will be affected too. Together, we can compare intel, form a plan to obtain treatment…' The words falter, her eyes rolling. The blaster tumbles to the floor as she collapses.

'A port,' I order the pilot, hauling her upright. 'Take us to a port.'

His gaze slides sideways again, first to the General, then to the gun on the floor. 'Otroville is a day's flight east,' he says carefully. 'Or there's Landfall F—'

'No. No towns, no army bases. No Accord.'

'Accord's everywhere.' The man frowns. 'There's a freight port out west, towards the Edge. Depot Twelve. Dirtrat sort of place, used for mining goods, mostly, but you might be able to barter passage there. You got money, anything to trade?'

I don't even have my medkit anymore. It was lost in the scramble from the Pit. For some reason, that thought hurts worse than my injuries, like a thorn, lodged deep in my chest. What good was I, without it?

'Yes,' I say vaguely, remembering the General's words about money, in off-world accounts. 'We can pay.'

'Well, in that case…'

He swings the chair around. One leg crossed casually over the other, displaying the pistol strapped to his ankle.

'See now, I'm in a tricky situation.' He reaches into his jacket pocket and pulls out a wad of dried century leaves, which he packs into the pipe. 'I am down a cargo, and the folk expecting it will not be best pleased if I show up empty-handed. But if you were to pay *me*, I can restock in the U Zone, you get your ride, and we forget this whole hijacking business ever happened.'

When I don't reply, he shrugs. 'Or you look kinda tired. If you fall asleep, I might be obliged to try and kill you, at least throw you off board. Leave you out in the middle of nowhere for the Seekers.'

In my grip, I feel the General's muscles trembling.

'Fine,' I say. 'Fine. We will pay. Just get us there.'

The man brings out a battered silver lighter – a relic from the old world. He flicks it a few times before a flame catches, and the bowl begins to smoulder. The pungent scent of dried century fills the cabin.

'Lady,' he smiles, 'we have ourselves a deal.'

•

Night falls as we fly. I sit in the co-pilot's seat and watch: the gathering dark, the marbled pink of Brovos in the sky, the rainbow shimmer of Delos, the many winking lights of orbiting ships. And beyond the lights… nothing. Just the Void, an unfathomable web of dark matter. It tugs at me. None of the probes sent in have ever returned. Was this how mariners once felt, standing on the farthest spit of land, facing unknown oceans? Knowing that to venture was, in all likelihood, to never return?

I look away from that sky. Below, the ground slides past as quiet as the shifting of a hand across a pillow. Here in the ship, the night seems still and untroubled.

The pilot – Silas – flies smooth. Maybe it's the lingering century smoke, drifting like a spider's web about the flight deck, but soon I forget all about him. I lose myself to the drone of the engine, the distant pattering of grit against the hull of the craft, like rain on a tin roof. I place one hand against the cold, thrumming glass of the window. Part of me wants to be like this ship, calm and functional, empty of blood and feeling.

'Low?'

The pilot looks over at me. The shadows beneath his eyes merge with the warm brown skin of his cheeks. He jerks his head.

'She's calling for you.'

The General is lying on a makeshift bunk in the tight space that doubles as infirmary and storeroom. I squeeze in next to her.

The filth of the past few days is gone, blasted away by the ship's vapour shower. Without the grime in the premature wrinkles on her face, she looks younger than I have yet seen her.

'How do you feel?' I ask.

'Weak. And tired. I have never been this tired before, not even during campaign.' She opens her eyes to look at the ceiling and I sense she is struggling to keep the emotion from her voice. 'It's not just physical. I'm experiencing atypical reactions, visual distortions.' She looks at me, her eyes pink-edged. 'You were right. I saw something, when the Rooks attacked. And back there, with the Augur… I don't want to lose my mind.'

When I speak, it's all I can do to keep my voice steady. 'The physical weakness may be your body adjusting to the terraform, still.'

'Or I could be dying.'

There's no hiding from it. 'There is something wrong. But without the proper facilities to run tests—'

She shakes her head. 'Even if we found somewhere, my enhancements are too complex for anyone on this moon to understand.' Her forehead creases. 'I need to see them. The others from C Class. If it's true, if we're all in the same situation, we might at least face it together.'

The resignation in her voice frightens me. 'And if it's not?'

She gives a bitter smile. 'Then they still want me dead.'

I busy myself with looking through the ship's medkit. 'Have you no family?'

'No. My parents ran security, on Felicitatum. Our warehouse was destroyed in one of the first Limiter strikes. They were killed, along with my baby sister.' She looks me in the eye. 'Do you remember where you were, when you heard that news? Did you celebrate?'

I break her gaze and look into the medical box. 'I am sorry.'

'For me, or for the war?' She lets her head fall back. 'Doesn't matter.'

I work without speaking, patching up her knuckles, trying to push down the clash of hostility and grief, trying to remember Peg's words about how easy it would have been for any parentless child to become like the General. Like it or not, I had played a part in her creation.

'What about you, traitor?' she asks hazily. 'Do you have anyone?'

'No.' I take out an ampule of painkiller. 'I have been dead to them for years.'

'I'm not surprised,' she says, but there's little aggression in her voice, only tiredness.

'Even if it's useless,' I say awkwardly from the doorway when I am done, 'I am sorry, for what the Accord did to you.'

She doesn't reply.

I don't know how long I stand in the ship's corridor after that, my palm pressed to the metal wall. Eventually, I rouse myself and go back to the flight deck. The pilot is still in his seat, the ship on auto, his feet propped on the controls. He's drinking from a tin mug, flipping through some years-old almanac.

'She alright?'

I drop into the co-pilot's chair with a wince. There's a bruise across my stomach the size of a dinner plate from the impact of the bullet through the armoured vest.

'She's asleep. Neither of us have slept much, recently.'

'I can believe that. You look like you've had the devil on your heels.'

I laugh, running a hand over my scalp. 'If it was only the devil.'

'Back there at the Pit,' he says idly. 'I heard gunfire—'

'Please. Don't ask.'

He shrugs and turns back to his almanac. A minute later I hear rummaging, and open my eyes to see him pull an unlabelled bottle from a hidden compartment.

'Here,' he says, glugging some into the cup he's been drinking from.

I take it and drink without questioning, I'm that tired. As soon as it touches my lips, I almost splutter it out for shock. It's whiskey. *Real* whiskey, not adulterated benzene or home-brew. It fills my mouth like rich, stinging amber.

'Where did you get this?' I wheeze, as it sears its way down my gullet.

He shows his teeth. 'Good stuff, huh? Payment for a job, few cycles back. I thought turning a hijacking into a cushy chauffeur trip demanded a celebration.'

I take another sip. Although it stings my cracked lips, it tastes clean and pure, like so little on Factus ever does. Like the first breath of icy morning air on a real planet.

'Thanks.'

'You're welcome, Low.' He nods. 'That what you go by?'

I swallow another mouthful.

'I'm called Ten.'

'Ah.' There's an awkward silence, before he sits back. 'Never met a Ten.'

His tone is easy, almost careless. There's none of the judgement I usually encounter when people find out my sentence. He sees my surprise and laughs.

'Look, whatever you did, whichever side you took, it's nothing to me. We're all born again out here, right? All equal in dust.' He tops up the cup. 'You've got as much right to a new life as anyone.'

I try to smile. 'The Accord would disagree.'

'The Accord should look to their own problems. Good intentions don't mean shit to people dying of thirst. They got what they wanted and it's more than they can handle. Life would be better if they could admit that.'

I look at his face, lit by blinking panels. Not Accord, not FL... What is he doing, on Factus? There are signs of hardscrabble about him, but only at the edges. His clothes, worn as they are, speak of somewhere else, far from the border moons.

For a second, we lock eyes.

'You should get some rest,' he says.

I nod, draining the whiskey. 'I'll sleep in the cargo bay. If you have a blanket?'

He waves a hand. 'Take the bunk. I'll be here, anyhow. One of us should get a good night's sleep.'

His fingers touch mine as he reaches for the cup, and for an instant I'm tempted to hold on, to ask him to come and lay with me and lose myself in smoke and in another person's warmth. But then I see myself reflected in his eyes, my bruised face, the scarf wrapped high around my neck, and I remember what I am.

'Thanks.' I turn away.

His voice follows me. 'May your thoughts be clear, Ten.'

•

I wake to an unusual feeling. I am warm and drowsy; I can't remember the last time I felt so safe. There's a soft drone from somewhere, like bees or a low, gravelly voice, endlessly humming. I press my head further into a pillow that smells of someone else's hair, not wanting to wake.

But wake I do. Reality needles at my body; first my aching ribs, then the sore skin of my face, then the memory of where I am. I open my eyes.

The bunk is in an alcove, shielded from the rest of the ship by a thick curtain. Light filters through the weave, illuminating the walls and ceiling not far above my head. I smile and reach up. I was too tired last night to look at anything, but now I see that the bunk is a patchwork of colour; old-fashioned postcards from a century ago, shiny wrappers from food that can only be found on the home planets, a poster for a one-night-only concert on a satellite I've never heard of, a hand-drawn sketch of secretive Voivira with its protective satellites, even some of the better designed Accord and Limiter propaganda, torn from walls. A magpie collection, from across the known system.

Gently, I touch a very old real photograph. It shows a sandy beach, where people with brightly coloured bathing costumes sit smiling on striped towels. Then, as if the image comes to life, an unexpected sound catches my attention: laughter.

Pulling boots onto my bare feet, I head for the tiny galley kitchen. Silas is there, the pipe hanging from his lips as he shovels at something on a grease-thick stove. The General leans in the doorway, listening.

'—and he told me, "son, I ain't never seen a jackrabbit."'

The General snorts into the mug she's drinking from. They both turn as I enter.

'Morning,' Silas greets. 'Hungry?'

'About time you dragged yourself up,' the General says. She looks much improved; the grey pallor is gone from her face, though a trace of weariness remains in the wrinkles about her eyes. She nods to the stove. 'You might be crazy, but you picked the right ship to hijack. One with coffee and eggs.'

'Vulture eggs,' Silas says apologetically, sprinkling some very shrivelled green chillies into the pan. 'Still, they're not bad. Better than protein.' He swings around to pour from a battered pot. 'Here, saved you some.'

I take the cup. It is indeed coffee – oily and bitter, but real.

'Thank you.'

'All part of the service. For what you're paying me, I should be laying on a buffet.'

I glance at the General and she shrugs. So, they have evidently worked out the details of this arrangement. How much money does she have, stashed away?

The horrors of the Pit remain on my mind, but – as always – my body is a traitor. A mug of coffee and a full belly make the memories easier to push aside.

'We'll reach At Least by noon,' Silas says, scraping oil from his plate. 'We can refuel there, then head onwards to Depot Twelve, the mining port I was talking about.'

'At Least?' The General raises an eyebrow.

'It's the only trade post in this sector for miles, nearest civilisation to the Edge. Place is hit so often by Seekers and bandits, only thing people can say is "at least it's still there".'

'Seekers again,' the General complains. 'They're a menace. They should be dealt with.'

Silas laughs at her. 'I'd like to see you try.'

'If I'd had a gun when they attacked us, there would be a few less of them.'

'You actually saw them?' Silas asks, alarmed. 'How close did they get?'

'We managed to get away before they could land,' I interrupt, before the General can say anything. 'We were very lucky.'

Silas is frowning, and no wonder. I've never heard of anyone facing the Seekers like we did and walking away. I can tell he is trying to figure us out, whether to believe a word we say.

'Will there be many other ships in At Least?' I ask quickly.

'Should be quiet there,' he says. 'I reckon the Accord has forgotten the place exists. Far as I know they don't even drop water anymore.'

'Sounds wonderful,' the General mutters.

'Quiet or not, we shouldn't leave the ship,' I tell her.

'I'll do as I please.'

I glare at her, but she just glares back. Friendly as Silas seems, I don't know how far we can trust him.

Rook, the Augur said, *Longrider…*

'It's not only the Seekers I'm worried about.' I sigh. 'We had a… run-in with the Rooks a few days ago. We need to stay away from them too.'

'Moloney's Rooks?' Silas whistles. 'What did you do?'

'Shot down one of their filthy birds.' The General smirks. 'Bastards had it coming.'

Silas looks impressed. 'I don't doubt that. Look, don't worry. *Charis* might not be faster than a Rook but she's well equipped. I'll know if someone is following. And it's unlikely anyone could have gotten ahead of us.'

When he goes back to the controls, I take the General aside.

'We have to be careful,' I tell her sharply.

'Of *that* hophead?' She snorts. 'I'm amazed he can even fly straight.'

'Not just him. We don't know how far the Augur's influence stretches. And if Moloney finds out we were at the Pit, what we did—'

'We? I seem to remember *you* did the lion's share of the killing. Or have you forgotten?'

'I didn't have any choice.'

She lets out a noise of disgust. 'Typical Limiter.'

'What does that mean?'

'There is always a choice, Low. You cowards never had any idea of consequences. You had your theories and romantic notions, but when it came to action you whined and moaned and said we pushed you into things you didn't want to do. But still, you did them. The Accord taught me to live with my decisions before I was even allowed to pick up a gun.' She sneers at me. 'People don't care about your reasons for killing them when they're dead.'

With that, she stalks back towards her bunk, leaving me alone.

Numb, I wander onto the flight deck. As I enter, Silas is putting down the transmitter.

'Just checking in with At Least,' he says. 'They've got fuel, and the good news is, they haven't seen anyone else for five days.'

I nod.

'Gabi alright?' he asks.

'Gabi,' I repeat, unable to hold back the bitterness in my voice. 'That's not what she usually goes by.'

'Maybe,' he shrugs, 'but like I said, this is now, not the past.' He pokes at a loose wire in the transmitter. 'How did you come to be travelling together, anyway? And from the Pit? Doesn't seem like there's much love lost between you.'

'Things just worked out this way.'

After a while he takes a pouch out of his jacket. Breath. My muscles jerk in anticipation and longing. I watch as he places one between his teeth and shatters it. I clench my palms, to stop myself from reaching for them.

'Reckon you'll go with her, if she can buy passage off-moon?' he asks.

The question strikes me. In truth, I haven't thought about my own fate. If the General can get access to her money, if she can pay me what she has promised – enough to buy more supplies, a new mule – should I take it? Ride alone back into the Barrens and continue as before, patching up desperate settlers, adding each life to the tally, like trying to repair a crumbling dam with paper? On the other hand, if I leave Factus, will *they* follow?

People don't care about your reasons for killing them when they're dead.

'I don't know.'

'Well, if you want a lift back east, I'll give you one. Wouldn't even need to hijack me this time.' He holds out the pouch of beads.

Laughing a little, I take one, and Silas laughs too.

I stare out at the horizon. As the shards melt on my tongue and dextro rushes through me, bright and pure, what I see looks a lot like hope.

•

Silas was not lying about At Least. It's the roughest trade post I have ever seen, and that is saying something on Factus. The only buildings are the temporary living containers dropped years ago by the Accorded Bureau of Land Development to get people started.

Only out here, there is nothing *to* start. It's so arid that seeds and crops just blow away; the monthly water distribution is barely enough to keep the throats of the inhabitants from closing with thirst, and according to Silas even that has stopped. Without crops, they can't access a legal water subscription, and without a legal subscription they have no access to the seed banks for crops. That's the Accord way of doing things.

We land in a whirlwind of dust. Everything looks as though it's been used and reused a dozen times. In the middle of a rough square stands a wire tower festooned with wind catchers that flap madly in our wake.

'Nice place,' the General says, as we step from the ship. 'What's that stench?'

Silas pulls the tattered collar of his flight jacket up and over his mouth. 'Muckbrick. You get used to it.'

'Muckbrick?'

He nods at the latrine.

'Ugh.'

'Look on the bright side. After this place, travelling on a mining freighter will seem like a luxury.'

He winks at me. I fight down a smile of my own. Half a dozen beads and I feel better than I have in weeks; my head's clear, my thoughts sharp. I stride towards the main building that seems to serve as store, bar, wire office, and everything else besides.

'Who the hell would live out here?' The General's face creases in disgust.

'Someone who doesn't have a choice,' I reply.

As she glares at me, Silas quickens his step to open the door for us.

'Only person here is Gilli. Used to be her husband Pike too, but he walked into the Edge one day and never came back. She's been a bit… odd, ever since. Don't pay too much attention.'

Of course, the place is empty, but as we enter an ancient buzzer sounds. There's a creak from the back room, shuffling footsteps, and a woman appears. She looks ancient, desiccated as a dried lemon, and yet she can't be more than forty. In her shoulder holster is a very old pistol.

'Afternoon, Gilli,' Silas says. 'May your thoughts be clear.'

'And yours,' comes the suspicious reply. Her eyes land on the General and stay there for some time, before drifting back to Silas. 'Seen you before. Not these others.'

'That's right. Silas Gulivinda, came through a few months back. Bought a pressure converter from you that fell apart within a week.'

The woman nods. 'So.'

'Alright if we refuel?'

'Alright if you can pay.'

'Do you have a wire booth?' the General asks.

The woman's eyes narrow even more, but eventually she jerks her chin. 'In the back, next to the shit filters.' As the General hurries away, she looks at me. 'She uses it and you don't pay, I get to keep her. That's only fair.'

'We can pay. Do you have any medicines? Breath?'

'No breath. Medicine's there on the shelf.'

I don't listen to the rest of her conversation with Silas – about water rustlers and Seeker scouts – and inspect the medicines instead. I should have known what I would find. The bottles and boxes bear their original labels, but the contents have been emptied long ago, replaced by god knows what. Snake bile, fermented urine… I unscrew the lid from a sticky bottle of expectorant and smell engine-cooling fluid. I put it back in disgust.

'These are worse than useless,' I mutter, turning back towards Silas, 'we might as well—' I stop. He's gone.

'At the pump,' the woman says, her dry eyes on mine. 'Said you should have a drink on him.'

A bottle of something brown and cloudy stands on the counter before her. I can't see the pump through the scratched windows, and the General is still occupied with the wire, clacking away at its keys.

'What is it?' I ask, leaning on the counter.

'Mezcal,' the woman says, glugging some into an ancient plastic cup.

One sniff tells me that it's not mezcal, just cactus juice left to ferment in the sun, with a drop of benzene mixed in. But the woman pushes the cup towards me, her withered lips twitching, and I know that to refuse it, when she has so little, would be unforgivable. Bracing myself, I knock it back in one. It goes down my throat like rat's claws.

'Much obliged,' I wheeze.

'You walked a long way.' There is a strange expression on her face, as if she's seeing straight through my head, to the desert beyond.

'We didn't walk. We flew here, in—'

A crash makes us both jump. The woman drops the cup, her hand flying to the gun. There's another crash and the sound of something splintering, followed by a stifled cry. I run before the woman has the gun from the holster.

I find the General crouched beneath the wire booth. The device is smashed to pieces, the cords ripped out, the box hanging from the wall like a tooth from sinew. The floor is littered with carbon printouts.

'What the hell are you doing?' There's no one else, no signs of a fight, only the General kneeling on the floor, her knuckles bleeding as she clutches the broken receiver.

I kneel beside her. In her other hand is a notice. I wrench it away, smoothing the creases from the flimsy paper.

LEADER OF THE NORTHERN AIR UNIT ASSASSINATED

General Doe Thackeray, Leader of the Northern Minority Unit of the Accorded Nations, was killed yesterday in a terror attack on the Spargo Waystation. Six individuals affiliated with a radical offshoot of the Free Limits, have been apprehended...

I scoop up another notice, then another.

CHIEF OF THE MINORITY
PEACE FORCE AWOL

Captain Uma Roche, Chief of the Minority Peace Force has officially been declared missing. She was last seen a cycle ago on her way to reparation talks with representatives of Delos's new administration. Roche's private physician has been treating her recently for a nervous condition. She is urged to contact...

WING COMMANDER GIANG PHAN
LOSES BATTLE WITH ILLNESS

We have been informed that Wing Commander Phan finally succumbed to the debilitating illness that has affected their health for many months. Phan passed peacefully, at a private hospice clinic in Bleu Shallal on Prosper...

Twelve notices, with dates spanning the past weeks and months, from different publications all across the known system.

'C Class.' The General finally looks up. 'It's the whole of C Class.'

I stare numbly at the papers. The deaths and disappearances are too many, too varied to be coincidence; this was calculated.

'The Augur was right,' the General chokes. 'I am already dead. They've killed me.'

I toss the bulletins aside. 'You don't know that. Whatever they have done to you, there might be a way to undo it. If we can find an Accord hospital, one with a good laboratory—'

'They'd kill me before I got through the door.'

'There are other ways in. There are always people who will help, for a price.'

'How do you know?' The General's eyes are red.

'Because I've done it before.'

She stares at me. 'If you were FL, why were you anywhere near an Accord hospital?' Her eyes go to my temples, to the scars there, hiding what had once been inked into flesh. Slowly, her expression drops into realisation.

'You were a spy? You were a goddam *rat*?' I say nothing, and she swears. 'I should have let you drown in that cesspit. How many of my comrades did you betray? How many died thanks to you? Do you even know?'

The tally waits, vast and bloodied. 'Yes. I know.'

Her face twists in rage but before she can speak a ship's engine roars outside, followed by another and another. Our eyes meet.

'We have to get out of here,' I mutter, looking about for an exit. Whoever is outside, if we go through the store, we'll be seen immediately. But there's a back door, half-obscured by empty crates. I shove them aside.

'You think I'll go with you?' the General spits.

'Do you have a choice?' I kick the door open.

Too late. A figure stands in our path, a shadow against the blinding desert light. I reach for my knife.

'Ten!' It's Silas, his face tense.

Trembling with relief, I let go of the weapon. 'I heard ships. What's going on?'

'Dunno.' He looks anxious. 'Sure it's nothing. Other travellers. Just need to pay up, and then we can go.'

He's cut off by the sound of a gun being armed.

'No one's going nowhere.'

A man stands in the doorway behind the General. Short and stocky, his face has been whipped to leather by the winds, his eyes blue and too bright. He smiles and grasps the General's shoulder.

She twists. 'Who the hell—'

He pistol-whips her across the face. 'That's for my ship,' he says.

Silas takes a half-step forwards as she curses, blood running from her cheek. I meet the man's eyes, fear making my hands shake. 'Moloney,' I say. *Longrider. Hell.*

He turns his smile on me. His teeth are brand-new fibreglass and shimmer, like oil on water.

'You must be Low.'

'Now look, man,' Silas starts.

'Stow it, Silage.' With his free hand, Moloney digs into the pocket of his long leather coat and produces a thin wallet, tossing it down at Silas's feet. 'There's your fee, as agreed. We'll take it from here.'

●

Gilli cowers behind the bar, her pistol gone. Eight Rooks, all in greasy black leathers, are busy looting anything of use and smashing what isn't. The place stinks of unwashed bodies and spilled liquor and engine oil.

I walk stiffly, pushed along by the mouth of a pistol, sick with fear and rage at my own stupidity. The hope I felt earlier in the day curdles into bitterness as I look at Silas.

'What you going to do with them?' he begs Moloney, following at his heels like a dog.

'What do you care?'

'They're wanted alive, you know.'

The bandit smirks. 'One of them is.'

'Maggot,' the General spits at Silas. 'You didn't even have the decency to take us in yourself. How much did you get for this?' When he doesn't answer, she turns to Moloney. 'What bounty have the Accord put on my capture?'

He seems amused by the question. 'Ten thousand credits, ma'am.'

'I'll better the offer. Twenty thousand for my freedom.'

Moloney laughs, a noise like cracking plastic. 'Poor Silas.' He reaches out to pat the younger man's cheek. 'Sold the pair for two hundred credits when you could have had twenty thou. How much gear could you have bought with that?' Silas jerks back as the Rooks laugh too.

Two hundred credits. And I had thought of taking up with him. I turn from him in disgust.

Moloney scratches at his face with the mouth of the charge pistol. 'You know, I'm thinking on it. What if I said forty thousand? You owe me a ship, little lady.'

'Thirty-five.'

'Haggling for your life?'

The General snorts dismissively, and I can tell what she's thinking. *Whatever might be left of it.* 'I've played higher stakes.'

The bandit nods in appreciation. 'Souped that brain up good, didn't they? Alright, sweetheart, it's a deal. But I want my money now and if you try anything, you'll wish I killed you quick.'

He spits oily foam onto his palm. In disbelief, I watch as the General does the same, as she clasps his hand in agreement.

When she looks at me, her blood-smeared face holds some expression I can't fathom.

'You lied,' she says. 'All that talk of wanting me alive... what was it for? So you could use me?'

'You don't understand—'

The world spins and I stagger, grabbing onto a shelf. Something goes tumbling. I blink but can't focus. What the hell is wrong with me?

'You gave it to her?' Moloney asks, and dimly, I see Silas nodding. The mezcal burns my throat, threatening to come back up. *Not just mezcal*, I realise.

'Don't worry, Low,' Moloney drawls. 'Just a little sedative. We heard the stories about you. About what you used to be. This way you'll be nice and quiet, all the way to Otroville.'

Even as the drug scrambles my system, something within me freezes.

'Otroville?' That's Silas's voice. 'But Ten's only wanted in the Barrens, look—' The sound of paper, being unfolded. 'Here, it says: "Wanted, the Woman Low, for theft, attempted murder and the kidnapping of a child".' He stops as Moloney laughs. 'What's so funny, Dru?'

'Her name ain't Ten.'

I look up, my vision blurring. Three Rooks stand between me and the door. I take off, running low like I was trained to, but the world tilts like a craft in a storm. A hand grabs my shoulder and I duck and twist, lashing out, landing a blow in someone's stomach, but from nowhere a fist smashes into the side of my head, sending my hat flying; a kick drives the air from my lungs and I fall to my knees.

No, I try to cry out as Moloney stands over me.

'Her name ain't Ten,' he says. 'It's Life.'

•

Life.

The word pulses in the air; a bullet stopped short of its target. I glare at the bandit through streaming eyes. I would have cut out his tongue to stop him speaking and he knows that. Savours it.

'What do you mean?' the General is asking. 'Who is she? Who the hell is she?'

Moloney kneels, taking my chin in greasy fingers. 'She's Prisoner 00942X. Life W.P. Lowry. That's Life, Without Parole.' I try to wrench my head away, but he grips tighter. 'Escaped from a max-security hulk, what, eighteen months back? Killed half a dozen guards and a couple of inmates and took off in an escape craft before they could stop her. Gotta hand it to you, sweetheart, that took stones. In another world, where we accepted women, I'd ask you to join.'

I close my eyes against the horrible clash of memories: blood on the infirmary floor, gunfire ricocheting from the metal walls of the prison, the sickening drop down three gantries, firing point blank into the stomach of the guard who tried to stop me at the airlock... I attacked the way I had in the Pit, no mercy, no hesitation, as if there was only one clear path and I had no choice but take it, whatever the cost.

What are eight lives against thousands?

Fighting the drug, I raise my head and spit at Moloney. He just smiles and wipes his hand on my jacket.

'Life?' I hear Silas ask, incredulous. His voice sounds distant. 'For what?'

Moloney shrugs. 'Spying, treachery, murder, you name it. Dedicated agent of the FL, this one.' His blue eyes narrow. 'Don't pay to be on the losing side, huh?'

My lips shake with anger. *It was war. I did what I had to.*

But then comes the pain, the terrible crushing guilt that never grows old, that drove me to madness in my cell. *You had a choice. You could have walked away.*

'This can't be true,' Silas stutters, 'there's no way, they would have found her by now.'

Moloney climbs to his feet with a grunt. 'The brass put it about that she died in the escape craft wreck, to save face. But those of us with connections know they want her back bad. A hundred thousand credits bad.'

'But—'

Moloney reaches towards my neck. I struggle, but three Rooks hold me firm, and there's nothing to stop him from ripping the scarf away to reveal the livid scar.

'There,' he says. 'Max-security prisoners wear full collars, not partial ones. They have to be surgically removed. She must have cut her own throat to get it off.'

Tears of rage fill my eyes. *You don't understand.*

The wind howls, slamming the door against the wall, and an empty drum clatters to the ground.

'Enough of this,' Moloney barks. 'Weather's turning. Cuff her, get them all to the hold.'

Hands sticky with engine grease bind my wrists behind me.

'I'm not going with you,' the General protests. 'We have a deal.'

'Deal's not done 'til I get my money, sweet cheeks. And since you did for the wire here, looks like you'll be our guest for a while. Jax, where's the nearest wire?'

'Prob'ly Depot Twelve,' one of the Rooks answers. 'Chances are we can score prisoner transfer there too.'

'Good. You too, Silas, you taplicker. You'll ride with us 'til I'm sure you ain't going to run to the Accord.'

'Moloney, I'd never.'

'Shut up. Get to the ship.'

Hands pull me to my feet, dragging me through the broken wares. Past the beating of blood in my head, I hear the wind, I hear the voices that ride upon it, swirling from between the stars.

The Rooks haul me out of the post to where a large ship waits, guarded by men with guns. Through the swirling dust, I see the name, scratched into the oil-black paintwork.

Longrider.

Whatever the Augur saw – whatever *they* had shown – it's coming true. The light turns thick and yellow as paste, the seconds are becoming unstuck, the skin of the world sloughing away. *They* are here.

'Rook,' I whisper. 'Longrider. Spindigo. Hell.'

'What she say?' a Rook asks, but the question is lost in the roar of the wind.

They crowd into my body, numberless, nameless, ravenous.

A grease-black Rook crashes from the sky towards the earth. Moloney's blue eyes are wide in death, sand clinging to the wet blood on his face. The General and I walk away, into the desert…

And then I know; *they* are showing me the way.

I laugh as the sedative does its work, dragging me into the void.

•

I wake to a hum in my ears, and for a moment think I'm still on Silas's ship, that any moment I'll smell eggs frying and coffee brewing and hear the General's hesitant laugh. But when I move, I feel cold metal beneath my cheek and smell nothing but stale oil and fuel and desert air. I open my eyes.

I'm lying in the hold of a ship, one that is thick with grease, stacked with tangles of wires and parts. Pain flares in my shoulders; my wrists are bound behind me, tied to one of the ship's girders.

It's Moloney's ship, the *Longrider*.

The name brings back the Augur's words – *Spindigo, Hell* – and the vision of the king of the Rooks, dead in the desert. I don't understand, but *they* don't seem to care about that.

When I try to roll to my knees, my stomach gives a violent lurch and I retch, vomiting bile onto the hold floor. Afterwards, I struggle upright and lean against the wall, trying to think as my head throbs.

What will the General do, now that she knows the truth about me?

Part of the truth.

She is Accord, right to the marrow. No matter that they want her dead, she still believes in them. Even if we do escape the Rooks, as *they* promise, will she let me go?

'Ten?' a voice calls across the hold. In the gloom, I see the worn sheen of Silas's flight jacket. He comes forwards cautiously, the way someone might approach a dangerous animal, a cup in his hands.

'You're—' He clears his throat, nodding at the vomit on the floor. 'See you're awake.'

'No thanks to you.'

He hunkers down on his knees. Out of my reach, I can't help but notice.

'Here,' he holds out the mug, 'they're eating. Not much, just soup.'

I laugh, a painful noise from my raw throat. 'You think I'm going to drink that?'

Even in the dim light, I see the strain on his face. His black hair is even more of a mess than usual.

'Nothing wrong with it,' he mutters. When I don't move, he takes a sip. 'See?'

My throat is crying out for liquid. 'Alright.'

He comes closer, until he kneels beside me and can hold the mug to my mouth. The soup is weak; a few spoons of unidentified savoury powder and long-desiccated vegetable flecks mixed with treated water. How long ago were carrots harvested from the hydroponic fields of Prosper? Three years? A decade? But as soon as the liquid touches my lips, my body responds and I drink greedily. Silas tilts the mug, careful not to let any spill.

When I'm done, he sits back, and we stare at each other.

'Is it true?' he asks at last.

'Which part?'

'That you killed people?'

I wipe my mouth on my shoulder, wincing as one of the cuts on my lip opens. 'You see, your theory doesn't work.'

'What theory?'

'What you told me before, that people can escape the past on Factus. They can't. The past is at our heels, even here, at the edge of the system.'

He takes the pipe out of his pocket but doesn't light it, just fiddles with the stem.

'I didn't fight,' he says eventually. 'I'm from Jericho. My mothers are both warehouse bosses there, farming and pharma. Meant we stayed out of the war and in on all the trade.' His lips twist. 'True neutrals. Original green. We made a fortune.'

It makes sense now: his once-costly clothes, his own ship, his lack of tattoos. Still, to run from that much wealth, from the security of a powerful home…

'Why?' I croak.

He shakes his head. 'Parents wanted me to take charge of one of the businesses, but I… couldn't stay. Thought I should come out here, see what life is really like, the places behind the names on all those shipping manifests. See freedom.'

I can't help but laugh, at my beaten state, at the greasy, brutal ship, at the vomit on the floor. 'And what do you think of it?'

'Not exactly how I imagined.' He tries to smile. 'You ever been to Jericho, Ten?'

He's still calling me that. Out of habit, or denial? 'Once or twice,' I say cautiously.

'Then you'll know how everything there is so vast, but there's no *space*. Just the warehouse walls, and a ceiling somewhere miles above with solar bulbs instead of the sky.' He squints at the ship's metal walls, as if he can see through them. 'I used to see those posters of Factus and Brovos, you know, the Land Dev ones. All that openness, it looked so beautiful.'

A hopeless smile twitches the corner of my mouth as I think of the pamphlets and bulletins that led me to leave the Congregations and join the FL. It had all seemed so *true*, their manifesto; the idea that these new planets and moons should be no one's property, that they should be shared, places where new laws could be made, new societies that relied on each individual to do what was right, rather than being yoked to a system that failed so many.

But the General was right about consequences, and Silas was right about intentions – and I have seen the depths you can fall to, so long as your actions are justified. And the longer we fought the harder every choice became, until the fire we started to light our way began to consume the future.

I look up, and meet Silas's eyes.

His face crumples. 'Ten—'

'Still talking to the traitor?'

The General stands at the edge of the hold. How long has she been there? Someone has patched up her face with a few sterile strips. One of the Rooks, I suppose.

'Moloney says we'll reach Depot Twelve within the hour,' she announces. 'He says if you put up any trouble, he'll shoot you.'

I let my head fall back. 'We will not make Depot Twelve.'

There must be something strange in my expression. Even Silas draws back a little.

'Why the hell not?' the General snaps.

'Unless Moloney lets us go, he will be dead before nightfall. Tell him that.'

Silas glances uncertainly at the General, but already footsteps are echoing towards us. One of the Rooks, the tall, lanky one with the shaved smooth head, appears at the hold doors. 'Not a word from any of you,' he barks. 'We're being hailed.'

'Hailed?' Silas frowns. 'By who?'

'An Accord patrol.' He smirks at me. 'Don't worry, Life, we'll get rid of them. Moloney won't risk losing your bounty to a bunch of privates.'

A shiver runs through me, then another. It's happening. Whatever it was *they* showed me, whatever path they chose, this is it. I listen hard. After several long minutes I hear the sound of other engines, faint but drawing closer.

'Screw this,' the General says, agitated. 'They're my people. They'll listen to me.'

But before she reaches the door, Moloney bursts into the hold. He is sweating, his face red, like meat pearled with fat.

'Untie her.' He jerks his head towards me.

One of the Rooks comes forwards, a knife in his hands. 'What's going on?' I ask.

'We're making a detour.' Moloney wrenches open a trapdoor in the floor of the hold. 'Think I'm going to let some scratchtooth border scouts take the rewards for both of you?'

The hatch clangs open, letting in a roar of wind, the sound of engines, closer now. Outside it's grey, approaching night.

I gasp in relief as the cords are loosed. Before I can massage my wrists, the Rook is tying them again, this time in front of me. My heart beats hard, blood humming in anticipation of whatever is to come. Moloney stands before me, violent with life. It seems impossible that soon it will be snuffed out. And yet. I've seen it...

'Keep the *Longrider* on course,' he orders. 'We'll slip away in the shadow.'

Longrider. The wind shrieks through the hatch. It leads down to one of the smaller crafts, I see; one of the oil-black, agile birds that pursued us across the desert.

Moloney turns to me. 'You try anything and the kid's got permission to stick you in the spine. Nothing to me whether you get to the Accord in one piece or not.'

Everything is too fast. The images in my mind keep coming. *Rushing ground, fire in the night. Hell.* I look around in panic and see Silas, his hair whipping in the wind. He reaches out and catches at my shoulder but the Rook rips his hands away.

'We rendezvous at Depot Twelve,' Moloney calls, as he slides down into the cockpit. 'No one do nothing 'til I get there.'

'Sure, boss.' The Rook hands the General into the craft. 'What if they open fire?'

Moloney shows those shimmering, fibreglass teeth. 'Shoot back. They might be Accord but they're on their own out here. Nothing but us and the Edge.' He grins up at me, and the next thing I know I am being shoved down the steps into the rear of the craft. It's tiny, built for two people and I'm pressed awkwardly against the General. The cockpit hatch slams closed, sealing us in with Moloney and the stench of sweat and grease.

'Hold on, ladies,' Moloney says, as he flips switches and starts the craft's engines. 'We're flying.'

·

The stars are just beginning to glimmer in the twilight, like rips in the terraform. The winds encircle the craft, slavering at it. I stare at the back of Moloney's head, at the vein pulsing in his neck. How many more beats does his heart have left in it?

'Think we shook them,' he calls into the comms, and wheels the craft, correcting our course. 'We'll skirt the Edge far as we can, then cut east. Double back around to Depot Twelve.'

For all the relief in his voice, my own heart hasn't slowed. I feel as if I've been thrown into a river, swept along by a current too strong to fight.

A flicker of movement, and I see Moloney's eyes, reflected in the cockpit glass.

'You're too quiet,' he says. 'If you got a plan to cut my throat you can forget it.'

'She reckons her invisible friends will save her,' the General calls, mocking.

To my surprise, Moloney only grunts. 'You mean the Ifs? You seen them?'

'I've felt them.'

'You and that mad Augur both.' He shakes his head. 'Charlatan predicted my death once, you know. With a dead bird.'

He looks at me in the glass. Something – wordless – passes between us.

'What's that?' the General's voice is sharp. On the radar screen, a moving point appears, closing in on us from above.

'Shit,' Moloney swears.

He stabs at the controls, preparing to boost the ship, but there's a high shrilling noise.

'They're hailing us.' The General peers up through the roof. 'Binoculars?'

'They can hail all they like,' Moloney yells, throwing a pair back to her. 'I ain't answering.'

'Then they'll open fire after three attempts, that's protocol.' The General trains the binoculars on the sky. 'There, I see it. A mark-seven Swift. They're fast ships—'

'Fast? That bucket?' Moloney barks a laugh. 'Hold on!'

He smashes the booster, throwing us back against the seat. The General disentangles herself from me, trying to see through the rear window.

'They're following!' she cries.

'They can't be.' Moloney glances at the radar, where the point is closing in once again. 'What the fuck?'

The craft roars above us, the noise of its engines deafening.

'Wait,' the General yells. 'Wait, I can see the insignia. It's not a normal scout. It's Air Fleet. Company Four, the *Spindigo Drift*...'

Her voice falters, and something within me lurches. *Spindigo*. I stare in horror through the fibreglass roof at the dark shadow of the ship, like a huge bird of prey. *Spindigo. Hell*.

Realisation strikes.

'Hel,' I murmur.

'I don't give a shit which company they are,' Moloney is bellowing, 'we got to lose them.'

'You don't understand,' the General shouts back, 'when I was at Landfall I saw the notice: Company Four have been missing in action for over a year. They're dead.'

'That's not the Accord,' I call. 'It's the Seekers.'

•

We hurtle across the sky, burning with fear-heat, with the quickness of a hunted beast, sinews straining an inch away from death. Bullets and charges strafe the darkness, sending the Rook wheeling crazily.

'What do they want?' the General yells.

'They want your heart, your guts, your tongue.' Moloney's face runs with sweat. 'Mine too, and they won't stop there—'

He lets out a cry as a blast shakes the ship, and we plummet rapidly, before he rights us again.

'We can't outrun them,' I shout over the roaring of the engine, the shrilling of the instrument panel, 'they'll push the engines until they burst.'

The bandit's face is livid. 'Then we have to outfly them.'

He sends the Rook into a nose-dive, hurtling towards the earth.

'They're still coming!'

A hail of charges rains down, and this time there's a sickening explosion, a hissing of smoke.

'We're hit!' the General yells. 'Damage to the starboard wing spars.'

Moloney swears over and over again, trying desperately to stabilise the craft. I stare into the darkness, lit by the flash of charges.

You and the dead General must walk to hell.

'Bastards!' Moloney screams as something shatters. In the reflection, I see his eyes open to the whites. 'Quick, one of you.' He stabs a thick finger at the nav screen. 'See a bank of interference to the right?'

I scramble forwards with bound hands. 'Yes.'

'How far off?'

Fear shoots cold through me as I realise what I'm looking at. 'But that's the Edge.'

'How far dammit!'

'Twenty klicks.' I'm shaking, the cords around my wrists slick with sweat. 'You can't.'

'I can.'

His fingers are white around the craft's yoke. I see his pulse beneath the grimy skin of his neck, beating, beating. 'One more boost,' he yells. 'Then we black out and dive.'

'Moloney—' I grab his shoulder.

For one brief second, he meets my eyes. Whatever he sees there, it makes his face blanch, his pupils contract. Then he lets out a curse and shoulders me back, wrenching at the yoke and slamming his palm onto the control panel.

'No!' I scream, too late; we are diving, the craft breaking up around us as it tears through the air. And then I see it, a bank of gloom ahead, where even the stars are blotted out. The Edge: the place no one comes out of alive.

Dust and sand splinter the glass of the windshield. We plummet towards the earth, but there is no earth, only whirling sand in the craft's lights and we are tossed and spun as the wind claws metal from the craft's wings, shredding it to bone.

Beside me, the General screams, but I can't hear words. I look up and – for a heartbeat – see the ground, hurtling towards us.

I throw my arms across the General as the world is torn apart.

THREE

THE
BOOK
OF
LIFE

IN THE RED light blood looks black, shining terribly bright, like oil. There is so much of it. Too much. It means I have minutes, perhaps seconds.

I drop the scalpel, but do not hear it hit the floor. The alarm is too loud, bouncing from the metal walls. In the red light nothing looks real. I trip, sprawling over the examination table, blood spattering in great dark pools. Across the room Darius the medic lies unconscious, his eyes rolled back, the saliva of the last word he uttered still fresh in his mouth, the needle in his neck where I plunged it. Poor Darius. Too young for this assignment. Too trusting.

I fall against the counter, sending the broken halves of the collar skittering across the floor.

My hands fumble desperately among the instruments, smearing everything with blood. There, the cauterising rod, used for much of the quick and dirty prison medical care, the only thing we deserve. I grab it and slam the button to charge it. It sputters, then begins to heat up. Black clouds roll in at the edges of my vision and as I raise it I think I see someone watching me; someone with my face but the eyes of a bird of prey.

I jam the iron against my throat. The hiss and the smell and the pain is too much and I know I'm going to black out, that all of this will have been for nothing. But, just as my eyes roll, the thing with my face grabs my arm, jerks me upright.

When I retch, dark sand pours out of my mouth.

•

The first breath is the worst. Pain flares through my chest as my lungs struggle, useless as empty sacks. Then air, laden with grit and smoke, but air all the same. I heave it in, sand spraying from my lips. Somewhere, a voice curses, saying my name.

'—sake, Low!'

I open my eyes. One of them obeys, the other remains stubbornly closed. Darkness all around, lit by a strange, muted red light.

'Low?'

I raise my head a painful inch. A small figure looms out of the shadows, smeared with blood and smoke. I try to say her name, but my mouth is too full of dust, the air too weak in my lungs. She unties my hands and hauls me up to a sitting position, even though I want her to leave me here, because I feel as if my body is going to snap.

'Are you listening to me?' She slaps at my face. 'Low, we have to move. This ship is like a goddam beacon, and… I keep hearing things.'

My head is so heavy, but I blink and try to focus.

The craft lies wrecked on the sand, its nose buried in the dirt. Parts are scattered around it, like gobbets of flesh. The red light comes from its belly. An emergency light, I realise, growing dimmer and dimmer. And beyond it…

No stars, an endless black void. I shrink from it, cowering in fear of being sucked into that emptiness.

We are in the Edge.

'Moloney?' I whisper.

'Dead.'

I close my eyes but the General will not leave me be. She slaps at my cheeks a second time.

'That light is going to die any second,' she pants. 'And then—'

She doesn't need to go on. Lost in the dark.

I haul myself to my knees, then to my feet, though the pain almost makes me vomit. One of my arms feels badly sprained, and I'm sure several ribs are broken. More besides. I have no mind to count the damage then. I lean on the General and feel her shoulders, stronger than any child's should be, bearing my weight.

'Why are you helping me?' I gasp.

'In crisis conditions two individuals are of more use than one. Even if one of them is a rat.'

We make it to the smoking carcass of the craft. Moloney slumps at the very front, still strapped in his pilot's chair, like a figurehead on the prow of an ancient sea ship.

His skull is broken open. Blood drips from the end of his nose but his eyes are wide and blue and glassy. Just as I saw. Just as *they* promised.

I had hated him. In another time, another place, I would have killed him myself, but – confronted by the end of that ferocious life – something like grief surges through me.

'He knew,' I hear myself say. 'He knew it was death to come here.'

'He couldn't have,' the General wheezes. 'Now stop gibbering and help me.'

She is searching through the wreckage for anything of use. I paw at the remains of the pilot's seat with my good hand. Tools and old cans and disgusting rags tumble out of every pocket and compartment I search but, at last, I find what I'm looking for: an ancient, scratched tin box marked with a single red star. A guerrilla medkit.

I shove it inside my shirt. The emergency light flickers and dies.

In the darkness, *something* shifts, like a snake's belly over sand.

When the light blinks back on, the General's eyes are huge.

'Water?' I croak.

She nods, still staring about. 'Half a canister. Stale.'

'Rope?'

'There are cables—'

'Get one.' My body threatens to give up, pain pulsing in waves, but there is one more thing I have to do. Clumsily, I reach down and drag the long, leather jacket from Moloney's corpse. It is ripped and blood-soaked, but I persist, though my muscles are as good as useless.

The General returns and lets out a noise of disgust. 'What are you doing?'

I thrust it at her. Her own jacket is ruined. 'Night is cold.' *And we have a long way to walk.*

Wincing, one hand clamped to her side, she puts it on. It swamps her, down to the ankles.

'Now, tie us together.'

'What?'

'If one of us takes a wrong step…'

Her gaze flickers to the impenetrable darkness. She swears and loops the cable around her waist, teeth clenched.

'Roped to a traitor,' she mutters. 'This is not how I'll die.' She squints ahead. 'By my reckoning, that's the direction we came from.'

I sway. The emergency light is little more than a faded glow, and beyond us, all around, is the unknown.

'Low?' the General says uncertainly.

In the last struggling flickers, I meet her eyes.

The light goes out.

•

The controls flash, the comms channel blares over and over as the hulk tries to reach me. The warden: she makes her voice soothing, makes it stern as she orders, entreats, bribes… *Life, come back and we'll be lenient, we'll see that no more than another quarter is added to your sentence, we'll overlook the assaults, come back now or we'll have to give the Accord Forces permission to strike.*

They'll send out scouts faster than this pitiful escape craft. My hands are caked in blood as I paw at the controls. There's enough power for one full acceleration and no more.

I scan the navigation screen, trying desperately to see where I am. They keep the hulks isolated, away from any major planets or moons, do not even tell us which sector we are in. There is nothing I recognise, just satellites and the dots of distant ships.

Life, think about the families of the victims, think how they'll feel when they hear you tried to escape. Stop now and we'll—

I wrench the control panel open and reach into the tangle of wires. One yank and the comms link dies. I am on my own. My body shakes, hot and cold with pain and panic and blood loss, my vision throbbing and swimming. I can't fly, in danger of passing out at any second, but I force myself to hold on.

There, at the edge of the screen, something comes into view, a far-off planet and a cluster of moons, stuck right out on their own, and beyond them…

Nothing. I scroll further but the nav system flashes a warning: beyond that point, no other bodies, nothing as far as signals can reach. Just the Void.

A shudder runs through me, fear and longing knotted together. I flip switches, overriding programs.

Everything; I will need to divert everything into the boost, including life support systems. It will buy time, perhaps minutes only, but maybe enough to lose any scouts.

And then?

The stolen medkit is on the seat beside me. A talisman, a reminder. I close my eyes and see the walls of my cell, every inch covered with a line, a life. The tally.

I strap the medkit to my waist. Even if I make the moons, it will be a crash landing, and if I overshoot…

A laugh breaks from me. I activate the boost and send the escape craft hurtling towards the Void.

·

I open my eyes. How long have I been staggering, lost in time, asleep on my feet? No way to tell. The darkness is absolute. I can't even see my hand before me. When I stretch it out into the air, all I can feel is the wind stinging my skin, twining between my fingers. The cable around my waist jerks and sways as the General forges on.

Sometimes the ground rises steeply and I feel as if we are scrambling upwards, the General's boots kicking sand back into my face. I have given up calling out to her. What breath I have I need for myself.

My head reels with pain and exhaustion. I can't keep going. The next thing I know, there is a gasp from ahead and the cable snaps taut, pulling me from my feet. I cry out in pain as I fall but something drags me down a slope – the General's weight. I grab at the sand wildly, and for one heart-stopping second, I feel fingers beneath, gripping my own.

I scream.

'Low,' the General calls from nearby, 'what is it?'

'Hands,' I splutter. 'Something under there, pulling me down—'

'You *fell* down. Why would there be hands? Come on, get up.'

She clasps my forearms and drags me to standing.

'There.' Her voice is urgent. 'Look, there, can you see it too?'

I blink, before I realise I *can* see something: a faint, fitful grey line – like a black cloth washed too many times.

Light. There is light on the horizon.

I laugh. 'It's the end of the Edge, we made it.'

Together, we stagger towards the rising sun. As we walk the light increases, casting a sickly yellow-grey film over everything. The moment it is bright enough, I look over at the General.

She is holding her side, below where the cable loops her waist. Behind us, in our wandering tracks, there are bright red spatters, soaking into the sand.

'You're hurt,' I croak. 'We should stop.'

Her eyes are fixed on the horizon. 'Not now. We are nearly there.'

Step by step, it grows hotter, night sloughing off its empty cold. I focus on walking, one foot, then another. Finally, the cable jerks taut. The General stops, staring ahead.

'What?' I rasp.

The pale line hasn't moved. There is no sun on the horizon, just the same horrid yellow half-light. Fear floods my body. I have been here before.

'We should be out by now,' she says desperately. 'We didn't fly far before we crashed. If that's east, we should be out.'

'It's not east.' My voice shakes. 'It's nowhere. The Augur said we would have to walk to hell—'

'The Augur is completely mad.' Her eyes are frightened. 'We don't need stories. We need to keep walking.'

She pushes on, and I stagger behind. *Hell, Hel*, the words beat through my head. Are they one and the same? What is hell? Faces. I close my eyes, feet sliding in the sand. The faces of the dead stare back at me in their thousands and I can do nothing to escape them. *People don't care about your reasons for killing them when they're dead.* I remember the feel of the fingers, trying to drag me into the sand, and painfully swallow a noise of terror.

I'm almost glad when the General stops again, so I can look at her face, flushed and frustrated and still full of life. Not dead. Not yet.

'This is absurd,' she gasps.

I follow her gaze, hoping to see something, anything. But the harder I look, the less I see, until I realise that even the trail of our footsteps is gone.

'There must be something,' she says. 'A base, a settlement?'

'There is no one here. Except the Seekers.'

'I refuse to believe that. An entire area of this moon lying empty? The Accord would have—'

'No.'

'What do you mean, "no"?'

There's something wrong here and whoever walks in never walks back out. Only the Seekers can bear it. Only Hel.

'We have to get out,' I say.

'We would be out already if you had not pulled us off course.' The General glares at me, her eyes reddened. 'Check the compass again.'

I fumble around my neck, searching through the bag of things we snatched from the wreckage. Finally, I find the craft's compass, trailing wires.

East, I pray and hold it out in front of me.

The needle points dead north. Swearing, I stumble a few steps in the opposite direction, but still, the needle doesn't swing, just wobbles up and down. With a cry of rage, I throw it into the pale dust.

A hand breaks through the sand and catches it. A hand with splintered nails, corpse-grey flesh.

I choke and try to run, forgetting I'm tied to the General. The cable snags and I fall, face first. As I scrabble for purchase I feel something cold and yielding beneath the sand. A human face.

Terror takes me, and I don't know anything until the General seizes my shoulder.

'What is it?' she demands.

Frantically, I search the sand around me, but it is just that, just sand, hot to the touch and cold underneath from the night.

Tears burn my eyes. 'We'll never find a way out. This is hell.'

Face twisting, the General shoves me away. 'You don't *want* us to find a way out. You know what's waiting for you, back there. A prison cell for the rest of your days. You'll wait until I'm dead and then—' She wheezes, and coughs. Eventually, she gives up on her accusations and sits down beside me.

'What are we going to do?' she mutters.

I look at the sky, yellow as marrow.

'Walk.'

•

'Something's coming.'

The words are urgent, jolting me out of a stupor. My head throbs with every beat of the sun, my mouth dry and foul-tasting.

'What?' I ask, and turn just in time to see the General collapse. I stumble towards her. In the thick light her face is ghoulish, and when I open Moloney's jacket, I see the reason why. Her pink shirt is soaked with blood, as is the makeshift bandage wadded there.

'Idiot,' I say, fumbling for the medkit stowed in my shirt. Why didn't she tell me? I flip the lid open.

The medkit is empty, save for a bottle of liquor and some rags.

'Moloney, you bastard,' I hiss.

As quickly as I can, I peel the bandage from the General's torso. There is a wound in her side, no telling how deep through the blood. I grab the bottle and twist off the top. The smell of cheap, raw mezcal almost makes me sick.

'Sorry,' I mutter, and tip some over the wound.

The General comes to, swearing violently, before immediately passing out again. I wad the rags against the wound, before binding them down with the only thing I can – the cable that ties us together.

I sit back, gasping for breath. The heat is unbearable, hammering down like noon in the Barrens, and for a moment I think the shape in my vision is a sun-spot. But there is no sun. When I look again, I see a figure in silhouette, standing there, watching me.

Fear shimmers across my skin.

'Who's there?' I croak. The figure doesn't move.

Shaking, I grope behind me, searching for something, anything to use as a weapon. But instead of the glass bottle, my fingers touch wet flesh, splintered bone. I recoil in horror.

Moloney lies beside the General, his head bleeding. His eyes, blue and piercing, swivel to fix upon me.

'No—' My voice is rough with fear. 'You're dead.'

The bandit grins. 'Takes one to know one.'

'We're not dead,' I whisper.

I close my eyes, digging my nails into my palm, willing my mind to return to reality. But when I finally look again, it's the same viscous light, the same fibreglass grin.

'I'm losing my mind,' I say.

The corpse laughs. 'Losing?'

'What is this? What is happening?'

The dead bandit rolls his eyes to the blind sky. 'This is the Suplicio.'

'How do we get out?'

'You can't.' Moloney flops on his side towards me.

I seize the General by one arm, dragging her across the sand. It must hurt, because she wakes with a shriek, loud enough to make me stop.

'What—' She struggles, before looking at her side. 'Ow.'

I can barely breathe, staring at Moloney. 'We have to get away.'

'Away?' The General struggles upright. 'From what?' She looks around, her eyes passing right over Moloney's corpse.

'You can't see him?'

She looks confused, before laughing weakly, reaching for the mezcal bottle where it lies in the sand.

'This will drive you mad faster than the heat.' She sways as she stares at it. 'But perhaps you're right.'

Before I can stop her, she unscrews the bottle and swallows a mouthful of the burning liquor.

'Thank you, Moloney,' she wheezes.

Beyond her shoulder, Moloney frowns. A bit of his brain falls out.

'That's my coat,' he says.

I take the bottle.

•

'You know what I hate? Shoes. And the army boots, they ruined our feet y'know. Put us in them so young, they changed the shape and now I can't wear anything else. Feet like tree roots, Giang used to say.' She takes a swig.

'Who's Giang?'

'Wing Commander – my best friend.'

I've long given up on trying to fathom a direction; there's no point, not when there's no sun and nothing moves.

'Where are you going?' Moloney whines, a few paces behind us. 'We won't get there like this.'

'Get where?'

'To hell.'

'Leave me alone. You're dead.' I reach for the mezcal.

'I'm what?' the General slurs.

'Moloney.'

'Still see him?'

'What do you see?'

She is silent, but something makes her eyes flood, makes her raise the mezcal bottle and drink deep again. 'Nothing,' she mutters.

I nod as I take the bottle. I told her about Moloney, but not about the corpses beneath our feet.

'I'm sorry.' I stagger to avoid a leg protruding from the sand. 'I'm sorry about this. If it had not been for me, you would be—'

'Dead,' the General finishes, making a grab for the mezcal. 'Augur was right, I have been dead since you found me, just delaying the inevitable.'

She takes a few weaving steps around something I can't see. 'Should have let the Commander do it,' she says. 'Would've got a funeral at least, a cremation. Never thought I'd go like this.' She tips up the bottle, spilling most of it over her chin. 'Eight commendations. Two of the highest order. Thought that would be my legacy. But now, I'll be lost forever out here, with a convicted traitor, no family to remember me, no friends even...'

'Still.' I sway. 'Better than drowning in a cesspit.'

She lets out a loud laugh and holds the bottle towards me, only to overbalance and land heavily on her side.

Fingers emerge from the sand like worms and crawl towards her. I grab the bottle first and her arm second, hauling her away from the reaching dead.

'No,' she groans.

'Got to keep moving.'

'… take orders from a Lifer,' she babbles, her eyes rolling.

A corpse comes yawning out of the sand, and I stumble away from it. If we can just escape the dead, if only they would only *stay* dead, then maybe we can make progress.

'Just a little longer,' I mumble.

'And then what?' Moloney is ahead of us now, bending to examine an arm that crawls from the sand. He slaps it as it grips weakly at his leg. 'I told you, there's no way out. You have to wait for *them*.'

'*They're* here?'

'Of course.' The bandit slides a glance at the sky. 'They made this place.'

I stop. Something has appeared on the horizon ahead of us; a black, crooked shape, like a ruined building or…

'General.' I shake her and her head lolls. 'There's a craft up ahead.'

When I look again, it seems to move further away.

'No,' I mutter. My body is disintegrating; with every step another cell blinks out of existence, and I can no longer carry the General. I let her crumple to the sand. But the craft is coming into view, just a bit further…

I stumble to a halt, letting out a cry. The craft is a wreck. Worse, it's *our* wreck. It sprawls across the sand just as we left it, Moloney's corpse slumped at the front. As I watch, the whole thing shifts, sliding across the sand with horrible slowness.

'Told you,' Moloney says, watching his own corpse inch away.

Half sobbing, I stagger back to the General and drop down beside her.

All around, the light is changing, turning the colour of old teeth.

'Low,' the General slurs, and I hear the frightened child she might have been, in another world. 'I don't want to die.'

'I don't think we have a choice.'

'Always… a choice.'

The light is fading fast. Or is it my vision? I close my eyes, because from all around I can see limbs rising, corpses dragging themselves painfully across the sand from every direction. I know who they are; all eight thousand, four hundred and forty-seven of them. An entire cohort of new trainees from the Accord camps, wiped out.

'Tamane,' I whisper.

Moloney looks down at me, with his glassy eyes. 'That was you?'

'FL told me it would save lives,' I murmur, 'told me the Accord would use the virus on the border moons if we didn't steal it. Didn't say they would use it instead, and I didn't ask, just followed orders…' I open my eyes to look at the corpses, the victims of the bio-warfare attack who had died, drowning in their own lungs. 'She was right. There is always a choice.'

The bandit says nothing, only watches the distant and lamentable parade of his ruined self disappear into the desert, as the dead come to claim me.

•

Death is not the release I thought it would be. For one thing, the dead are not satisfied by my act of dying. It is not enough for them; they want to open me up and number my bones, unspool my nerves and stretch them out to measure against their own lives, inch to inch. I let them. Didn't I carve each of their lives into my cell walls, before I realised what I must do? Didn't I keep the tally for this?

A needle enters my flesh, siphoning blood to add to the measure of me, a blade presses into the skin between my breasts, to take my organs and pile them on the scales.

Only, there is pain and that's wrong because the dead should not feel pain. I open my eyes and see darkness, full of red pointed stars and moving shapes so vast they blot the light. *Them?*

Yes, *they* are here. And through the chaos, a face is looking back at me. The skin is marked, thousands of lines scored into the flesh in the same pattern: four lines and a slash.

Are you Hel?

The figure leans closer. Their hands are gloved in blood and when I see their eyes I try to scream, because they are my own.

The dead hold me down so the thing with my face can work. They speak, words I should understand but can't and the stars pulse vermillion, and the thing with my face keeps cutting and

213

they – *they* – sway the universe and beat worlds together until realities come loose.

I find myself looking into those eyes, dark mirrors of my own, the pupils huge and black and fathomless as a raptor's. Then, with a decisive nod, Hel the Converter lowers the scalpel and cuts the last thread.

•

'—could be alive, for all we know. And we won't know until she talks. And she can't talk if you've put a bullet in her head, Amir.'

'It ain't right. *She* ain't right. No one walks outta there. Look at her.'

'And you'd look a peach after days in the Edge?'

'I'd look like I was missing a vital organ or two, that's the point.'

Something brushes my arm. 'She could have just been lucky.'

'Luck's a bad word, on Factus.'

Silence follows. I open my eyes. Everything is blurry and for a moment I see only a greasy film of light. No vermillion-toothed stars, no darkness. A shadow looms over me and I shrink in fear, remembering the thing that wore my skin and cut my heart from my chest.

'Ten?'

The faces come into focus. Gentle eyes, one of them reddened and swollen, an untidy black beard…

'Silas?' When I try to speak, nothing comes out and I panic. Hands hurriedly cross my vision, removing something heavy and stale with breath. Air – not clean, but living – rushes over me.

Silas steps back, holding the helmet from a flight suit. 'Put it on you for the oxygen. We didn't know…' He stops.

I blink, my head pounding. Silas hands me a tin cup and I drink without tasting, coughing out most of it.

'What…?' The only word I have.

'Good question.' He shows his teeth in a smile, but looks nervous, hunting through his pockets. 'You're back on the *Longrider*. We found you and the General last night, a quarter mile from the Edge. Just lying there. No tracks, nothing. Thought you were dead.'

I look down at the body the Suplicio had broken. My arm is bound in a clumsy sling, my wounds swabbed with iodine. My hand goes to my chest. A dressing is plastered there, my tank top stiff with dried blood.

'Yeah, sorry about that.' Silas gestures at the bandage. 'I'm no medic.'

I touch the edge of the dressing. The memory of the thing cutting into me returns.

'Don't.' Silas reaches to stop me.

Too late. I rip the bandage free. Scored into my flesh are two sloping lines, forming a deep V from collarbone to breastbone and a horizontal line that crosses the middle. Even swollen and crusted with blood and iodine I see the cuts are precise, sharp-edged. Deliberate.

'Didn't want the others to see,' he mutters, not looking at me. 'They're already spooked. Heard the Edge can do things to your mind, make you crazy. Wasn't sure if you…'

I shudder. Had I done it? The Suplicio, the dead beneath the sand, Moloney. Had any of it been real? I press the dressing back down.

Silas holds out a pouch of breath. Very few left, I see. I take one, trembling. He waits a while before speaking again.

'What do you remember?'

I crack the bead, allowing the shards to melt before I speak. 'I remember the ship. The one that hailed us. It wasn't the Accord. It was the Seekers.'

Silas gestures at his bruised face. 'No shit. They were on us too. We fought them off and eventually they just… turned around.' He pauses. 'Never heard of them doing that before. Crazy as it sounds, I think they were more interested in you.'

'They opened fire.' Charges strafing, the craft falling apart around us. 'Moloney flew straight into the Edge, said it was our only chance. But it was too dark, too fast. We crashed—'

'Moloney's dead?'

'Yes.'

'Then where is he? His body?'

I see it again, Moloney's grim expression as he watched his corpse borne silently away across the wastes. Something inside my mind shudders and threatens to give.

'We left it in the wreckage.' With a groan, I straighten and swing my feet to the ground, the breath doing its work, giving me a spike of energy. I have been lying on a stack of crates, I see, covered with a blanket. 'The General?'

'Alive. Though she hasn't come to yet. From her clothes it looks as if she lost a lot of blood.' He stops, worrying at his split lip.

'What?'

'She should be dead. Both of you should.' When I look at him again, his face is almost imploring. 'You really don't remember anything else, after the crash?'

I move my toes on the floor. It feels solid, greasy. Real.

'I remember walking.'

'And the Seekers? They didn't find you?'

'If they had, would we be here?'

I push myself to my feet and when I stumble, Silas catches me. Up close, I see how exhausted he is. 'You shouldn't go out there, Ten.'

'Why not?'

'Rooks didn't want to bring you aboard. They're only alright with me because I helped them fight. They think you killed Moloney. And they think you're cursed. Keep saying no one comes out of the Edge alive.'

'I am not sure I did.'

Outside the storeroom, the *Longrider* is in disarray. It bears the marks of a brutal fight; holes blown in walls, wiring hanging loose like entrails, badly bandaged with tape and rags. Blood too, embedded in the grooves of the metal floor that no one has yet washed out. Looking down into the hold, I see the shapes of bodies wrapped in blankets. Five altogether. Though Silas tries to dissuade me, I have to see for myself whether the General has come through alive, as they say.

There are three Rooks on the flight deck, survivors of the attack. From their expressions, I know that Silas is right. They are afraid of me.

Moloney's second-in-command pulls out a pistol. There's a dressing taped to his bald head. 'Get back in there,' he says.

I ignore him and limp on, towards the bunk room. No one stops me.

The General lies on one of the lower bunks, covered in a blanket. No storeroom prison for her. Her face looks terrible, sun-scorched and drained of blood, but when I feel for her pulse it's strong, almost violent. Pulling back the blanket, I search for the wound in her side that should have killed her, bleeding out as she did across the sand. Someone has placed a dressing there and, carefully, I peel it away.

The wound has been cauterised with brutal efficiency, as if by a field medic. Someone, or something, treated us; preserved us and left us to be discovered. But the only people in the Edge are the Seekers, and Seekers... My hands go to my chest again, to the carved mark. *They* had been there, in whatever darkness I had thought was death. Them, and the thing that wore my face.

I return to the flight deck.

'How long were we gone?' I ask.

Silas takes the pipe from his mouth. 'Four days. We had to land, after we shook the Seekers, and repair the ship. Then we went to Depot Twelve and waited, but Moloney never showed. So we came back, flew patrol near the Edge and,' he glances at the others, 'saw you.'

'Moloney's gone,' I tell the Rooks. 'He flew us into the Edge and crashed. That was what killed him, not me.'

The oldest of the three Rooks turns away, placing a fist against the wall.

'And we're just meant to believe that?' the second-in-command snaps.

'Believe what you like. I told him it was suicide. He did it anyway.'

'Sounds like Dru,' the older Rook chokes. Tears slick his grimy cheeks. 'Where is he? His body?'

Ghosting across the desert, a ghastly figurehead. 'I don't know.'

'If he's dead,' the second-in-command says, 'I'm in charge. And I say we carry on to Depot Twelve, hand this bitch over and get the cash.'

I laugh coldly, stepping close to him. 'If you try, Hel the Converter will come for you too.'

Evidently, they are as spooked as Silas said, because not one of them says a thing after that.

'The General will perhaps keep her word and pay you, *if* she lives,' I continue. 'And for that we will need more medical supplies.'

The second-in-command won't look at me. There is sweat on his upper lip. 'Dabb,' he barks at the younger of the Rooks. 'Where the hell are we?'

'Middle nowhere, boss. Somewhere back between the Depot and At Least.'

'At Least?' Silas sounds hopeful. 'The *Charis* is there. I have some medical supplies on board.'

'Fine,' the second-in-command grunts. 'Fine, but keep *her* away from me.'

•

We make At Least by nightfall. The Rooks push their patched-up ship hard, ignoring its groans and splutters. They want their money, but more than that they want to be rid of us, rid of me. I hear them muttering that I'm a witch, that I'm not right. For some reason, it makes me smile. A thousand guns wouldn't have shaken fear loose from these men, but two women walking out of the Edge has. Besides, without Moloney they are fatherless, rudderless. I don't want to give them time to gather their strength and crush their fear with the thought of a hundred thousand credits.

'You think they'll let us go?' I ask Silas, as the weak guide lights of the trade post come into view.

He laughs around his pipe. 'I think they're too afraid to do anything else. They're convinced you're cursed.'

'And you?'

'I think you're lucky.'

'I meant, will you let us go? Or will you try and sell us again?'

He looks away, his jaw tight. 'Saved your life, didn't I? They would have left you out there.'

'We wouldn't have been out there if not for you.'

'Look,' he won't meet my eyes, 'I'm sorry, okay? I assumed you were just some two-bit rustler, that they'd give you a month's labour and that would be all. If I had known who you were, if I'd known they'd send you back for life I...'

'Would have asked for more money?'

His nostrils flare, and he falls silent.

'Did you earn it?' he asks eventually. 'That sentence?'

My hand strays to my neck, to the legacy of my escape. 'Yes. I am still serving it.'

We do not speak again until the ship touches down. The oldest Rook carries the General from the ship, gently, I notice. In his arms she looks smaller than ever. The trade post looks small too; a place of scant humanity and strained hearts in the pitiless desert. I look up at the winking lights of orbiting ships, only to realise that night will never seem dark again, not after the Edge. The terraform makes the starlight ripple strangely, as if seen through the skin of a great, invisible beast. It seems a fragile membrane, compared to the endlessness beyond.

In the landing pen, the *Charis* hunkers, grey and dusty.

'Hello, baby.' Silas hurries towards it. 'I was afraid that old hag might have sold you.'

We make it within twenty paces of the trade post before a shot breaks the night open. The door flies back on its hinges and a figure steps out, a shotgun in their hands. All around, red eyes blink into life, guns whine, like dogs ready to attack. We are surrounded.

The shotgun jerks. Whoever holds it is tall, wearing a mask and night-vision goggles. 'Hands where I can see them.'

Behind me the Rooks are swearing. At any second, one of them might do something stupid…

'We are just here to refuel,' I call, raising my hands, 'and we have an injured child. We do not want trouble.'

There's silence where there should have been a gun blast.

'*Doc?*' an incredulous voice calls.

The figure rips the goggles free. One brown eye glints at me in the near-darkness.

'Falco?'

•

'Thought you were dead.' Falco laughs. 'Gilli said you got nabbed by Moloney.'

'I was.'

She looks over my shoulder, and the joy on her face drops into hostility; more than hostility, to a rage that I have rarely seen in her.

'These the ones that took you?' she snarls, raising the weapon again.

Then I realise. It isn't just rage on her face. It is grief.

'Where are the others?' I ask.

'Peg's inside.' The shotgun does not leave the Rooks.

'And Boots?'

'Where the hell do you think?' Her eye is bright, face creasing with pain. 'She's back there too, buried in the goddam dust with a dead century tree for a marker. And all because some shitbirds got greedy and wanted a chase.'

'Look, Falco—' Amir begins.

She arms the shotgun. 'Did I say you could speak?' She nods at the General. 'Is the kid alive?'

'Last time I checked.'

'Put her down.'

The older Rook holds the General closer, like a shield. 'No way, you'll shoot me.'

'Meet your death with dignity, scum. Pegeen,' she orders behind her. 'Get ready to fire.'

'Moloney's dead,' Amir calls.

That gives Falco pause. She flicks a look my way. 'You kill him, Doc?'

I shake my head.

'We got targeted by Seekers,' Amir continues. 'They got the rest of the boys too. We're all that's left.'

Falco doesn't look away from the men, her eye narrow, pitiless, calculating.

'Get into the light.' She jerks the shotgun. 'Let me look at you.'

Sullenly, the Rooks move forwards, dragging Silas with them, until the faint light from the trade post falls upon their features. After a minute, Falco lets out a cold laugh.

'The three musketeers,' she mocks, before looking Silas over. 'And who the hell is this gutspill?'

'He's just some hophead smuggler, Falco—' the older Rook says.

'You keep talking without permission.' She turns her piercing gaze on Silas. 'So you're the one sold them out. Should've known. Say the word, Doc, and he's grub meat.'

Silas meets my gaze, half-defiant, half-pleading. Slowly, I shake my head.

'He saved our lives. Guess it makes us even.'

'If you say so.' She hefts the gun. 'Alright. I had sworn to kill every last one of you, for Boots, but since Moloney's gone, I might, *maybe*, be willing to entertain an offer for your worthless lives. What's it to be? Death or a deal?'

Amir's jaw clenches. He's furious, but at least seems smart enough to realise the truth of his situation.

'A deal,' he grunts.

'A deal *what*?'

'A deal, please.'

Falco laughs at him. 'Doc, take their guns. And then I suggest we all get cosy. We've got a lot to discuss.'

•

The seven of us sit around the single table in what serves as the trade post's saloon. Pegeen leans in the corner, a revolver propped on their boot, pointed at Amir. Gilli looks in warily from time to time from the curtained doorway that leads to her bedroom, where the General rests. She is obviously resentful that the same Rooks who smashed up her store are now sitting, watching Falco and Pegeen and I eat dried snake meat and airtight pears, drinking ersatz coffee laced with cactus syrup. More than once, I see the youngest Rook stare longingly at the food and lick his dry lips.

'I want sixty per cent,' Falco says, delicately scooping a watery slice of pear from her plate. 'Of any take. Your territory will be from Wilson's Ridge to Naz Peak. If I catch you working outside it, you will be shot. If you go after any of my G'hals, or informants, or associates, you will be shot. If I hear you have been undercutting me' – she wipes her fingers on a rag – 'you get the picture.'

'Alright.' Amir's lips twitch. 'Ma'am.'

'You're heading back to the Rookery?'

He jerks his head. 'Got to bury the ones the Seekers didn't snatch, before they start to stink too bad.'

'Well, when you're done there, come and see me in Landfall and we'll discuss the matter of your recruiting.' She smiles. 'You understand all that?'

'Yes, ma'am.'

'Good.' She sits back. 'You may go.'

The Rooks stand and shuffle towards the door, the youngest glancing nervously at Pegeen's revolver.

'What do you say?' Peg's voice stops them.

'Thank you,' they each mutter, before shoving their way outside.

Falco turns back to the table where Silas sits awkwardly, fiddling with the pipe that she had refused to let him smoke.

'I, ah, think I should go check on the *Charis*?' he says hopefully.

Falco nods in permission and he hurries out, not without a lingering glance at me. She laughs when she sees that.

'You sure pick them, Doc.' She takes a slurp of her coffee. Without the Rooks the small room seems cosier, with the stove sending out an orange fug of warmth and my belly full, the sugar of preserved fruit tingling in my blood. And yet there is talk to be had, painful though it is.

'What happened back at the Pit?' I ask them both softly.

Falco shakes her head. 'We got out. Don't ask me how. It wasn't pretty. Would have headed for Landfall, but some pit fiends laid chase, pushed us clear in the wrong direction. Fifty klicks before they gave up.' She sighs, setting down the mug. 'Had to use the fuel out of Peg's mare to get us even halfway here. Pushed the wagon hard as I could, for Boots's sake, but…'

She trails off, staring down at the peeling tabletop. Peg holsters the revolver to put an arm around Falco's neck, leaning their head against hers.

'I am sorry,' I say. 'If I had been there…'

Falco sniffs hard. 'No use wishing on it now.'

We sit in silence for a time, listening to the wind lap at the edge of the door.

'I'll go check on Gabi,' Peg says quietly, leaving a kiss on the side of Falco's face.

I fill our mugs from the pot on the stove and stare down into that weak, sweet brew that tastes like the ghost of coffee, waiting for Falco to ask about Moloney, and the Edge and how the General and I are alive.

But to my surprise, she doesn't. Instead, she leans forwards with a grunt and takes a battered tin from her pack.

It's some kind of cream, I see, smelling strongly of artificial violets. She scoops some out and works it across her strong, scarred knuckles, pushing up her sleeves to rub it into the ashy skin of her elbows. 'Damn moon,' she mutters. 'Makes everything dryer than a drunk's eyeball.' She holds out the tin. 'You should use some too, before you turn into Gilli.'

I laugh at that, the first proper laugh I remember for a long time, and scoop some up, smoothing it over my hands, flaking and cracked by the desert winds as they are.

'Listen, Doc,' Falco says. 'We've been here for three days, waiting on someone to rob. While we were waiting we helped Gilli get the place straightened up. Peg even fixed the wire. We read the news.' She works cream into a spot on her wrist. 'Afraid Moloney's boys were less than discreet about your capture.'

So, she knows about me, about the past. I meet her gaze.

'What,' she says, 'think I never suspected you were a Lifer? Scar like that?' She sighs. 'So far, the news is only out on the tangle, not the proper wire. But once folk hear Moloney's dead, you're going to have every scalper in this quadrant down on this place, looking for those hundred thousand credits.'

'And you?' Falco has a price – she has never denied that – I just don't know what it is.

'Don't know what you did to get put away for that long. But if it was done during the war, you're not special. We all did bad things. Difference is, you lost.' She smiles a little. 'Accord can keep their bounty. I'll siphon it from them some other way.'

'Mala!' Pegeen bursts through the curtain, their face white beneath the sunburn. 'It's Gabi.'

Gilli's bedroom is cramped, barely a cupboard. The General lies twisted on the bunk, convulsions shaking her skinny frame while Gilli watches from the corner, hands over her mouth. 'Get Silas,' I tell Peg, 'tell him to bring whatever medical supplies he has on the ship.'

The General's boots clack and thud against the boards of the bed, and I do my best to hold her steady, to make sure she's not biting her tongue. She's a terrible colour, like old ash, running with sweat. The wound in her side is burning hot, even through the bandage. Infected.

'Don't you dare,' I hiss, as her breathing becomes more laboured, horrid wrenching gasps escaping her throat. 'Don't you dare do this now.'

Silas comes running. His eyes go wide when he sees what's happening, before tumbling an armful of medicines onto the rag rug beside me. 'What can I do?'

'Hold her,' I bark. 'Tranquillisers?'

'Ampules of Jix and a bottle of blockers.'

I hunt among the mess of drugs, much of it alley-grade, cut and watered. But I find the ampules of J-I10 he means, load up an injector gun and shoot one into the General's arm.

It doesn't help, and she's getting worse; I can hear the breaths clack and stop, clack and stop in her throat. 'Is there anything—' I ask desperately, but Falco appears, holding out another object. The medkit from the abandoned mare.

I swear with relief when I see what's inside. Silas's drugs might be cheap, but Falco's are proper army supplies, unwatered and pure.

'She's not breathing!' Pegeen cries.

I grab up an adrenaline syringe and stab it into the General's thigh, before snapping a defib coil against her chest. The jolt goes through her, hard, and after one terrible second, her eyes fly open.

I sag back on my knees as she heaves in a breath, then another, wheezing and coughing. From the corner of my eye, I see Silas slump with relief.

'Fuck,' the General gasps, blinking at me through reddened eyes. 'Are you trying to kill me?'

Pegeen laughs, wiping away tears.

'Welcome back,' I say.

•

The next morning at dawn, I stand outside the trade post, beside the old, dead century tree where Boots is buried. Tied to the tree are offerings; a bouquet Falco made from dried agave stems and plastic wrappers, a scattering of bullets from Boots's revolver, a plaited lock of Peg's pale hair. Sand blows in small eddies across the ground, like the softest waves at the edge of a calm sea.

I let a handful of it trickle through my fingers. I don't need to try to remember the words of the prayer; they were scored into my brain by eighteen years of repetition, as if into stone.

"'Creator, maker of planets and moons, who dwells in the space between thoughts, the breath between words, the eternity between the beats of a heart, give us the grace to walk this world of matter, and to shape it in your name and to your will, until we may meet with you, beyond substance, beyond breath, as one, in the place beyond all reality.'"

The wind takes the grains, gathering them on the currents, bearing them away. I look to the west, the direction of our prayers. There, the sky still clings to night. Further out, beyond the edge of the terraform, beyond Factus, lies the Void, from which no exploration vessel has ever returned, in all the decades since humans had first crept into this corner of space. Back on the Congregations, my fathers believed that God the Creator dwelled in the space between atoms. What then, might live in that web of dark matter, of ultimate potential?

I open my hand. Where before there had been sand, now there's a dice, old and yellowed, its pips rimed with blood.

Kneeling, I roll it in the dust.

One.

I roll again.

One.

Again.

One.

Six times, all the same. I give up, and place the dice in a hollow at the root of the tree.

'So as we are, we shall not be.'

From the west, a breeze licks the salt from my eye. Another offering. I turn away, before it decides to take more.

In the saloon, I find the others breakfasting on coffee and protein grits and peaches. Falco has given any airtights she can spare to Gilli, as well as a promise to arrange regular water drops with one of her black-market contacts, saying that the Accord might have left At Least to rot, but *she* won't, not while one of her own and best is buried there. Gilli cried, and asked Falco and Peg to stay, for all she knew they wouldn't.

I stop in the doorway. Beside me, Gilli is arranging the tins of fish and beans and tomatoes proudly on the shelf. She catches my eye and smiles.

'You walked a long way,' she says.

I frown at her, when a bang makes me jump. The General is knocking the cactus syrup tin against the table, drowning her grits with the last of the stuff.

'One thing is for damn sure,' Falco says, in the middle of a conversation. 'The Doc needs to get off this moon. You too, Gabi.'

'Agreed,' the General says, shovelling grits into her mouth. 'But if you think I am going to travel with *her*—'

'She saved your life again, you little rat.' Peg snatches the syrup tin away. 'Or have you forgotten already?'

'That was her choice! Can I have that back?'

'No, you may not,' Falco says, taking the syrup. 'You owe her. And if your money's getting you off this moon, it's getting her off too.'

The General huffs, slumping back in her chair.

'That's not going to be so easy,' Silas says. 'Every passenger port's going to have eyes all over it.'

'What about you?' the General says sweetly. 'Couldn't you take us off-moon?'

He shakes his head, rubbing at his untidy beard. '*Charis* isn't built for long distance. She could manage a short hop, no further than say, Waypoint Ninety-Four.'

I must make some noise, because he looks up, and sees me in the shadows.

'Ten,' he says loudly. 'Come and have coffee.' He pours the dregs from the pot on the stove. 'We were just deciding where to go.'

'"We"?' I ask, with a half-smile.

'Seems I have been hijacked again.' He passes me the mug, and his hand is warm against my chilled skin.

'East,' I tell them. 'We should fly east.'

•

It's obvious from the moment we take off it is not going to be an easy ride. Falco stalks around the *Charis*, poking at the wiring, inspecting every hiding place and cupboard.

'Amazed it stays in the air,' she mutters, but there's a note of amusement in her voice, something like respect. Until we have been flying for an hour or so. Then, a torrent of curse words pours from the corridor, followed by the sound of clanging, and the hiss of the vapour shower turned to full.

'Hey!' Silas yells, straining away from the nav controls. 'What the hell are you doing? We can't waste water, we need it for the cooling systems.' He gives me a pleading look. 'Ten?'

I find Falco standing outside the bathroom pod, hosing it down with vapour.

'Revolting, hophead slob,' she mutters. With a laugh, I leave her to it.

Later, after changing the dressing on my chest and helping Pegeen take a weapons inventory, I go to look for the General. I find her at one of the portholes, staring at the hot, hissing desert that slides by below. She does not look up when I join her, but takes a deep breath.

'You, Low, are a traitor and a murderer who didn't even have the courage to answer for her crimes.' She shifts uncomfortably. 'But, if we ever find anyone mad or stupid enough to take us off this moon, I will pay your passage. In return you… will do your best to keep me alive. Until I can find an answer for whatever is happening to me.'

Her hand is pressed to her side again. She's suffering, not only from the wound, I realise. Were the artificial enhancements within her breaking down, like the Commander had said?

'Agreed.'

We look out at the passing desert.

'We shouldn't be here,' she says.

'I know.'

'We were dying. I couldn't have walked another step, let alone crawled out of the desert.' Her hazel eyes are still bloodshot. 'How are we alive?'

I remember the way the dice had fallen, *one, one, one, one*. 'I wonder if we are.'

'What do you mean?'

I hesitate. It's one thing to let such thoughts whisper through my head, but to voice them? 'What if we did die, there in the Edge? But somehow, we have moved across to another reality, one where we lived.' I cannot look at her. 'All I know is that when I feel the Ifs I see different futures, or different possible futures or… realities that are happening, simultaneously. What if *they* lifted us from one to another, crossed two worlds over? How would we know? We wouldn't, perhaps we would only *feel* that something is wrong.'

She stares at me. 'Those… *things* you're obsessed with, they don't exist. They're just superstition.'

I catch her arm as she turns away. 'They showed me Moloney's death before it happened. It's why I went with him. I knew he would die.'

'And they didn't mention that we would too?'

'The Augur did. Don't you remember? They said we had to walk through hell.'

'You're insane, you know that?'

But there is something in her face, guarded and fearful. The mark carved into my chest prickles.

'What did you see,' I demand. 'In the Suplicio? I saw Moloney. I saw bodies. I know you saw something.'

'Nothing,' she says, trying to pull away from me, her voice shaking. 'Nothing, it was just an hallucination.'

'It was more than that. What did you see?'

'I didn't.'

I shake her. 'Tell me!'

'I can't!' she bursts, her face reddened and terrified. 'Don't make me, please.'

Abruptly, I let go. I see it then, in a way I had not before; how much she carries for someone so young, a weight and responsibility she should never have had to bear, but does, all the same.

Hesitantly, I reach out again and place a hand on her shoulder. 'I'm sorry. You were right. We were just hallucinating.'

She wipes at her eyes. 'Don't patronise me, traitor.'

I smile a little. 'I wouldn't dare.'

'You'd be dead before you got the words out.' She sniffs. 'Now, what the hell is Peg doing with those weapons?'

She hurries away.

Rubbing at the pain in my chest that seems to come from within and without, I follow.

•

The sun is setting and across the endless stretch of the Barrens every rock casts a distorted shadow. Silas stealthily lights his pipe, taking advantage of Falco's temporary absence from the flight deck, and my eyes are heavy with the bitter smoke. The light drips like hot honey through the windshield to where I sit, a battered almanac in my lap.

It's only five years old, but might as well have come from another century. In it, there is an article about Factus, filled with alluring pictures of majestic sand dunes and spectacular sunsets, an image showing the vibrant, free-wheeling architecture of Otroville's main street. Is this what had drawn Silas here, from his safe, comfortable, enclosed life on Jericho?

I let out a breath of laughter, turning the page. What the article does not mention is that the buildings in the photograph of Otroville are not real; just facades stuck to the front of container stacks, Accord propaganda built to reassure new arrivals. Anyone arriving at the port these days can see right through them, literally, to the grit-blasted metal beneath. Neither does it mention the Market of the Innocents – a gauntlet run between port and town – where quick tongues and nimble fingers wait, ready to strip any new arrivals bare as they gasp, dizzy and sick from the lack of oxygen. It fails to mention how Accord disbursements go missing, how aid drops arrive gnawed to the bone, skimmed by every hand they pass through, until there is barely anything left. And lastly, it fails to mention the simple fact that – when it comes to Factus – the Accord are too far away to care. In that one respect at least, the Free Limits were right all along; a whole system is too much for a single power to govern.

From somewhere in the ship comes talk and the occasional thump; the General, Peg and Falco sparring in the hold.

'Again,' I hear Falco say, over the blare of raucous music.

'Show me the other one,' the General asks. 'The eye-gouging.'

'Not until you have this one learned.'

'I know it already!'

There's a scuffle of footsteps then a heavy *thud*.

'That was cheating,' the General complains. 'I wasn't ready. Try it again, I'll show you a move I learned from a brawler from Delos—'

'Enough for now. You should rest.'

'No!'

'Yes. You're tired.'

'I am *not*.'

Smiling to myself, I look across, studying Silas's profile. The golden light brings out the warmth of his skin, and the saturated blue-black of his hair. He looks over, catches my eye, and smiles.

A second later the ship lurches sideways, almost throwing me from the seat. Instantly, the drowsiness is gone, replaced by alarm.

'What's going on?'

Silas's teeth clench around the pipe stem as he hammers at the controls. The ship lurches again, with a sickening drop. 'Boosters aren't firing.' He swears and spins around, wrenching open a panel to reveal a mess of wires. 'Goddam it.'

Pegeen staggers onto the flight deck, followed by Falco as the ship bucks and sinks.

'What the hell?' Falco shouts.

'Yeah, what the hell,' Silas shoots back. 'This is what happens when a crazy woman with a shotgun uses all the water that we needed to stop the system overheating.'

'If this was a real ship, it wouldn't overheat.' She leans on his chair. 'What can you do about it?'

Silas flips some switches, shaking his head. 'Nothing. We gotta land, let her cool down.'

I scramble to peer out of the windshield. The view is not comforting; we're flying above a long, desolate canyon between plateaus. Bad terrain, unless you were planning an ambush.

'Where the hell are we?' I look at the nav screen, scrolling it rapidly, hoping that I'm wrong. 'Shit.'

'What?' Falco asks.

'I think we're in the U Zone.'

She swears, with greater energy than me. I know why. The Unincorporated Zone is part of the Barrens even she avoids, unless absolutely necessary. Sometimes, in my lowest moments, I have thought about the U Zone, about driving the mule past the signs that tell me I'm leaving Factus's official territory and that I will have no recourse to the regulations of the Accord, or of any land. But every time, I remembered the stories – cults, loners, communities who hated outsiders, hostile to the point of madness, too much space between them and no one coming, no water or medical or food drops, no Air Line Road for hundreds of miles – and turned back.

'You got a map?' Falco demands.

The tattered and stained thing that Silas produces is less than promising.

'This is out of date,' she accuses, peering. 'Look, it has White Cat listed. That place burned down two years ago.'

'What's happening?' The General stumbles onto the flight deck.

'We have to land,' I tell her.

'Why?'

'System's overheating.' Silas lets out a noise of frustration as the ship drops, a horrible whining noise filling the flight deck. 'This sounds bad. Might mean repairs.'

'Have you tried opening the secondary air-cooling ducts?' the General asks.

'Of course I have!'

Falco jabs at the map. 'Here, I think we're at the end of this canyon.'

I look over the host of Xs hatched across the desolation, marking dead towns and no-go settlements and ghost ranches.

'Think we could reach Tidhar's Dozen?'

'How far?'

'Eighty klicks.'

'Too far!' Silas hangs on as the ship sways.

'There.' Pegeen is at Falco's elbow. 'What about Bliss?'

'I heard the headman went crazy, killed everyone but himself.'

'There's a ranch here— ah forget it, it was the Mbelas's place. They upped sticks six months ago.'

'What about Gally Town?'

'Gallowtown? We'd be dead and this ship stripped in minutes.'

'There.' On the map, just beyond the canyon's lip, a dotted line has been hashed in. 'What's that? It doesn't say what it is, just...' I peer, 'Esterházy.'

Falco and Pegeen look at each other.

'That's Angel Share,' Pegeen says. 'It's a port, kind of.'

'A port? So we could land there?'

'Not a good idea.'

'Why the hell not?' Silas yells as the whining increases. 'I've heard of that place, a clearing house, isn't it?'

Falco's jaw is tight. 'It's a clearing house that will be crawling with bounty hunters, and what's more, has a Marshal who is an asshole and a psychopath.'

Silas swears. 'We're going down fast, it's there or fry in the desert!'

Pegeen takes Falco's arm. 'Pec would give us shelter, surely?'

Falco's noise of disagreement is lost to the terrible lurch of the ship as it sinks. 'Looks like we've got no choice.'

•

How Silas manages to limp the *Charis* the last few klicks to the edge of Angel Share I have no idea. By the time the settlement comes into view we are already flying too low, wallowing towards the ground like a drunk vulture. Through the tilting windshield I make out an ungainly metal structure: a port, with as many as thirty rusted docking platforms spreading across the dust. Behind it is a forest of containers, some new and shiny with paint, others dented and battered as if they have crossed the system a dozen times. A handful of buildings stretch beyond them, on either side of a dirt street, as if the port opened its great steel maw and belched them out onto the sand.

There are one or two other ships on the wharves, pilot birds and a pair of freighters, by the look of them. Not the reputable kind. I raise an eyebrow as Pegeen arms a pair of pistols. We'll have to deal with whatever's waiting.

The *Charis* flounders down onto the very last platform, almost taking out a gantry before fishtailing in the dirt and crashing to a stop against the buffer. Silas sags back in the pilot's chair, hair matted with sweat.

'That's my girl,' he gasps, patting the yoke.

'Alright,' Falco says, buckling a gun holster beneath her jacket, checking the one at her ankle. 'Let's get things straight. We get in, get the ship repaired, get out. We keep our heads down. We do not invite trouble.' She shoots a meaningful look at the General.

'It is never *me*,' the General complains.

Falco grunts doubtfully. 'Cover those tattoos, *ma'am*. And Low…' She sighs, looking at my filthy, blood-stained clothes.

'Here,' says Silas wearily, shrugging out of his flight jacket. 'Wear this. Then perhaps you can be the pilot. I've had enough of it.' He goes back to packing his pipe with shaking fingers.

Gingerly, I slide my arms into the garment. The lining is torn and still damp from his perspiration. It's heavy, and smells strongly of him: century smoke and sweat and old coffee. I turn the collar up to hide my wrapped throat, and for some reason, immediately feel better.

'Good,' Falco says. 'Ready, Peg?'

Pegeen ties back their tangled hair. 'Ready.'

Outside, the wharves are quiet. The only noise comes from some bit of metal squeaking in the breeze, the occasional groan of the platforms and, from somewhere, a low buzzing. The late-afternoon sun hammers down, as if the terraform here is thinner, as if even that has been pared to the barest minimum by the Accord, above these people who will not pay their land tax. Between the rising wind it's eerily still. Nothing lives this far out. The air is too thin for vultures to venture far from the larger settlements that are their food source. Even the snakes that escape the ranches don't survive long, with nothing but the dust and howling wind to sustain them.

'No guards?' I whisper to Pegeen, as we clang along the walkway.

Peg's grey eyes scan ahead to where the ugly freighters squat, like great eyeless toads. 'Ships got their own. Everyone for theirselves, out here.'

At the end of the walkway sit two low metal buildings with a gate between them. A sign reads:

U TOMS O ICE

'They took the Fs,' a voice says. A man sits in the wink of shade beneath the roof of the second building. His face has sunk in on itself, beetle-like eyes watering in the breeze. He wipes at them with a filthy rag, before going back to fixing something on his lap.

'What?' I ask.

'Said they took the Fs.' The man winds a screw into place with agonising slowness. 'Crew wanted them for their ship, the *Fine Fandango*. C fell off on its own. Never did comprehend what happened to the S.'

The General rolls her eyes. 'Is there one place on this moon where people are *normal*?'

'I'm sorry,' I say, but the man doesn't seem to be expecting much of a response. Instead, he puts the item he was fixing on the floor. A mechanical dog. It takes four steps, lets out a bark and falls over.

'This the stable?' Falco demands, peering into the building behind the man, filled with a jungle of cables and parts.

The man looks mournfully at his dog. 'Yes.'

'What happened to Horse, the old mechanic?'

'I am Horse.'

Falco grimaces. 'Alright. We just landed in that Orel.' She jerks her thumb towards the *Charis*. 'Pilot reckons the booster valves are all chawed up. You can take a look? Clean 'em out?'

'I can take a look, clean 'em out,' the man says, picking up his dog.

Silas starts forwards. 'There's no way—' he protests, but Falco shoves him so hard that he wheezes.

'We're obliged,' she says. 'And if you mess it up, I'll cut off your hands.'

'Hands,' the man agrees.

We walk away across the dirt. Behind us, I hear the whirring of the dog's steps, another half-bark and a clatter.

Silas is furious. 'If you think I'm going to let that crazed landgrubber loose on my baby—'

'He'll do the job.' Falco's face is set. 'He used to be the best mechanic from here to Prodor.'

'So what happened to him?' I ask, glancing back.

'What do you think? Factus happened.'

We make our way towards what passes for a town, here in the U Zone. The air is so heavy and sullen a bullet could have sunk and crawled along the ground.

Buildings flank a rough dirt road. They look like most on Factus, built from century wood and old freight containers, sand blown in drifts against the walls. A series of them welded together announces itself to be the General Store. The doors are closed, a faded sign in the rough plastic window states: *WITCHETTY GRUBS: FOUR FOR THREE*. Beneath it, fat, pale grubs pulse their bodies over a piece of rotting wood in a tank.

The road ends in a larger building – the only two-storey affair in the settlement – made of breeze blocks painted weather-beaten blue.

'What is this place?' I ask.

'Clearing port, from what I've heard,' Silas murmurs. 'Freighter crews stop here and get their planetfall stamp before going on to the depot in Otroville or the townships.'

'Why not straight there?' the General asks. 'The Accord have their own clearing houses.'

'The Accord tend to take issue with discrepancies on the manifests. But if the haulers come to Pec Esterházy for approval…' Pegeen shrugs.

'Banditry,' the General sneers. 'It's what keeps these goddam moons so backward.'

'It's what keeps these goddam moons from rotting altogether, little miss.' Falco narrows her eye at the General. 'Or do you think folk get by on what scraps the Accord bother to send?'

The General raises her chin. 'The provisions dispatched by the Bureau to useless moons like these would be more than enough, *if* smugglers stopped taking their cut at every rest stop along the way.'

'"More than enough",' Falco mocks. 'You need that Academy nonsense knocking out of you. If we had time, I'd take you to an Accord-run border town and leave you there for a week. Then you can tell me what is enough.'

'Shh,' Peg hisses, over the General's spluttered reply. 'What's that?'

We stop dead in the middle of the street.

For a long time, there's no sound beyond the distant metal groan of the port. Then, I hear it. *Tap, tap, tap.*

Falco reaches for her gun.

Tap, tap, tap.

'Two snipers,' the General murmurs, her eyes fixed on the curtained windows of the building. 'At eleven and one o'clock.' Her hand twitches towards her rifle Falco has lent her.

Tap, tap.

The front door of the blue building creaks open, and a woman steps out, leaning on a cane, shielding her eyes from the sun. I can't help but stare. She's old; possibly the oldest person I have ever seen on Factus. Her face is like the Barrens themselves, leached of moisture by the winds, scored by deep canyons and etched with fine lines, like abandoned mule trails. A faded tattoo of a crescent moon circles one eye.

'Who's there?' she calls, her voice stronger than I expected. 'State your business.'

Falco steps forwards. 'Afternoon, Pec.'

Like a squeezebox stretching, the old woman's face breaks into a smile. 'Mala! Come in, out of the sun.' She glances up at one of the curtained windows. 'It's alright, Bebe, Thrip, stand down.'

With a shiver, I watch as the mouths of two guns are withdrawn from the sills.

'Who is that?' the General asks, staring at the old woman. With a jolt, I realise that what I had taken to be a cane is actually a long rifle, its mouth resting on the ground.

'*That* is Ma Esterházy, the first and greatest smuggler on this moon,' Falco says. 'So watch your tongue.'

'Falco,' the woman greets, extending one arm as we approach. Falco responds with a G'hal hug, a gentle one. 'And Pegeen. It has been too long.'

'We would have been back, if you weren't plagued by that rabid Air Marshal. Or has someone finally put him out of his misery?' There's a note of false cheer in Falco's voice I haven't heard before.

'Sadly no,' the old woman says. 'And who have you brought?' Her eyes are amused as they land on Silas. 'New special friend, Falco?'

'In his dreams.' Falco smiles. 'Peg's my one and only. Silas is just our flyboy for the present.' She turns to me. Beneath the friendliness, I see a warning in her eyes. 'This is Doc, a medic we're taking east. And Gabi, her niece.'

'A pleasure to meet you all, I'm sure,' the woman says without hesitation. She has a slight accent I can't place. 'Do, come in.'

As the others step to follow her, a sudden pain stabs at my chest, like an insect sting. I touch my wound through the coat. Something has been carved above the door, scratched into the breeze blocks. Two sloping lines and one horizontal: the same symbol cut into my chest.

Fear sweeps cold across my skin, and I look down to find the old woman's eyes fixed on mine, dark as the space between the stars.

'Welcome to Angel Share,' she says.

•

Even a glance is enough to tell me that Ma Esterházy's joint serves a multitude of purposes. The walls are festooned with ragged maps and star charts, so full of pin holes they look as though they have been attacked by termites. Silas stares at them, his eyes bright with interest. There are wanted posters and bulletins that give me pause – though none of them look new – as well as goods tags, thousands of them in different colours and shapes, printed with the logos of every freight company in the system. It reminds me of Falco's place; a patchwork of anything that might be spared or stolen, each one a victory, however small.

A rough bar of beaten metal dominates the main room, surrounded by mismatched tables and chairs, and through a door in the wall I see what looks like an old-style jail cell.

'For folks' valuables,' Esterházy says smoothly, when she sees me looking.

I only nod. I want to grab the old woman's thin, papery arm and demand to know what the symbol means and who carved it into my flesh and who saved my life. But I know I cannot. As far as she is concerned, I'm simply "Doc", simply a medic and a friend of Falco's, travelling east. Would that I were. I take a seat at the table she shows us to.

'Excuse me?'

A woman is addressing me. Her black hair hangs limp down her back, and a battered holster, with two pistols, is slung over her faded floral dress.

I try to smile. She returns it. Her teeth are fibreglass, cheap ones.

'I was just wondering,' she says softly, 'would your niece mind spending a little time with my Franzi? It's so rare he meets another child, these days.'

'I'm sorry?'

A small boy peers from his mother's shadow. He looks to be around nine, but could easily have been older. Growth is often stunted out here, faces worn too soon, so that it's impossible to guess at ages. The boy's light brown skin is grubby, his dark hair close-cropped. He stares fixedly at the General.

'Ah.' I look across the table. 'Well, that is up to Gabi.'

'No,' the General says without hesitation, her eyes on the tray of tumblers being carried by the man who works as bartend. He's heavily muscled, his shaved head smudged with the shapes of tattoos.

'Manners, Gabi.' I give her a warning look. 'Why don't you go along and play with Franzi?'

The General stares daggers at me. 'Because I don't want to. I'm thirsty. I want a drink.'

The man with the tray hears. 'It's alright, sweetheart, I'll bring you out a soda. How about that?'

Franzi's face creases with envy. Soda is a rare treat indeed on Factus, sugared as it is. Shyly, he creeps around the table and grasps the General's hand. 'Come on,' he says, 'I got beetles.'

The General gives me an outraged look as the child drags her away. I shrug, trying to keep down a smile.

'Thank you,' the woman watches them go, 'it's been months since he saw anyone even close to his age.'

'Do not start crying, Bebe,' Ma Esterházy says, limping over from the bar, an unlabelled bottle in her hand. 'Not when we have friends here.' She thumps the bottle down and drops into a chair.

'It is only right,' she continues, pouring clear liquid into small metal cups. 'That we begin with a drink. Xenia, the ancient

Greeks used to call it, the sacred law of hospitality. Or translated for Factus, "liquor first, questions later".'

Bebe rolls her eyes good-naturedly as she takes a cup and leans back against a table. It seems compulsory that we all do the same.

'*Egészségedre*,' Esterházy announces, looking us all in the eye.

'*Egészségedre*,' I mumble, forcing myself to meet her gaze. Her expression flickers, just for a moment, before she raises the cup and drinks.

Whatever the liquor is, it stings my lips and makes my eyes water, but it's good, somehow clean, scouring the dust from my throat.

'Now,' Ma Esterházy says, refilling the cups. 'We may talk. What brings the great Malady Falco so far from Landfall?'

'Ran into some trouble at the Pit,' Falco says carefully, sipping at her second cup.

'So have many of late. I hear this Augur has a new way of seeing to business.'

'Valdosta's mad,' Silas says, cleaning out the bowl of his pipe. 'Anyone gets even a nick, it's into the Seekers' cages.'

'Was this your experience?' Esterházy asks, her eyes flickering over me.

'That or worse. They chased us clean the other side of the plateau before they left off.' Falco looks down into the cup. 'Lost a G'hal because of it.'

Esterházy reaches a worn hand across the table and clasps Falco's bare arm. 'I am sorry.'

'As am I.'

'You will seek retribution?' There's a tension in the old woman's words.

'The person responsible has already paid the price.'

'And that was?'

A shadow of a smile lifts Falco's lips. 'Dru Moloney.'

They all swear, Esterházy, Bebe and the barman, and Falco laughs. As we drink, Falco and Pegeen tell – if not the truth – a version of Moloney's death from which the General and I are carefully absent. I stay quiet, and look out the window instead, trying to avoid the old woman's gaze without truly knowing why.

Outside, the street is listless as before, but beneath the shade of what looks like a locked water tap I see the General and Franzi. The General drinks long from a cold bottle of soda before hesitating, then passing the rest over to the boy, much to his jubilation.

'Horse is seeing to your ship?' Esterházy says, so abruptly that I look back.

'Yes.' Silas grimaces. 'Can't say I am easy about it. The *Charis* is—'

'Capricious?' The old woman smiles at Silas's surprise. 'Do not trouble yourself. Horse is a good mechanic, if not a whole man, any longer.' She casts a look at us, suddenly commanding. 'You will have shelter beneath my roof for as long as the repair takes. Though I cannot, I'm afraid, promise safety.'

Falco nods. 'We will take shelter, gladly. Though I hope we'll be long gone by sundown.'

Esterházy shakes her head. 'Rest while you can. Night comes fast in the Barrens.'

•

For all the woman's words, I can't rest. Though – with a vapour shower and a change of clothes, courtesy of Esterházy – I begin to feel calmer. Less like a dog with hackles raised or a soldier who dares not remove their boots at night, for fear of waking to a screamed command.

Bebe comes by with some clothes for the General, and a box of make-up. I stare at the cosmetics. It's been so long since I wore any… I touch the little tubes and boxes, remembering how on Prosper I once had a bag, cluttered with these, had once patted and blended and buffed my skin, shared them with others among the chatter and good humour of a barracks bathroom before a rare evening's leave. I had made myself up for a night in Prosper's shining bars, painting a face over the mask I already wore every day: comrade, friend.

Traitor.

Slowly, I take up a tin containing a homemade mascara cake – soap, black dye and maybe oxides, if Bebe has been able to get any. I use it to black my lashes, then pick up a little pot of rouge and dab it on my cracked lips. For a moment, I glimpse the woman I once was, the one who made the choice that led me here.

I sit on the bed, listening to the gentle clank and hum of Esterházy's establishment. Could I stay somewhere like this?

Would I be satisfied with it, or would the tally drive me on? Would *they* find me, as they always do, and tamper with the workings of my life to spin it off course? Is that what they had done, in the Edge?

The door creaks open and the General slopes in, grimy and smelling of cooking fat.

'I should kill you,' she says, sinking onto the bed, but she doesn't seem to mean it. Seeing me, she frowns. 'You look... different. Like a person.'

I smile, nodding to the bundle of clothes at the bottom of the bed. 'Bebe left those for you. And there's wash water in the bucket.'

'Thank god.' The General sheds the filthy jacket and shirt, wincing at the pull of the wound in her side. On her chest and arms I see, once again, the scars of making and remaking, criss-crossing her flesh. 'Poor kid,' she says, scrubbing at her neck. 'He showed me his battle beetles. I will admit, they're better than those sorry-looking ants. These actually fought. They threw each other onto their backs, and he won three fights, but I won the last. And he let me name one. I called it Voivira after the camp.' She stops, looking at me. 'What?'

'Nothing. I just forgot, for a moment.'

'Everybody does, when I want them to.' Awkwardly, she pulls on the too-big, flowered dress Bebe has given her and holds out her arms. 'Look, who would suspect a thing?'

A moment later she sways, catching herself on the wall.

'Give me a shot. That kid has worn me out.'

I grab the medkit, brought from the *Charis*.

'I should check the wound too,' I say, as I inject a booster into her arm. 'Does it still feel hot?'

'Don't fuss, medic,' she snaps, looking around. 'Is this the best command could come up with? I'm not accustomed to such quarters.'

With dismay, I see the confusion on her face, the heightened colour, the racing of her pulse. 'You should rest, General.'

'No, I must review the consignments.' Her eyes cast about the room blindly. 'Where are they?'

Pity jabs at my insides, like a pin worked loose. 'Here.' I hand her a tattered almanac from beside the bed.

She takes it solemnly. Then, her face clears and she stares up at me in abrupt, terrible clarity.

'Low?' she whispers.

'I know.' The pain jabs at me again, as I fill the syringe with cognitive enhancer. 'Don't worry. You'll be alright.'

She's quiet, after that. I let her be. In any case, the time to rest has passed. It's as Esterházy promised; like insects that favour the coolness of the night, dusk brings ships to Angel Share.

Not many, but enough to make me anxious. Some seem to stop only to refuel, others to visit the ramshackle stores, which open their doors at sundown. Most come for Ma Esterházy's. From the second-storey window, I watch them swagger or hurry up the dirt drag, towards the blue house. This is the beating heart of Angel Share, giving out as it does sex and drink and news and authorisation; relief and warning in equal measure.

Bebe and Thrip run the brothel between them, renting out rooms to freelance workers who arrive on the ships. Ma Esterházy sits in her office off the bar, dispensing stamps brought to her by the consignment runners. The cargoes themselves come from all over; meat and dairy from Brovos, oil from the great floating belch of the Delos refineries, scrap from Tin Town, airtights and water from Prosper... Among the tags, I even spot the austere white and blue symbol of the Congregations, though what anyone on Factus would want with the handcrafted prayer beads and religious pamphlets of my home planet I have no notion.

Falco is right; this is a dangerous place for us to be, and yet I feel small enough to be lost in all the activity. We soon find ourselves seated around Ma Esterházy's private table, set in an alcove from where we can see the whole bar. Silas smiles when he sees me; he's also cleaned himself up some, washed his hair and trimmed his beard and moustache into what is more or less a style. Falco looks more herself, scalp freshly shaved, wearing bright orange lip-paint that she must have found somewhere. Peg too is clean, hair brushed for once, frizzing thanks to the dry air. And yet, each time the door creaks on its hinges, I see the two of them tense.

I was expecting the usual Factus fare of protein steaks in old fat and grains hard as teeth from long-storage, but I'm mistaken. Esterházy obviously has access to wares that most do not, and has spared no expense for her guests.

For the first time I understand where Falco's seemingly limitless supply of airtights must come from; here are tins of sardines from the fishvilles of Prosper, and blue corn from the vast roof fields of Jericho's agri warehouses. There's a bowl of long-fermented greens, soft-shell smoked beetles, and meat, actual meat: huge Brovian steaks, cut into slivers. And – in a nod to local custom – there are dishes of cooked witchetty grubs, their skin crisp and their innards soft as boiled egg yolks, and dishes of real salt.

Esterházy sits at the head of the table, quietly watching us eat. She herself eats little, picking at the odd piece of sausage and drinking cups of liquor from her unmarked bottle. Every so often one of her workers appears and whispers to her. More than once, I realise I am staring only when she catches my eye. I look away and drink down the beer in my glass – miraculously cold – and try not to rub at the marks on my chest.

The others forget their tension with each bite. The General, who was at first silent and troubled, eats ferociously, like a feral cat who fears her meal might be snatched at any moment.

'My god,' she says, mouth smeared with grease from the steak, 'real food.' She takes a slurp from the cup at her elbow. It seems she has forgotten her sulk at not being allowed beer like the rest of us. 'Real milk.'

'If you call rat milk real.' Silas shrugs.

The General stops dead, the cup halfway to her mouth. 'Rat milk?'

'Sure.' Silas spears another beetle. 'Milked from Chansatorian udder rats. Most useful creature, very popular here on the border moons.'

'Ha ha,' the General says, but I notice she takes a surreptitious sniff of the milk.

Falco is the only one who doesn't fully let her guard down. Her eyes keep flicking to the door, to the darkness outside the windows.

'Problem?' I ask her quietly, as I reach for the dish of grubs.

'Horse said he won't be done with the ship 'til midnight at the earliest.'

'Ah well.' Silas drains his cup. 'The night is young.'

'Exactly.'

Silas ignores her. 'Hey, Ms Esterházy, aren't you worried about the Seekers out here?'

Esterházy looks at him hard. 'The Seekers?'

'Yeah. I hear other settlements in the U Zone get hit hard.'

The old woman gives a small, dismissive smile. 'They tend to leave us alone.'

'How come?'

'There was… an agreement made. A long time ago.'

Silas snorts. 'An agreement with the *Seekers*? Right, and Hel the Converter signed it in blood.'

'Don't be silly,' Esterházy says lightly. 'Hel doesn't exist.'

'Falco said you were among the first to come to Factus.' The words are from my mouth before I can stop them. 'Were you…'

I look at her neck. Sure enough, among the crinkled flesh I see the two round scars.

'Was I a convict?' Again, the woman meets my eyes with that gaze I find so hard to hold. 'Yes. Does my name not give it away?'

'Your name?'

'Pec. It's short for Peccable. That means, "one capable of sinning".' She smiles widely, showing worn, real teeth. 'The prison warden who released me fancied himself a scholar.'

'If you were one of the first here, and before that served time, you must be…' The General frowns. 'Just how old *are* you?'

'Gabi,' warns Falco.

'It's alright.' Esterházy laughs. 'To answer your question, Gabriella, I am almost eighty. Quite the record for Factus, I'm told.' She sits back. 'I have seen many things in my years. I was born on Earth, you know, in a city on a great river, what feels like a thousand lifetimes ago.'

'On Earth?' Pegeen's voice is shy, almost awed. 'And, is it true that you once ran a brothel, on Quaker's Gasp?'

'Quite true. There were not many opportunities for work out here, then, except on the terraform rigs. And a great many lonely people.'

Her voice is soft, and in another time or place I might have been soothed by it. But when I look at her closely, what I see makes me wary. Beneath the wrinkled skin and the pinned-back grey hair is a woman as tough as wood hardened over decades into iron; into a substance quite unlike what it once was. I stare, fascinated, wondering how I might find a moment to speak with her alone, and if I do, whether I can ask...

'I wonder—' I begin.

'Excuse me.' She rises stiffly, leaning on her gun. 'I am afraid my attention is required in the office. But please, eat, drink.' Her eyes find mine. 'We will speak more soon.'

•

As soon as she's gone, Falco pushes her plate away. 'Peg, go check on Horse, would you? See if you can't hurry him along.'

'What's the rush?' Silas helps himself to Esterházy's unmarked bottle. 'It's alright here.' He smiles at me, pouring a shot of liquor and pushing it in my direction. The General promptly grabs it and knocks it back, making Silas laugh.

'Lay off that,' Falco says to her. 'You're too young for it. And we'll need to be on guard if things get ugly.'

'Why would they get ugly?' Silas asks easily. 'We're causing no harm.'

'Yet,' Falco mutters. 'Listen, that Marshal I spoke of, his name's Joliffe. He's entirely mad, and what's worse, won't admit it. Makes him dangerous.'

'Franzi told me about him,' the General says, scraping her plate. 'Said he flies an old buzzard, fitted out with a hanging net to transport prisoners. Apparently, he once let the net drag behind the buzzard for forty klicks. Nothing but a bag of raw meat left of the prisoner by the end.' She smirks at Falco. 'Franzi said last time you were here you shot him in the thigh, and he went berserk.'

Falco smiles humourlessly. 'Gutspill deserved it. A whole system of people scattered from every goddam corner of old Earth and there are still some white people who want to see us under their boot.'

'Can't Esterházy do something about him?' Silas has lost some of his levity. 'She said we were under her protection.'

'She said we were under her *roof*. It's different. Even she can't go too far against the asshole. For one thing, he's not employed by the Accord. He works for the insurers.'

Silas groans. 'Should have known.'

'Just keep your eyes open, alright?' Falco orders.

'Yes, ma'am.' The General makes a grab for the liquor bottle. 'If he comes in, he's carrion food.'

It's not until some while later that I realise that the General is drunk, or rather, we all are.

'If this is a port,' the General says, her eyes on a woman who has just entered, wearing the uniform of Provo Swift – *fleetest fleet in the system* emblazoned across her back – 'why can't we barter passage here? Get off this stinking rock? That's what we want, isn't it?'

I've been wondering the same thing myself. I tap the cup on the sticky table, listening as a cargo tout bawls out the list of wares available to be "handed on" to another courier.

Fifteen gallons of pure liquid Brovian shit, seven crates of accelerated, artificial, top-drawer amylase. Five thousand kopeks of primo-grade grub spawn...

'Go ahead and barter.' Silas shrugs. 'Without a trusted contact you'll be handed over to the Accord at the nearest satellite outside of atmos. These haulers care about one thing, and that's profit.'

He fills my cup once again.

'What about you, Ten?' he asks softly. 'What do you want?'

'It's not about what I want.'

'But if it were?' There is a question in his voice. His hand grazes mine beneath the table, and I meet his eyes. His face is flushed with drink and the heat of the place, even as the desert night shivers outside.

'Well as long as someone within the upper echelons wants me dead, I have only one option,' the General interrupts. She squints at me, one eye closed. 'I will have to invoke the Last Accord, like some common criminal.'

'No extradition from a home planet,' Silas muses. 'Would that work for you, Ten?'

I shake my head. 'I was exiled from the Congregations when I joined the FL. And after sentencing I was registered to the hulks.' I laugh into the cup at the horrible irony of it. 'The only place I am physically safe is in prison. And I am not about to break back *in*.'

'Too bad for you,' the General slurs. 'But if *I* can get to Felicitatum…'

'You're from Jericho?' Silas's face brightens. 'But so am I. Which warehouse? I grew up in Braxoco, then Gul-Kline-Sun.'

The General snorts at him. 'Should have known you're a greener. *I* was born in Frontera.'

As they bat insults back and forth, Pegeen hurries into the saloon, covered in dust from the winds that must be spluttering outside. Their eyes roam the place for Falco, quickly, urgently. Something's wrong.

I half rise from the table. Falco has already intercepted Peg and strides back towards us.

'What is it?' I ask.

'Well, the good news is, I might have bartered you passage for tomorrow,' Peg says, breathless. 'Uan said he could take you both as far as one of the transport satellites, with a shipment of rat pups heading for Prodor.'

I nod, trying to ignore the stab of reluctance and fear in my belly. 'The bad news?'

Falco is tense. 'The Marshal's in town. Peg just saw his craft.'

'The crazy one?' the General says sharply. 'He know who we are?'

'You'd better pray to anything you believe in that he does not.'

Instinctively, I turn to look at the saloon. It's crowded now, the tables filled with people playing stabberscotch and Chuck-a-Luck; folk from off-moon who don't know or care to fear the Ifs with their games of chance. Franzi goes from group to group with a box that contains his fighting beetles, taking bets, his mother is working the tables and Esterházy... Through the crowd I see the limping, wavering shape of the old woman. A wind I do not feel blows, whipping her dress, and for a moment I am back in the Suplicio, back in that endless waste of sand, and she's coming towards me across the dunes...

Tap, tap, tap.

The hand that grips the cane is dripping with blood. The eyes that bore across the distance are my own.

I push myself away from the table. Someone catches me. Silas.

'Ten, what is it?'

I look back again. There's nothing there.

'We have to get out of here, now.'

Even before I finish speaking, I hear it: the cackling drone of a low-altitude engine, coming to rest outside the saloon. We all look at each other.

'You three,' Falco says, 'get back upstairs—'

The door crashes open. A man stands on the other side, swathed in a long coat. When he pushes it back, dust cascades from his shoulders. Beneath, a rusted metal badge glints, in the shape of a gibbous moon. He spits and looks around, eyes quick as flies.

Peg swears. 'Too late.'

•

The bar goes quiet, as more than one pair of hands hurriedly slip cargo tags into boots or pockets and come to rest on weapons. The Marshal's face is wind-burned to leather, white creases fanning from the eyes, as if his skin is splitting to reveal a pale and grub-like body beneath.

'That's Joliffe?' the General whispers.

'Peg,' Falco's lips barely move, 'go find Esterházy.'

The man has not yet looked our way, half-hidden as we are. As slowly as I can I slide one of the steak knives from the table. Silas's stare is hostile, alcohol hot within him. My own head thumps with liquor and adrenalin. Not a good way to fight. And yet, my muscles tense, ready.

'Where is she?' the man bellows into the room. 'Where is the old bitch?'

No one speaks, but I see a ripple of undisguised loathing run through the patrons, as the Marshal walks towards the bar. That gibbous moon badge – symbol of the Consortium of Freight Underwriters – is the only thing keeping him in one piece. Sullenly, the bartend thumps down a cup and pours a shot of something brown into it. The Marshal seizes it up and knocks it back.

'Now, Peg,' Falco hisses, and the G'hal slips from the table into the corridor beyond.

The click and whine of a gun charging makes everyone freeze, including Peg. The Marshal aims a pistol at them with one hand, the other clamped around the cup.

'Another step,' he says. 'And I blow that sweet face off.'

Falco moves in front of Pegeen. 'Joliffe,' she says derisively. 'Still sucking air?'

He sets the cup down, and brings out another pistol. 'Malady Falco,' he sneers over its whine. 'Lady Sickness. Heard you were in town.' Lazily, he jerks the second gun at her. 'You gonna come in quiet, or do I gotta damage the old woman again? Her leg still ain't recovered from the shot I gave her last time.'

'What?' Falco spits.

The Marshal's lips twitch. 'Old Pec didn't mention where she got that limp, huh? See, when you didn't stick around, *she* had to answer on your behalf. Leg for a leg, as it were.'

'If you touch her again, I'll slice your guts open and leave you for the Seekers.'

Through the open door, a tendril of wind creeps, like a wild animal into a house. It sets the tags on the walls rippling, raises the hairs on my arms. I close my eyes as a sweat breaks out on my neck. *Not now*. The sound of a gunshot that has not yet been fired echoes through my head, the pressure building.

'Big words for a woman with empty hands,' Joliffe jeers. 'Reach for a weapon and I shoot. I'm taking you in, along with that trashcan out there you call a ship.'

'That trashcan is mine,' Silas starts. 'You have no right—'

'I have every right!'

Perspiration cuts channels through the dust on the Marshal's face, and I feel it in my blood now, how his mind is slipping, how control is leaching from the room with every breath. Soon, something will happen and the paths across realities will spill and tangle and *they* will be here, waiting to gulp down all those different worlds.

'If she don't come with me,' the Marshal yells to the room, 'I'll burn this shithole to the ground, and all your goods with it!'

A flash of movement: Falco reaching for her gun. I leap up, just as the Marshal fires.

With a cry, Pegeen crashes back against the wall, clutching at their chest. Falco screams in rage and grief and sends two charges flying, hitting the man twice in the shoulder, before dropping to her knees beside Pegeen. But the Marshal is still standing, and – with a wild grimace – aims the pistol directly at Falco's head.

A path opens before me.

The knife is in my hand as I lunge, throwing myself across the room. He is not expecting me. The moment before he pulls the trigger, I lash out, slicing him across the face.

He screams, staggering back, dropping the pistols. Stepping behind him, I seize his greasy collar and bring the serrated blade against his throat. I see Falco stand and level her gun.

'Stop.'

The voice cuts through the beating of the blood in my head, and at once I feel it, the violent shaking of the man's body, the hot, clean iron of his blood, the stench of him: body odour and stale breath and urine. The blade has bitten into the surface of his skin, and it wants to bite deeper. Falco's teeth are bared, her finger on the trigger.

'Let him go.'

Esterházy stands in the doorway, the night behind her, a rifle levelled at the man who is almost a corpse in my arms.

At once, the clear path vanishes, leaving me stranded in a place without roads. I let the Marshal go.

He sinks to the floor, clasping at his bloodied face with his good hand. The bullet wounds smoulder in his shoulder, my knife cut him from chin to eyebrow, splitting one of his nostrils.

'Get out,' Esterházy tells him coldly. 'And do not forget to tell your employers that I saved your worthless life.'

Shaking and gasping, the Marshal snatches up the guns and flees.

•

'Will they be alright?' Silas asks, as I close the door of Pegeen's room, where Falco sits, her face tear-stained.

I nod wearily. 'Peg is lucky. The bullet lodged under the collarbone. I was able to get it out. If it had been a charge pistol…' I don't need to say it. Instead, I stare down at my hands, rimed with dried blood.

'Here,' Bebe says, handing me a damp cloth.

The blood will not come off. For a few hours I had forgotten myself and what I was. What I had done. I feel tears rising in my chest and know I won't be able to keep them back.

'Come on,' Silas says suddenly, guiding me away. 'You can wash up in my room.'

As soon as the door closes behind us, the first sob escapes. I press the blood-stained cloth against my mouth, but more rise, hot and violent.

'I can't outrun it.' The words come out thick. 'I try to keep the tally, I try to preserve life, but everything I do…'

Silas doesn't answer. Instead, he sinks onto the bed, lights the bowl of his pipe and takes a deep drag. 'You think that bastard didn't deserve it?'

'It's not that.' I let the cloth fall to the floor. 'I swore that I would *save* lives, not take them.'

'A man like Joliffe doesn't give a damn about what you swore.' He looks at me through the smoke. 'You did what you had to, Ten.'

'You're still calling me that.' Wearily, I sit down beside him and when he offers the pipe, I take it. 'Why? You know it isn't real.'

'Real or not, it's what you told me, that first day.' He shrugs. 'I can call you Low, if you prefer.'

'It doesn't matter now.'

Slowly, the terror and pain ebb from me, the century fills my head, making everything soft and distant.

'I should go,' I murmur at last, but don't move. Silas's arm presses against mine, so that I feel the warmth of his skin through the threadbare shirt.

'I don't want to be alone,' I say. 'Not tonight.'

'And tomorrow? Will you leave?' He traces a pattern on my knuckles. 'I meant it before. If you wanted to stay on the *Charis*…'

There's no good answer I can give. Instead, I turn towards him, so close that I feel his breath on my cheek, sticky with smoke and liquor. I lift a hand to touch the fading bruise on his eyebrow. In turn, he reaches out to brush a hand across my scalp, the scars on my temples.

'Who are you?' he whispers.

I lean in and meet his lips.

•

I'm back in the desert, in a storm of sand, and around me something terrible is happening. Cries, screams. One by one, figures appear from the murk, some fumbling for guns, others peppered with blood and burns. I look behind me and see Pegeen, lying empty-eyed; Falco spinning to the ground, lit up by a hail of charges; the General, face down, blood seeping from her middle. I watch the Charis crash horribly into the sand, all the trash and clutter of the flight deck spilling out around Silas's lifeless body.

A figure looms above me, her eyes dark and merciless as a raptor's, her hands gloved in blood…

I open my eyes and the dream fades. I'm shaking, my naked back slick with cold sweat. What have I seen?

Silas stirs in his sleep, reaching for me. I look down at his shape in the sheets, wishing that I could separate this small corner of reality from the rest, tear it away as easily as paper and live within it, forgotten.

But I can't. Quietly, I pull on my clothes and boots and slip from the room.

The saloon is silent. It's dark outside, but I sense that night is losing its grip, beginning the slow slide towards morning. When I open the back door, the wind picks up, like dogs that have been waiting for someone to come, tangling about my ankles. I breathe it in, wondering why I've left the comfort of Silas's bed.

'It's as I thought.'

The ragged voice comes from the darkness. On a bench against the wall, Pec Esterházy sits, a cigarette burning dully between her fingers.

I feel no surprise. Somehow, I knew she would be here.

My shirt hangs open at the neck, the raw cuts illuminated by the momentary glow of the cigarette.

'What does it mean?' I ask.

'It means you have been marked.'

Sweat is cold on my torso. 'Marked.'

'By *them*.'

'The Ifs?'

A flare of the cigarette. 'Is that what you call them? Yes. Perhaps by them, indirectly. Human hands cut your flesh. Though many would not call them human any longer.'

'The Seekers did this?' Her head dips, and in the scant light I see one of her eyes, bright and black as opal. 'Why?'

'Because they know you belong to *them*.'

'Do you… feel them too?'

When she speaks, her voice is like the scraping of sand across the roof. 'You remember what Mala said, about my being one of the first to arrive on Factus?' The bench creaks as she leans back. 'The moment I set foot in the dust, I felt them. We all did – soldiers, engineers, convicts – no matter what people say now, we all felt them, and we knew instantly that we were not alone on this moon.'

I shiver as she voices the thoughts that I have always been too afraid to acknowledge.

'I can't describe how it felt,' she continues, 'to come face to face with another life force, to finally have proof that we are not all there is in the universe, and to be summarily dismissed. The wardens didn't believe us, neither did the Settlement Bureau; no one did. They put it down to mental strain, fatigue, low oxygen levels, mass hysteria, bad food. But they were far away, on their bright stations, or on Prosper. They were not here.'

She shakes her head, her eyes fixed on me. 'While we stayed on Earth, *they* were spread thin, ranging so far to reach us. But here.' She points towards the Void. 'Here is where they are born, where they are strongest. And in those early days we were like sheep that had wandered to the mouth of a wolf den. *They* could not help themselves. They flocked to us, they lapped and gnashed and clawed at our lives and everything that could have gone wrong in those first years did. Many people died, many more fled Factus, driven mad by fear.' She pauses, her jaw working. 'It was how we began.'

'We?' I'm held in place, desperate to hear.

She nods. 'A group of us – all convicts, all deemed expendable – were assigned to Search and Rescue. It was our task to scour the reaches of this moon and bring the lost workers home. Only, their tracks went into the Edge. We followed them in.'

Cold runs through me, deep as the marrow, as I remember the endless dunes of the Edge, the pitiless darkness; the horrible fear that I had not emerged the same.

'I was in the Suplicio,' I whisper.

'Then you know what we experienced.' Esterházy's eyes are haunted. 'Just when we thought there was no hope, *they* came. They showed us a path, a way out, and for the first time, we knew the truth of what they are. How they are made of nothing and everything: pure potential. They let some of us live, and we knew why.'

She looks at me, without seeing. 'What use is a heart in the chest of a corpse when on another moon a child will die for want of one, and take a life's potential with them? *They* feed upon those latent futures, and so we had to save as many as we could. That's how we justified what we did. What we became.'

'You're a Seeker?'

'I was,' her voice is barely a whisper, 'perhaps I still am. We never truly let anyone go, once we recognise them as one of us.' Stiffly, she rolls up her sleeve. There, in the wrinkled flesh, is an old scar, the mirror of the one on my chest.

'No.' I take a step back. 'No, I'm not like them. I never joined. I promised to *save* lives.'

'And they don't? Tell that to the young man who will die without a new lung, or a mother who needs blood for her child's transfusions. The Accord won't help them, out here. So who can they turn to? The land barons? The mine owners?' Her voice is sharp. 'I saw it in you, tonight. You would have cut Joliffe's throat, had I not stopped you.'

I can't deny it, and she smiles. 'You see, the only difference is that the Seekers would not feel remorse, knowing his death would bring new possibilities into the world, would be a gift to *them*.'

'I have seen them kill innocent people—'

'How do you know they were innocent? We never did anything without reason.' When I don't speak, she continues. 'We believe the Ifs grow stronger, every time they influence the world. And if we continue to feed them, soon we'll be able to see what *they* can see. We'll be able to escape the boundaries of this reality into a multitude of others.'

'Are you Hel?' I ask.

She laughs, her sunken eyes bright. 'We are all Hel.'

I'm not looking at Ma Esterházy. I'm looking at the thing that wears my face, the bloodied hand that reaches for me, skin scored with lines. Her eyes are a bird of prey's, filled only with purpose. In her hand is a scalpel...

I stumble away, and am back in the yard of Angel Share. Except now, all around me the air is thick with something that makes my stomach churn.

'*They* are here,' Esterházy says breathlessly. 'Something's coming.'

I hear the scuffing of footsteps in the dirt, the clanking of gun-belts from the front of the saloon. Without a word I run into the dark building, until I can see the street outside.

The flickering light of the solar lamp above Esterházy's door illuminates a posse of a dozen figures, vigilante Peacekeepers, heavily armed and armoured. And at their head, his face swathed in stained bandages, eyes blazing with hatred, is Marshal Joliffe.

•

'Esterházy!' the Marshal bellows. Blood oozes from the bandage, down onto his lips and teeth. 'Esterházy, give the bitches up or this place burns.'

'You cannot touch us, Joliffe,' Esterházy calls through the door. 'Every crew from here to Delos will seek retribution upon you.'

'Let them!' The Marshal is crazed. 'Let them come! I'll kill them all.'

Flames, breaking glass, Bebe's bloodied face, the bartender screaming… I stagger and Esterházy catches me, gripping my hand tight.

'I saw—' I gasp.

'I know.'

In the front of the saloon, the Marshal continues to bellow. Around him, the Peacekeepers are arming their weapons. I see one woman pull out a smoke flare from her belt, ready to light it.

'Go,' Esterházy says. 'Take the others and run.'

'We can't leave you.'

'You must.' For a moment, she presses her palm against my chest. 'Now go!'

I run for the stairs. At the top I look back and see Esterházy, her back against the bar, the long rifle loaded and trained on the door.

'Out!' I bellow into the corridor, as the shouts from the street grow louder. 'Everyone, out!'

Bebe stumbles from her room, eyes puffy with sleep, the gun holster slung over her nightgown.

'The Marshal, he's back,' I gasp, and she goes running,

screaming for Thrip to arm himself, for Franzi to hide.

'Ten?' Silas is there, naked and dishevelled. 'What's going on?'

'Get dressed, we have to get out.'

I burst into Falco's room. She's already standing, buckling on her guns. I realise she has not slept.

'Trouble?'

'The Marshal. With a posse. We have to run.'

Her face hardens. 'Esterházy?'

'She told us to go.'

Peg stirs groggily in the bed, the bloodied bandage wound around their upper chest.

There's a cry from downstairs, an explosion of gunfire and shattering plastic.

'General!' I yell, and run.

Together, half-dressed and rattled from sleep, we tumble onto the landing, Silas and Falco holding Pegeen between them. Rapidly, I give Peg a shot – a cocktail of amphetamine and analgesic – so they can run and not feel pain.

'Now me.' The General holds out her arm.

No time to argue. I shoot a dose into her as well.

'Falco, how many guns do we have?' I ask.

'Four. Flyboy, you got that peashooter?'

Hurriedly, Silas scrambles for the pistol he wears at his ankle.

'Five then.'

I hold out my hand. *They* have chased us onto a path of chaos; if I want to live, I have no choice but to walk it. Falco places a pistol in my palm.

As we round the stairs, gunfire lights the darkness; the bright flashes of charges, the duller flare and *thunk* of old metal bullets. The windows are already smashed, as are most of the bottles behind the bar, where Esterházy, Bebe and Thrip shelter.

'Out the back!' the bartend yells. 'We'll cover you!'

'Pec!' Falco cries.

The old woman looks up. In the fitful light her face is that of a younger woman, the tattoo stark on her skin, her eyes like scorched metal. She smiles.

Then there's a scream, and a smoke grenade arches in through one of the windows.

'Go!' she orders.

We run, smoke billowing at our heels. And yet it works in our favour, because in the confusion of dust and smoke the posse doesn't see us stagger around the corner and onto the road behind them.

Two of the Peacekeepers kick at the saloon's doors. With a horrible clatter, they give way, the metal bent inwards. A rifle shot rings out, and one Peacekeeper staggers back, holding their middle.

Vehicles block the road ahead of us; a dozen buzzards and mules and mares ridden by the posse.

'We'll never make it to the ship,' Silas gasps, staring at the distance between the town and the port, a stretch of darkness with no cover, nothing but empty dirt. Pegeen sags, clutching Falco's shoulder and breathing heavily.

'We will,' Falco retorts. 'Get ready to run. Peg?'

'Ready.'

As the gunfire and the shouts from Esterházy's place increase, I meet Falco's gaze. She nods.

Lowering my head, I sprint out into the middle of the road, to draw the Peacekeepers' fire. The wind is with me as I run, as I raise the pistol and fire once, striking a Peacekeeper in her shoulder. Across the road, I see Falco push the others on.

Four Peacekeepers open fire on me; I scramble behind a parked mule, sparks flying as charges smash into the metal. Reaching up, I fumble for the ignition, praying it's still engaged. It is – I jam the lever, punch the accelerator with my fist and leap away as the vehicle shoots forwards, straight at the posse.

I sprint, Silas's jacket whipping behind me. Gunfire spits dust at my heels. Ahead, I see the others, heads bent against flying charges. If we can just make it out of range…

From nowhere, an explosion sends me sprawling to the dirt. There's smoke, and a ringing in my ears, but I force myself to my feet. Up ahead, Silas drags Pegeen up from the ground. Falco, her nose bloodied, reaches for her guns. Then, in the light of the gunfire, a small shape comes running towards me, a pair of pistols in her hands, her eyes fixed.

Without stopping, the General sights and fires. The Peacekeeper on our heels sprawls backwards, a bullet hole in his skull. She seizes the weapon he dropped: an ex-army blaster.

A louder explosion, and flames paint the night. I look up, eyes stinging with acrid smoke and dust. Esterházy's place is on fire.

'No!' I scream, but it's too late. The Marshal's buzzard bursts through the smoke and speeds towards us.

I run. Somewhere up ahead I hear the rabid snapping of Falco's pistol as she fires over her shoulder. I turn to do the same when a volley of charges sends me diving for cover behind the stands outside the General Store. Glass shatters and witchetty grubs fall tumbling and writhing into the dirt all around me. Then, someone fires out from the window over my head: the store owner, screaming insults.

It's just enough cover. I stumble forwards, onto the stretch of dirt before the port. Fear rattles through me. There's no way we'll make it. Over the sounds of gunfire, I hear the awful cackling of the buzzard speeding towards us. I look back: Marshal Joliffe is at the wheel yelling something, his bandages scorched and bloody. Behind him, a Peacekeeper sights a rifle.

A blast and the Peacekeeper falls, throat spraying blood directly onto Joliffe, who swerves wildly off course. Falco lowers her pistol.

'Come on!'

There – up ahead – I see the shape of the docks, the looming bulk of the *Charis* at the end. Falco puts an arm around Pegeen and staggers behind cover of the stable, where a terrified Horse cowers in the doorway, clutching his mechanical dog.

Other crafts in dock are joining the fight, thinking themselves under attack, guards and freight shotgunners opening fire on the

Peacekeepers who come roaring from the fire-licked darkness of the town. Bullets tear past as I draw level with the General and we throw ourselves behind the metal walkway. Her chest heaves violently, her eyes bulging and too bright.

'Lieutenant Okmulgee,' she barks, stuffing a new charge pack into the blaster. 'There are enemy snipers at six o'clock, we must draw their fire to protect the medical corps.'

'General?' I shake her, but she is not present, she's on some distant battlefield during the war, and as I watch, she scrabbles at her waist. 'Where is my ammunition? Lieutenant, send a runner to the supply line, we will mine the area for their retreat.'

Charges and bullets thud into the walkway. 'General, we have to go!'

Her face is slicked with sweat. 'We never run,' she says, and leaps up, firing the blaster again.

She catches the Marshal's buzzard on its nose, and snarls triumphantly as it flips in the air, careering into the metal barriers behind us.

No more time. I grab her arm and drag her with me as she screams about insubordination. With a desperate surge of relief, I see that the others have reached the doors of the *Charis*, that Pegeen is slumped safely inside the hold.

'Silas,' I yell, climbing aboard. 'Get us out of here!'

Blood soaks his shirtfront from a gash to his head, and he looks dazed, but he nods, staggering towards the flight deck.

A charge pings off the ship's hull, and something shatters.

'Limiter scum!' the General calls.

'Shit!' Falco ducks as a rain of charges slices through the night. 'Low, they've got us fixed!'

I look down in alarm. A generator is running at the edge of the dock and beneath the dirt I see it: the fine, mesh pattern of a gravity mat, fizzing at the edges, locking the *Charis* in place.

Deep within the ship I hear the rumble of the engines starting up, coughing and spluttering. The General fires the blaster again and the ship shakes, the metal of the walkway beyond buckling from the force of the explosion.

Through the blinding flare, *they* crash into my consciousness, unspooling the paths around me. Thousands of versions, but through it all the same terrifying images; *the desert, my friends lying dead, the thing with my face reaching out…*

My eyes clear. Falco is yelling, the General smacking the dead blaster. I see the Marshal stumble through the smoke towards us, his pistols raised.

I leap from the ship, back to the ground.

Shouts follow, but I ignore them as I kick at the dock's control panel. The ship strains against the pull of the mat, and soon it will overheat, the Peacekeepers will rush upon us and it will be too late.

Wrenching open the metal casing, I find the power lever. A shape looms from the smoke, not six feet away; Marshal Joliffe, his face lit with violence, a pistol pointed at my heart.

Too late.

I pull the lever, sending the *Charis* leaping into the air at the same moment that he fires.

•

The wind carries me in its jaws. I feel its breath rush past me, a continuous exhalation.

I remain motionless. The jaws are like a cat's; gentle while I don't move, while I don't remind it of my quick heart and thin skin, so easily broken. But it is already broken, and pain comes on in fast, red circles. Who has done this to me?

The memories are washed with darkness, merging into one another, but I remember faces; smoke-stained, fibreglass teeth, bloodied armour. Boots, metal-toed and thick with dust that drove into my body, that drove bile and blood from my stomach into the sand. Fists, thickened by the long exposure under the sun without water, that collided with my face and head until I stopped resisting and sent my thoughts to *them*, wanting them to take my body away, to make me like them, vast and hungry and untouchable.

But *they* did not. *They* set me on this path that was paved with violence, and feasted silently on their choice. Is this penance for Tamane finally visited upon me? If so, I can't fight it. Perhaps I have been wrong to fight death, all this time. Wrong to keep the tally when this is the only price I can pay.

I open my eyes. One of them obeys.

There is sand below me, sand and a shadow like a bird. I try to raise a hand to touch it, but agony redoubles through my limbs and oblivion takes me again. Too soon I return, and with me, realisation.

I'm in a net, folded like a calf and swaying in the air. A net made from tightly woven cables, too tough to think of breaking. The desert rushes by some distance below.

Blood coats my front, dried stiff on Silas's jacket. When I move there's pain, and the fabric grows wet again. I inch my fingers across my chest.

The Marshal may have missed my heart, but the bullet wound in my shoulder is deep and ragged. An old metal slug, dirty and vicious, not clean, not quick and searing like charges. The wound dribbles blood. Without care, it will kill me.

I roll my head away from it, though my neck screams like rusted metal. I try to open my lips. They are swollen too, crusted with blood that flakes into my mouth. How long has it been since I rose from Silas's bed, since we ran from Angel Share?

Inch by inch, I check my clothes. They've ransacked the pockets, pulled out anything that could be of use or aid. The only thing I find, deep in the lining, is a small, worn bone dice. I close my hand around it, and let my eyelids fall.

The ground wakes me, the hard thump and scrape of it bringing a fresh surge of pain. I cry out and my mouth fills with dust. Finally, we come to a stop. I lie still, ears ringing in the sudden quiet. Other sounds drift: the click of cooling metal, the clang of compartments, the scrape of boots coming towards me. I close my eyes, feigning unconsciousness.

Liquid splatters my face. For a brief moment I think it's water, but then the smell reaches me and I spit and gag, knowing it's urine. Above me, Marshal Joliffe laughs.

'Still alive?' he says, buttoning his trousers awkwardly. 'Just as well. If you can stay that way another day or two I'd be obliged. Wanted alive, that's what it said on the wire.'

I spit again, reaching up a grazed hand to wipe at my face. 'I'm dying.'

'Yeah, but dying is alive, isn't it? Until dead.' He peers around. 'We'd be making better time if that bitch kid hadn't maimed my buzzard.'

'Where?' I choke.

He kneels beside me. He looks terrible, the bandages that slant across his face gummed with pus and old blood, a bulky dressing on his shoulder.

'We're taking a trip to the Air Line Road.' His stale breath wafts across my face. 'Heard a rumour see, about what your carcass might be worth to the Accord, specially still sucking air. I reckon for a hundred thousand credits I can hold off on a killing blow.' He reaches out, and pokes the wound in my shoulder.

I retch in pain and he stops pressing, but leaves his hand there, fingers dabbed in blood.

'Hundred thou credits,' he says, gaze going somewhere else. 'I'll finally get off this backwash moon. Buy out my pension and retire, somewhere green, green as old copper.' He presses down again, absentmindedly.

'You will rot here,' I tell him.

His lips shake and he drives his fist into my head.

Hours later, I wake again. The same place? Impossible to tell. Night has fallen, and above I see the scattering stars, fading out towards the Edge. I smell smoke. A cook fire. The same as I lit many times out in this wilderness, hunching in its glow, trying not to feel the night at my back.

After half a dozen attempts, I manage to roll over in the net. A short distance away, Marshal Joliffe sits on an old ammunition box, his face lit by flames. He has removed the bandages and dabs at the livid cuts, muttering to himself. I clench my good hand. This pathetic, vicious, broken man will not be the one to destroy me.

'Hey,' I wheeze, barely able to speak. 'Water.'

He looks up as if, for a moment, he forgot I am here. With a smile, he takes his canteen and pours it over his mouth, slavering the liquid from his face.

'Water,' I beg again. 'I will tell you how to treat your face.'

'Treating it just fine.' He picks up an unmarked bottle from the ground. Liquid glugs out into his palm.

'The cuts need attention,' I say. 'You should clean them, close them with sealant, unless there is infection…'

I barely know what I'm saying, muttering medical words almost at random, but it doesn't seem to matter. Joliffe looks up suspiciously.

'How do I know if it's infected?'

'Let me out and I'll see.'

He snorts, but comes forwards to release the net from the buzzard. As he does, the stench of the wounds reaches me.

'You try and run,' he says, 'I'll slice your hamstrings.'

Free, I haul myself up on my side, but the Marshal takes hold of my coat and drags me the rest of the way, as I cry out in pain.

'Well?' He drops down onto the box as if at a lesson, his good eye bright and fixed.

'What… is that?' I wheeze, pointing to the bottle he's using.

He sets it down at the edge of the fire.

'Can't see,' I murmur weakly.

He moves it closer. *DANDICAT'S LINIMENT*, the label declares, *FINE FOR AILMENTS INSIDE AND OUT*.

'Good,' I whisper. 'Now, let me look.'

Frowning, the Marshal hunches towards me.

With all my strength, I grab the bottle and push myself from the ground, though the pain almost makes me pass out. He snarls and reaches for his gun, too late; I'm on him, digging my fingers into his wounded face until he howls in agony. The bottle, I raise up and bring down hard on his skull.

Plastic. It does nothing but spill foul oil over his face. Gasping, I roll away from him, kicking hot embers into his path as he lunges for me.

Get up. I force myself to my feet, though they shake under me. *Run.* Enough distance, enough darkness, he might not find me…

But my body is hurt, weakened by thirst and pain and blood loss and after a dozen steps I go sprawling. Frantically, I crawl one-armed, though I can hear him staggering after me, swearing and screaming, and I know he'll make good on his threat; he'll cut the tendons in my legs, and I will die hanging in a net above the desert, my blood dripping out across the miles to disappear like snakes into the sand. Is this the end *they* have been leading me towards? Have they saved me a dozen times from the hulks, the Seekers, the Rooks – for this?

My heart is loud in my ears as I crawl, as if it knows it is on its final beats. The Marshal is at my heels, rabid with violence. He grabs my boot and hauls me back, raising his knife.

The noise of my heart explodes, but it's not my heart at all, it's engines: the steady pounding strokes of engines. I look past the Marshal's oozing face to see four crafts hurtle from the night sky.

They open fire, charges of red and pure white lighting the desert. Joliffe staggers back, his arms shielding his head, screaming obscenities. As the crafts bank and wheel for another attack, he looks up. Fear twists his features as he realises what he is seeing.

Sleek and deadly, the Seekers' crafts roar over our heads once more. No charges this time, but a searchlight, blinding, inescapable. They have us in their sights now and won't risk puncturing good organs. Squinting through one eye, I see the shapes of gunners hanging precariously from the open doors, night-vision goggles lit red. The nearest one lifts a rifle, hair flying, ready to shoot.

Momentarily, among the noise and dust, I see Esterházy's face, her eyes hard as burned metal as she tells me, *it means you have been marked*. I drag the coat and scarf aside, baring my neck and collarbones. The searchlight blinds me, and I shut my eyes, waiting for the end.

Nothing. Just the savage cough of the overhauled engines, just the churn of the air. I open my eyes a crack. The Seeker hanging from the craft has put up their arm in some kind of signal.

Dimly, I'm aware of Joliffe hauling on my leg, trying to drag me out of the searchlight, back towards the buzzard, like a dog with a carcass. Then there is a single shot, and the tugging stops.

With an effort, I raise my head. The crafts have landed close by and figures emerge from the dust. Joliffe gibbers, crawling away, his leg pumping blood into the sand.

At the edge of the light, one of the Seekers stops. I can't see their face, covered by a mask and goggles. Their clothes are old and sun-faded, a patchwork stolen from the dead, tell-tale signs of stab wounds and bullet holes darned over and scorched closed. But there's something familiar about the way they tilt their head; did we meet before, out in the Barrens? Did they carry the General and I from purgatory in the Suplicio?

The skin of their hands is cracked and rough, the flesh marked with thousands of tiny black lines. A tally, I realise in horror and fascination. Beneath their ragged collar is an old scar: two longer lines and a slash across.

Silently, they raise a hand and point to the matching marks on my chest.

'Alive?' they ask.

I nod desperately. 'Yes.'

The Seeker gestures at Joliffe, who still crawls, spluttering towards the edge of the light.

'Him?'

I remember the torture he exacted, his threats to Esterházy and Falco, the way he hurt Peg, the feverish excitement in his eyes as he drove his boot into my flesh.

'No.' I look into the shadows where the Seeker's eyes should be. 'He's dead.'

FOUR

THE
BOOK
OF
HEL

I N THE STARK mid-morning light, Angel Share is desolate. Smoke still drifts in places, the dirt scorched and disordered. Few ships remain; no doubt they took what they could of value and departed.

One ship is familiar. The *Charis* waits on one of the docking platforms, unattended and silent. Nearby, Peacekeepers – four of the twelve who made up the original posse – guard the gate. There's no sign of Horse or his metal dog.

Beneath me, the buzzard cackles unhappily after being pushed so hard across the desert. I feel the same. With water and food and drugs I have deceived my body into forgetting some of its damage, its maimed flesh and pain and rising infection. An illusion, but one I need to maintain for a little longer.

As I approach the dock, I reach for the pouch of breath and carefully crack one between my teeth. A rush beats through me, the amphetamine in the beads more powerful than any I've encountered. A lawman's perk.

Joliffe's hat hides my battered face, his reeking coat covers the blood and filth upon my clothes. As I bring the buzzard to earth a dozen paces from the Peacekeepers, I check the blanket around the bundle at my side.

The engine dies away with a splutter. One of the Peacekeepers steps forwards, peering through the settling dust.

'Joliffe?' she calls. 'Where's the fugitive?'

I climb from the buzzard, taking up the bundle. Face lowered, I limp forwards.

'Joliffe?' another says uncertainly.

I throw the blanket to the sand. The cloth unravels and the Marshal's head – eyeless and tongueless – rolls to a stop at the Peacekeepers' feet.

I look up at them then, one hand on the pistol at my waist, the carved Seeker marks visible on my chest.

They scatter.

Gathering the head under one arm, I limp across the scarred earth onto the main street of Angel Share. My muscles fizz with artificial energy, head light from blood loss. All around are signs of the devastation wrought the night before last, yet to be cleared: a few dead grubs left in the sand, an empty window frame, a door sagging on one hinge, like a tooth on sinew. The air is thick with the wet-dog slap of sodden concrete drying in the sun.

The saloon is a ruin. The blue-painted walls are lapped with smoke stains and soot, the roof gone, the windows gone, only the breeze blocks remaining. A group works in the wreckage, pulling at what can be salvaged. Beneath the shade of the water pump are two blanket-wrapped figures. Swaying on my feet, I walk over and bend to turn back the cloth.

Pec Esterházy lies dead. Her arms have been folded onto her chest, her eyes closed. Soot catches in the strands of her grey hair, on the lined face of this woman who took her first breath on

Earth eighty years before; who journeyed across the universe and took her last on Factus, here, at the known system's limit.

I drop the Marshal's head before her lifeless body.

'For you,' I croak.

One of the figures in the wreckage turns. Falco. Her face falls into shock, as if she's looking at a walking corpse.

'Doc?'

Then Silas is there, hurrying towards me only to stop, uncertain. Something else is wrong. The General isn't among them. I look up in question.

'They got her,' Falco says, her mouth tight with rage and grief. 'The bastards got her.'

•

As Silas begins the slow work of patching me up, Falco tells me what happened. How the General, upon hearing the Marshal's gunshot and seeing me fall, went berserk, and – screaming orders to troops who did not exist – threw herself from the *Charis*, twelve feet to the ground, and attacked the Marshal with everything she had.

'By the time I made it to the flight deck we were already too far up to help.' Falco's jaw works as she soaks a cloth in water from the pump. 'We managed to reverse velocity, but then they opened fire and we had no choice but to get out. It was hours before we could land again. When we did, we found Joliffe gone, the place looted, whatever remaining Peacekeeper scum more interested in drinking than doing their jobs. We didn't know where you were. Then we found Pec.'

Savagely, she rips open a dressing. We are gathered in the General Store, broken-windowed and ransacked as it is. The man who runs it does not like our being there. But he can see the head of Marshal Joliffe out in the sun, and so says nothing, only turns his dry, goat-yellow eyes on us from time to time as he sweeps up shattered plastic and gathers dead grubs to feed to the insects that survived.

'The General?' I ask weakly. The pain makes my head spin. I feel in the Marshal's jacket for another bead.

'We think they took her east someplace,' Pegeen says, wan with exhaustion. 'Horse told us, before he died. Said two Peacekeepers rode off with her. Alive, or he thought so.'

Closing my eyes, I remember the General's strained tendons, the fever and frenzy as she disappeared into whatever battle she imagined she was fighting. If they beat her the way they had beaten me…

I try to stand, only to fall back against the wall, head spinning.

'Stop it,' Silas admonishes gently. 'You may have got the bullet out, but that shoulder's a mess.' He's been hurt too, his forehead patched up with sterile strips. I hiss as he eases the jacket away from my shoulder, exposing the filthy top and the tell-tale symbol that scars my chest.

'What's that?' Falco's eye is hawk-sharp.

'It's a special sign,' Franzi says. His head is on his mother's shoulder, his face bloodless. 'We had one over the door. Ma Pec always said it was for protection. But it didn't work, did it?'

Bebe strokes his hair with a grazed hand. 'It protects us from Seekers, Fran, not from people.' When she looks up, I see that she knows more than she's saying. 'Did it protect you?'

My hand creeps to the scabbing cuts. 'Yes.'

Falco only frowns. I nod at her wearily as Silas cleans the wound and re-dresses it. There is more to say, but first comes rest.

When I wake, hours later, I find the others kneeling outside Esterházy's place. From beneath the burned rubble in the yard, Bebe has dug up a strongbox. In it are credit notes: hundreds of them.

'Enough to start again,' she says, tears streaking the grime on her cheeks. 'As if Pec knew.'

I turn away, uneasy. What had Esterházy seen in the presence of the Ifs, the moment before she told me to run? What had she seen all those years ago, during her first encounter with *them* as they raged from the Edge?

We bury the dead – Thrip and Horse and four Peacekeepers – in the rough plot at the edge of the settlement, where a handful of rusted metal grave markers cluster.

HERE LIES WRETCH BARKER, one reads, A GOOD FRIEND WHO DIED IN JUNE.

One grave in particular is better tended than the others, a faded plastic bouquet fastened to it by a ring. MARIOLA DUROY, AND CHILD.

Sand blows in sheets at those who dig the graves. Bebe says it doesn't matter much if they're deep; the dirt blows away too quickly for anyone to stay buried for long. The weather will eventually do the work the earth cannot.

There is to be no grave for Esterházy. Instead, a wind burial, which Bebe says the old woman would have wanted. Together, outside the limits of Angel Share, we construct a makeshift shelter through which the wind can howl. Here she will lie until the wind has dried her flesh to thinness and it comes loose and is borne away across Factus, across the Edge and out into the unexplored vastness of the Void.

Will the Seekers come to her? I wonder, as I watch as the first mutterings of the night breeze stir her grey hair. Was that the reason for burying her out in the open, far from the town? In death, would she rejoin them, at last?

I look to the horizon, imagining this moon as it must have been when it was newly terraformed, imagining Esterházy leaving behind the oppression of the prison hulks, to fly into the unknown.

'She's here,' I murmur to Silas. 'In another reality, she's here.'

Carefully, he puts his arm around me, taking care not to bump my bandaged shoulder.

Bebe sings a song, an old one from Earth with half-remembered lyrics that speak of forests and mountains. Even the General Store man comes to witness the ceremony along with the other survivors, bringing with them what tokens they can spare. Falco makes another flower from protein wrappers; Silas drops a bit of scrap metal hammered into the shape of a crescent moon. Bebe pours a glug of mezcal into the dirt at the old woman's feet.

And then it's over, and people hurry back to their walls and roofs, chased by the gathering night.

In the shadow of the ruins of Esterházy's saloon, Bebe pulls me aside.

'She left this for you,' she murmurs, handing me something wrapped in a rag. 'Before she died, she said you were to have it.'

She watches me unwrap a scalpel; ancient by Factus standards, dented and tarnished, sharpened to thinness at its edge. The same sort of scalpel that hangs from the belts of the Seekers, that they wielded to take the Marshal apart with brutal efficiency.

We are all Hel.

'You understand what it means?' Bebe asks.

My fingers tighten around the blade's handle. 'I think so.'

I rejoin Falco and Silas and Pegeen in the General Store, where they poke dismally at plates of fried grubs.

'Here.' Silas hands one over. 'It's all the old tightwad will spare. They're better with some pseudosalt.'

'Better than what?' Falco grumbles, washing one down with a swig from a bottle of mezcal.

I stare at the plate without seeing it, imagining the expression of disgust the General would make now if she were here, confronted by a dinner of witchetty grubs.

'We have to go after her,' I say.

Silas shrugs helplessly. 'We don't know where they took her.'

'We know they went east.' I look up at them all, one of my eyes still blurry. 'Joliffe was planning to take me to the Air Line Road. Surely the Peacekeepers will go there too?'

Bebe watches me, a strange expression on her face as she nods slowly. 'The Air Line *is* the nearest place with an Accord presence. Doubt they would go much further than that, Peacekeepers don't like to stray outside the Zone. Most of them are wanted too.'

'What's the closest station?'

'Drax. About a day and a half's ride, on a good mule.'

I nod, and tip the greasy fried morsels into a twist of paper. Shoving them into the pocket of the Marshal's coat, I gather up whatever can be spared from the floor around us: a roll of bandage, the *Charis*'s medkit, a packet of dried snake meat.

'What are you doing?' Falco demands. 'We don't even know if she's still alive.'

'The Peacekeepers won't kill her, not while there is bounty to be had. And to execute her, the Accord will probably need to give an executive order.' I wince, picking up one of the guns abandoned by the window. A Peacekeeper pistol, it looks like. 'If they're travelling by mule, they'll be moving slowly. It means we have a chance.'

A hand grasps my arm.

'Ten,' Silas pleads. 'Look at you, you're half-dead. You need to rest. And if the Accord catch you…'

I squeeze his hand, before letting go and shouldering my pack with difficulty. 'Meet me in Drax?' I ask them all. 'You have to pass it to get back to Landfall, in any case.'

'And where the hell are *you* going?' Falco demands.

I stop. I'm tired, more tired than I dare admit, and yet I can't rest. My hand goes to the scalpel hidden in the jacket.

'To send a message.'

●

The ashes of the fire spiral into the air around me, before falling soft, like the snow I once saw in an old wire-and-picture show filmed on Earth.

Night has fallen as I sit on the sand. I add another piece of debris to the fire, making sparks leap high into the air. I know it will be visible for miles across the Barrens – a spark, a red pointed star. A beacon.

To my right, a vague shape beneath the shelter, lies Esterházy's body.

'Will they come?' I ask, over the crackling of broken furniture. There's no reply.

I turn the scalpel in my hands, tracing the tarnished handle, worn to smoothness. How many lives has this blade taken? How many arteries severed, how many hearts cut free? Or am I seeing it all wrong? The blade reflects a narrow strip of my face; just an eye socket, swollen from the beating, and an eye within it, dark as a bird's. How many lives have they saved, in their bloody trade? Can such things be measured and weighed and balanced in any meaningful way, whether one or a thousand?

I feel the lives that make up the tally rising around me, as they did in the Suplicio. Is this why the Ifs follow me? Do I carry the balance of all those unrealised realities? Or is it a debt that can never be paid?

In another world, Ten Low does not exist. In another world, a young army medic refuses to forget her name and wear another face to spy on the enemy. In another world she never goes to Prosper. She never accepts a mission from a contact on the corner of a lonely street. The virus research never leaves the medical laboratory. And Tamane is never a target, just another moon, home to thousands of young Accord trainees – fighters of the future. And the Free Limits still fight, gathering their scattered allies, forgetting why the fight ever began, and the war goes on.

I open my eyes, looking down to my chest. Which version of me was dragged out of the Suplicio?

When I look up I see a figure standing, staring at me from where the firelight fails. I see grey hair thick with ash and dust, wrinkled skin like the desert from above, eyes that are dark holes. I blink. The figure sways with the wind, always an inch beyond where the light falls.

'Esterházy?' I murmur. The fire flares, getting smoke into my eyes. By the time I open them again, the wavering figure is gone, replaced by someone else.

Night-vision goggles glow red, scarred hands grip a belt hung with weapons, reddish hair blows in the wind. As I watch, the darkness gives up other figures. Four, then six, ten. All masked, all staring.

A wave of fear courses through me. Picking up the scalpel, I push myself to my feet.

'She left me this,' I call, holding it out. 'She told me about you.'

They have come on the Seekers' heels; so silently, so softly, that I had not noticed. They take up space between atoms. One of the Seekers steps towards me.

'What does it mean?' I ask, the scalpel trembling in my hand.

The figure stops, six feet away. I can't see much of the face, only weathered brown skin. Among the hundreds of lines that score their arms, is a fresh one, just below the elbow. A new mark to the tally. An addition, not a subtraction.

Slowly, they hold out a hand in invitation.

'I can't,' I say. 'I have to find Gabi. I want her to live. *They* do too.'

The figure takes another pace forwards, until they are within arm's reach. I smell them; the faint sweetness of old blood, the chemical sharpness of disinfectant, the iron tang of clean metal, and something distant, like lightning-burned sand. The smell of the Suplicio.

'I need your help, one more time,' I murmur.

The figure inclines their head. When they speak, their voice is soft.

'There is a price.'

'I know.' My head swims as I look into the dark glass of the goggles. 'I will pay it.'

The Seeker nods, reaching for one of their knives. Fire flashes on the blade.

I open my eyes. I am sitting beside the fire, the dirt all around me undisturbed. There is no one, only the faint rustle of Esterházy's clothes stirring in the wind.

And yet when I look down I see the Augur's dice lying on the sand before me, resting on the number *two*.

•

I push the buzzard hard all night, running the aircraft to the point of overheating until, at noon the next day, I reach the station Bebe talked about. I land the buzzard in the holding pen near the stable, keeping my head low beneath the Marshal's hat. No one looks at me much, and if they do they recoil in distaste. With a surge of relief I see the *Charis* docked at the far end, looking shabbier than ever, but locked up. Shouldering the pack, I set off to find the others.

For a no-hope, hard-bitten place in the middle of nowhere, Drax is busy. There are miners from the mineral pits, leaving on rotation or reluctantly returning. Mica dust is engrained in the pores of their skin and the lines of their faces, so that they shimmer strangely in the light. There are traders with wagons of supplies – airtights and illegal water canisters and soil bulkers and pre-spawned fungus blocks – on their way to the settlements, and a snake oil salesman, displaying serpent wines labelled Rượu Rắn and coils of dried meat and vials of "restorative" venom. Two grubhawkers, hoping to outdo each other, snatching sales from the bored and the hungry.

But, to my dismay, the place is crawling with Accord. It doesn't take me long to realise there must be a fort nearby, and that the station exists mostly to support it. From here, the Accord draft in new recruits, promising decent food, pay, and most alluring of all, the chance to leave Factus.

The street outside the Air Line platform is crowded, folk jostling and pushing to get a look at something that gleams on the track. I stop among them. It's the strangest Air Line wagon I have ever seen. It squats on the rails like a huge, metal insect, windowless and armour-plated, shining with newness, sparking with small lights that tell of high-grade tech. It looks like something from another world. Which it is.

'What the hell?' I murmur, as figures in Accord uniforms start to emerge, filling tanks and checking panelling.

'It's an Iron Slug,' a woman in dark-lensed glasses beside me says, chewing hard on her century leaves. 'Came from Landfall before sun-up. We ain't never had one here before. Not even when they finally caught the Chow Baron. They transported him to trial on the regular Air Line, in a crate.'

'It's for prisoner transfer?' I look again at the soldiers. These aren't sun-worn, hungry, hastily instructed local recruits. They're Air Fleet: well-trained, well-armed. Well able to hold their own.

'Sure.' The woman sucks her green teeth. 'And I'll tell you this for free—' She stops, seeing me for the first time. I catch a glimpse of myself in her lenses, wrapped neck to brow in yellow-stained bandages. 'Ugh,' she utters, edging away from me without another word.

I can't help but smile, a little. Folk are so afraid of yellowrot, they never spare a thought for what might be beneath the bandages.

'You too, huh?' From the edge of the crowd, an elderly man nods at me. His flesh is bubbled with swellings, some of them crusted, the bandages stained a tell-tale bright yellow.

I nod back, and in silence we watch the soldiers about the Iron Slug.

'Look at that goddam thing,' the man mutters.

'Know who it's for?' I ask.

'Talk round camp is one of them war brats.' He lips at the bandage above his mouth. 'Gone mad, they say. That's why they sent the Slug.'

The Accord sent this wagon for the General, I'm certain, and this time, they are taking no chances. Is she aboard, even now? The dim, flickering departure board shows a noon train, but there's no sign of one. Either way, it's probable that we do not have long…

I hurry to the saloon. It's busy, humid with breath and steam from the kitchens, and reeks of disinfectant vapour and sweet, stale liquor. At a table by the window, one of the grubhawkers is displaying a tray of glitter worms to two women, poking at them to make them extrude the glimmering, seductive ooze that some people like to paint their faces with. Shards of plastic crunch under my boots as I make my way towards the bar.

A group of Peacekeepers have laid claim to most of the space, their weathered faces flushed with drink, their knuckles scarred and scabbed. Were they some of the crew who killed Pec Esterházy? Clenching my hand in the pocket of my jacket, I jerk my chin to the bartend.

'Mezcal,' I mutter quietly, but still, the Peacekeepers turn to look at me, their lips curling in distaste.

The bartend too looks uncertain, licking her lips and glancing at the crowd. Finally, she thrusts a tumbler in my direction, careful to avoid my bandaged hand. 'Drink it outside,' she barks. 'And throw the cup away.'

At that moment, the door crashes open. Two figures stand silhouetted against the blinding dust. Falco and Pegeen. The chatter in the place momentarily dips.

'Is that?' I hear one of the Peacekeepers murmur.

'Malady Goddam Falco,' the other confirms. 'What the hell's she doing out here?'

Ostentatiously, she elbows past me.

'Got any peaches?' she asks the bartend.

The woman gives a nervous smile. 'Lemme go check.'

Glancing into the scratched aluminium mirror behind the bar, I catch Peg's gaze and jerk my head, before making my way outside.

There, I almost run into a shabby figure, with a pipe in their mouth.

'Silas!'

For a second, he stares in confusion, before his eyes widen. 'Ten!' He grabs me in a hug. 'My god, we had almost given up.'

'Careful,' I say, pulling him out of sight around the corner. 'Folk are meant to think I have the rot.'

·

Falco and Peg soon appear, holding an open tin of peaches and a bottle of benzene. With them are two other G'hals, both weary and travel-stained.

'Gotta hand it to you, Doc.' Falco smirks. 'That's some disguise.' She motions the G'hals forwards. 'Rat you know, and this is Bui. They've been running a protection racket at Las Cruces. We managed to get them on the tangle.'

They nod at me. I remember Rat from Falco's bar; she's hard to miss, a muscular woman with bright red hair and sun-pinked face tattooed with stars and swirls, covering up the three dots, one at her temple. Bui by contrast is small and slight. She eyes me suspiciously, wiping at her cheeks with the end of the dyed scarf she wears over her hair.

'The General?' I ask.

Silas sighs. 'That thing was already on the tracks when we arrived. We've been watching, but if Gabi is here, she must already be on board.'

'She has to be,' Peg says. 'Soldiers out there are Air Fleet. Never seen them out here, before. Someone high up is behind this.'

It comes back to me; Commander Aline's face on the screen as she coolly ordered the General's termination, the General's expression as she looked her superior officer in the eye and blew out the camera, as if it were her brains. The back of my neck prickles.

Bui frowns. 'If those soldiers are so flash, why isn't the kid already dead?'

'She *is* a General,' I point out. 'Maybe they don't have the clearance level to do it. Either way, we need to get her off that thing.'

Falco says nothing. Thoughtfully, she fishes a slice of peach from the tin and eats it. 'What's in it for us?'

'How about the fact rescuing the child is the right thing to do?' Silas demands.

'You haven't been on Factus long enough, flyboy. If you had, you'd realise that everything has a price.'

I sigh, bone-weary. 'I have nothing to pay you with, Mala.'

But Falco smiles slyly, her eye narrowed at the rail tracks, where the Iron Slug waits.

'How many Air Line shipments would you say we've waylaid over the years, Peg?' she asks.

The G'hal shrugs. 'Fair few.'

'And how much is top-class Accord tech going for on the market these days?'

Rat grins, showing bright blue fibreglass teeth. 'Heard on the tangle that businesses on Delos are desperate for components.'

'Bet that Slug has all the latest modules and boards. If it were to somehow become decoupled…'

'What about the security?' Silas asks, serious. 'Those Air Fleet grunts are no joke.'

'Only as good as their fancy peashooters,' Bui says, flicking some dirt from her rifle.

Falco takes a long swig of benzene. 'G'hals,' she says. 'Saddle up.'

•

Beams of light streak my face, grit-laden air buffets through the thin gap that serves as a window in the side of the carriage. A prime spot this, away from the stink of the passenger cars. So far no one has dared asked me to move, cringing away from my bandaged face. Even the soldiers did not want to look too closely at me while boarding, not after I started to cough on them; they let me pass with a disgusted flick of the hand.

I take a scrappy piece of paper from my pocket and peer out of the window. A squat weather-eaten boulder is sliding past. *Toad rock*, Falco has scrawled on the hand-drawn map. Just past it, hatched in ink, is what I'm looking for. *Shade's Gulch*. According to Falco it's a long, narrow canyon, deep and shadowed enough to hide any activity from the satellites that might be tracking the Air Line from above.

My shoulder gives a sullen throb. I reach into the Marshal's coat for the small canister of oxygen Falco was able to score in Drax, and fill my lungs with a few deep breaths. I follow it up with two beads at once. I'm in a bad way, my shoulder burning and head aching, my whole body battered and sore.

It will have to be enough. As the rock slides out of view, I reach for the pistol hidden in my pocket. This is it. I close my eyes, knowing that somewhere, beyond the terraform, in the cells of my blood, *they* are waiting. I step forwards and shove open the wagon door.

Desert air blasts my face, sending the bandages flapping.

'Hey,' the shotgunner yells as I step out. 'You can't—'

I grasp his padded armour and spin, throwing him from the train. He's whisked away with a shriek, the shotgun clattering from his grip. The wound in my shoulder tugs as I seize the gun and arm it.

A second later the Air Line plunges into cold, ochre shadow. We're in the canyon.

Ahead of me, a guard carriage rattles and sways and after it, last of all, comes the Iron Slug.

The noise of the train echoes against the canyon walls, rebounding so that the world seems full of beating wings. But beneath that noise is another sound, a many-throated growl that grows louder until, with a roar, two G'hal mares burst over the ridge of the canyon, skidding down a steep path to race behind the train. The riders scream a battle cry.

I answer it, amphetamine smacking through my blood, making me forget the pain. Rat and Bui draw level with the guard wagon, screaming insults, pelting the sides with rocks and bags of the foul paste they mixed up back in Drax: grit and excrement and glue that explodes on the wagon's sides and coats the external cameras in a paste that can't be blown clear.

Gritting my teeth, I leap from one swaying platform to another. There's a whine as one of the automatic guns swivels my way, but I hit it with a shotgun blast, enough to knock the tracking out, at least. Shots rain down on each side of the wagon, targeting the G'hals, but Rat and Bui laugh and swerve away, leaving the armoured windows too smeared and filthy for the soldiers to see through. Grimly, I sling the weapon over my good shoulder and haul myself up onto the roof.

The wind strikes me with the force of raging water, but I keep my head down, squinting at the stretch of metal before me.

One gun turret, battered and dented and spattered with grime, but still operational. I claw my way towards it, breath snatched away, watching as the mechanism jerks and spins, as the red light declares me a target. With a surge of effort I throw myself forwards, using all my weight to push the gun down as it fires.

Charges ricochet from the roof, searing the air inches from my feet as the gun strains to right itself. I won't be able to hold it for much longer. With my bad arm I pull a knife and – gritting my teeth against the pain in my shoulder – jam the blade into the hydraulics, twisting and ripping at the cable.

There are sparks and a shock jolts through me, sending my arm flying, the knife clattering from my grip. The turret sags downwards.

My palm is burned from the shock, muscles fizzing, but there's no time to think about it. I crawl forwards, until I can peer down at the last platform before the Iron Slug.

It's miraculously unguarded. Breath heaving, I lower myself awkwardly from the roof, but halfway down my shoulder spasms and I fall sprawling onto the metal.

Before I can even swear, I realise my mistake. Two shotgunners stand in the open doorway, weapons pointed down at me. There's nothing I can do, nowhere to go except…

As they open fire I roll from the edge of the platform, catching myself by my fingertips.

The bright silver blade of the Air Line rushes by below. My boots scramble for purchase on the wagon's side and slip, my sweat-slick fingers giving out, my shoulder screaming in agony.

There's a flash of movement, and I look up, directly into the barrels of a shotgun.

'Doc!'

The soldier above me falls back, blood spraying from the inch of flesh where the armoured uniform meets his chin. His gun falls, almost striking me in the face before being swept away. I glance over my shoulder. Falco's mare races alongside, Peg balanced on the seat, hair streaming out, grimacing in pain as they aim the pistol again. Another cry and the second soldier goes spinning from the edge of the platform. With every scrap of strength I have left, I hook my fingers onto the floor panels and worm my way back on.

'Doc, hurry!'

Peg aims over my head, where at any moment more soldiers will appear.

I look up. Not six feet away is the Iron Slug, with its smooth sides, its narrow platform. I drag myself into a crouch, ready to leap—

My body, riddled with bullet holes, tumbles onto the tracks. A gun jams into my scalp from behind and bursts my head open. I hang from the platform as someone stamps on my fingers, kicking me away to be crushed beneath the Air Line. I cower, hands over my head as Falco and Peg are hit by a strike that sends them flying like rag dolls; my eyes fill with fire as the train is engulfed in an explosion...

No! I cry silently. *Show me!*

Just for a second, there is an overwhelming sense of being seen. *They* hear me, I realise, in a split-second of horror, before one image shines clear through the rest: that of a gun turret.

I flatten myself against the platform as a hail of charges bursts from one of the Slug's guns. I scream, expecting to feel the charges pierce my flesh but there's a roar, a flash of light and I open one eye to see the gun swivelling, locking on to another target…

'Falco!' I scream.

Her eye meets mine and she throws the mare onto its side, skidding through the dirt as the Slug fires, filling the air with deadly light and splinters of rock dust, charges thudding into the body of the vehicle. The mare explodes, the blast echoing from the canyon walls.

My cry is lost in the noise, even as the targeting beam pivots back towards me.

This time, I don't wait. I struggle up and leap, crashing clumsily onto the polished platform of the Slug. Before I can pull the pistol from my holster the beams split, one swinging to take me in its sight, the other flashing as it pinpoints a mare racing towards the flaming mess of Falco's vehicle.

I plunge my hand into the jacket and drag out the only thing I have left: the oxygen canister. I throw it into the narrow aperture around the gun and fire the pistol before I even think about what I'm doing. The explosion sends me reeling, the gun tumbling from my grip as I flail to hold on.

I can barely breathe, let alone stay upright, my head filled with ringing. Another panel slides back and a second automatic gun appears, smoke billowing around it. When it swings down to aim at me, there is nothing I can do.

A rumble, a glare of light and the beam swings away, pointing up at a dark shape that drops from the sky, flying terrifyingly close to the walls of the canyon. It's the *Charis*.

Silas! I try to shout, but there is no air in my lungs, and I watch in horror as the Slug opens fire, punching holes in the *Charis*'s belly, sending her pin-balling from one rock wall to another.

Then from above there's a sudden clank, and streams of water cascade from the *Charis*'s cooling tanks, putting out the fires that smoulder on her body, throwing the beams off course in the cloud of vapour and dust. Water hits me too, and though I gasp at the shock, it clears my head, giving me a last burst of energy.

As the *Charis* rises rapidly from the canyon, out of the line of fire, I wrench at the coupling that joins the wagons together. But it's useless, the thing is solid metal, the hydraulic screws locked tight and without my pistol…

There's a cry. Turning my head in the rushing air, I see a mare racing alongside me once again. It struggles to keep speed, overloaded with G'hals; Rat is driving, Bui is balancing on the seat and behind her, bloodied and torn but alive, are Malady Falco and Pegeen.

'Move!' Bui bellows, as the automatic gun spins. On her shoulder is a blaster. With my last strength, I scramble back onto the Slug's platform and cover my head as she pulls the trigger.

The explosion smashes into me, sending shards of hot metal and burning plastic flying. The coupling blows with an ear-splitting shriek and – with a crash that nearly sends me plummeting from the side – the Slug is free. I look up to see the rest of the Air Line carriages speeding away, the distance already increasing. On the mare, Bui aims the blaster once more, this time at the automatic gun.

The explosion shakes the Slug violently, and acrid smoke pours from the apertures, like a creature heaving out its dying breaths. A second later the door flies open and a gunner staggers onto the platform.

I trip them up, throwing them from the edge. Bui is ready; she pulls a smoke grenade from her coat and throws it towards me. I catch it and – before anyone can figure out what is happening – toss it inside the body of the Slug.

Within moments, it is chaos. There are cries from within, the whine of the malfunctioning gun systems, barked orders. Dragging the bandages over my nose and mouth, I stumble inside, trying to stay low. Screens and panels light the darkness a feverish red, more tech than I have seen for years. Eight soldiers: some of them crawl towards the air, others are arming weapons or trying to override the automatic guns. One sees me and brings up their gun, but I drive my elbow into their sternum and they collapse to the floor, wheezing. The smoke burns my own lungs, makes my injured chest heave, but I fight my way on.

There, at the very rear of the carriage, is an internal compartment protected by a thick door. I pull at it, trying not to breathe, but it's shut firm. In rage, I see a lock, flashing red.

I grab the soldier I sent down, dragging her back by the jacket. She fights back but I swing, driving my fist into her nose. She sags, groaning, but I haul up one of her limp arms, pressing her thumb against the lock.

With a hiss, the door gives.

'General?' I choke, pulling the mask from my mouth.

In one corner of the bare, black-walled cell, a figure huddles. The General, her face bruised and bloodless. She looks at me in horror, in hope.

'Low?' she whispers.

Smiling wildly, I pull her to her feet. The Slug lurches and jolts to a stop and she falls against me.

'What the hell are you doing here?'

'What do you think?' I say, my eyes burning. 'Come on, we must—'

She jerks back. 'Don't touch me.'

I look at her closer. She's shaking as if with fever. Lost in her memories again? As I reach out to take her arm, I hear it: a low drone from above, the noise of powerful engines.

'They're here,' she says, eyes huge. 'The Air Fleet. They have come, just as I ordered.'

Cold wraps my heart, but the General is already moving, stooping to grab the pistol from the soldier who moans outside the door.

I follow at a run.

Together, we stagger through the smoke-filled darkness of the Slug. Two soldiers slump over the panels, unconscious, I hope; the others must have fled the grenades. We burst into the light. The Slug has come to a stop at the very end of the canyon, and all around us is carnage; smoke and soldiers downed by the G'hals, blood in the dust.

'Doc!' Falco yells, staring above my head.

I turn. Six hard slaps of silver against the white sky and one dark blot; Air Fleet fighters speeding towards the *Charis*.

'No,' I gasp, but it's already happening, the terrible vision the Ifs showed me. Two of the fighters split off and strafe the ship's sides, aiming for the fuel tanks. With an explosion like a bellow, the *Charis* drops from the sky, engines screaming. At the last moment Silas pulls up out of the descent, but it's too late. The ship meets the ground with a sickening, deafening impact. I choke and stumble forwards. Through the pall of dust I see that the *Charis*'s windshield is shattered, smoke rising from the twisted metal of the sides, that in the pilot's seat, a figure with black, untidy hair slumps, lifeless.

Someone is yelling for me to run. Dazed, eyes burning with tears, I look around as the fighters bank and return, as one of them splits off, and – engines blasting – descends to the dust.

I can't see, can't think, all I can do is watch as the fighters fly low, strafing the area. The G'hals run for the mare, Falco covering them, firing wildly into the sky. Then, charges explode, and with a cry and a splatter of blood she spins to the dirt.

'Falco!' I lunge towards her, only to stop dead.

The cold mouth of a gun has been jammed hard against my skull, in the killing spot.

'Don't move,' the General orders over the engines, her voice breaking.

'What are you doing?'

'What I have to.' There's a whine, as the pistol charges up. 'If they'll pay a hundred thousand credits for your life, then maybe they'll agree to spare whatever's left of mine.'

'General, you don't understand.'

'Tamane.' The gun bites into my skin. 'They told me what you did. I knew you were a killer and a traitor, but that… Thousands, Low. All of them young. More left sick for life.'

'Please.' I try to turn around. 'Gabi—'

'Ortiz!'

The voice comes from everywhere at once, magnified over the roar of the ships.

'Ortiz!' the voice barks, louder this time. 'Stand down. That is an order.'

Automatic cannon beams break through the dust to fix upon targets. Rat and Bui raise their hands, staring up at the crafts above with hatred. Peg kneels by Falco, sobs shaking their chest.

We are surrounded.

Finally, the noise of the engines lessens as the lead fighter lands. A figure climbs from the hatch, followed by three elite soldiers. A woman with grey, tightly curled hair and the uniform of the Accord High Command.

Commander Beatrice Aline.

'General Ortiz,' she calls across the distance. 'I hereby order you to stand down.'

I feel the gun tremble. 'Gabi—'

'I said don't move!' the General barks. 'Commander Aline, this is the traitor Life W.P. Lowry. She's the one who stole the formula used on Tamane.' Her voice cracks. 'Do you even know how many you killed, Low?'

Bodies beneath the sand, each one a line carved in the metal cell wall. Each one unable to be measured.

'Yes,' I say. 'I do.'

'I propose an accord,' the General shouts. 'I will give up Low, and you will revoke whatever termination order there is upon me, allow me to live freely, for however long I have left. You'll let me look for a cure.'

Commander Aline smiles pityingly. 'You are not in much of a position to negotiate, Ortiz.'

'You want her alive.' Desperation creeps into the General's voice. 'And she knows things, about the Seekers and the forces here that people are afraid of. She can control them!'

Fear, greater than the threat of the gun sweeps through me. 'No,' I begin.

'Landgrubber stories,' Aline dismisses, but beneath the cool expression is another, one of intense interest, almost hunger. The General's instincts are right. The military know about the Ifs. And they want to know more.

'Grant me clemency,' the General says, 'or I kill the traitor and everything she knows goes with her.'

Slowly, Commander Aline inclines her head.

'Very well. I am willing to talk terms at least.' She motions two of the soldiers forwards. 'Stand by while we secure the prisoner.'

With a strange noise the General removes the gun from my skull. 'You'll live. You'll be a prisoner, but you'll live, damn you.'

I turn to grab her but beyond the two soldiers, I see Commander Aline raise an army revolver and know – too late – what is about to happen.

'No!' someone screams as she pulls the trigger.

•

I open my eyes. Yellow light falls thick into my vision, like bitter honey, illuminating endless sand and a heavy, unchanging sky.

There was somewhere else, before I was here. A place of terror, the sound of a ship crashing to earth, a scream. I feel my skull. My hand comes away coated with blood, but there is no pain.

The General... As I think her name there's movement, a grey shape shifting in the distance. I walk towards it. With each step, hands worm their way out of the sand to collect the blood that drips from my skull. They are welcome to it.

At first I think the shape is Moloney trapped in his endless parade, but I stumble over a leg protruding from the edge of the dune and realise there are others here. I bend down and brush at the sand, uncovering black hair matted with blood, a face that saw too much too soon. The General.

I shake her, wanting her to wake up, to blink and laugh at me for crying, but she is gone. Through tears, I look up. The Charis is a wreck, shot to earth. As I watch, another piece of trash flutters through the shattered windshield. Silas is there, dead.

Further away, half-buried in the stained sand I find Rat and Bui, and Pegeen and Falco lying close together, as if in sleep.

Something kindles at the back of my mind, like the first wisp of smoke before a conflagration. Those lives, so bright, so vivid, tearing through the world like comets and this is their end?

And where are they? I start to shake. They have haunted my steps, they have knotted and unravelled the paths of my life, for this?

I scream for them to answer and the Charis catches fire. I scream again and the sand flames, turning to dark glass beneath my feet, and through it I see them all, the fallen of Tamane. When I look up, the yellow light is almost gone.

'No.' I stumble away. There are other paths, a hundred other choices, realities that are not this one. I don't want this one. 'No!' I yell, as the light fades.

I stagger and fall. Hands catch me before I hit the ground. Hands that are gloved in blood.

The thing with my face stares back at me, her eyes like the web of matter between the stars. Every inch of her skin bears a line, bears a life. Slowly, she raises her hands, palms up. In one of them, Esterházy's scalpel gleams silver. In the other is a small, bloodied bone dice.

There is always a choice.

I look into her eyes and understand. The lines are not lives taken, not a debt subtracted from the world. They are different realities, a thousand versions of every life, a line for every choice. No one could see all that and hold on to themselves.

There is a price, *the Seeker said.*

I take the scalpel.

Hel smiles, and rolls the dice.

•

The bullet strikes.

The world is still, as if embedded in the yellow light of the Suplicio. Then, with a cry, the General falls.

I look down, the light of the bullet still streaking my vision. She lies on her side, shuddering. A pool of blood spreads across the sand from her middle.

'No.' The word escapes my lips. Without thinking, I go to my knees beside her. But her entire front is a mess of dark blood, and I can see one of her ribs through the sundered flesh. 'She's a child.' The words tumble from me as I drag the scarf from my neck and press it to the General's chest, trying to stem the bleeding. 'She was dying anyway, why couldn't you just let her live in peace?'

'She wasn't dying,' the Commander says, her mouth a hard line. 'Nor would she have lived in peace. They are too dangerous, these children, they can be turned against us as they age. It's for the good of us all that the programme is concluded.'

'They're your shame,' I spit as the General convulses. 'You want the world to forget they ever existed—'

Commander Aline's face creases as she raises the revolver again, levelling it at me. 'Restrain her.'

For all their training, the soldiers hesitate, their eyes fixed on the dying General, before coming forwards to drag me away even as I fight to keep my hands on the wound. Aline takes something from a pack. The sight of it sends terror and anger through me; it's a high security prison collar, with locking needles and embedded blades that will spring out and cut the throat during any attempt to remove it.

No, I tell *them. No, not this.*

They don't answer me; nothing stops Aline from coming close and lining up the needles with my scarred flesh. How could I have been wrong?

'Do not feel bad, Low,' she murmurs as she works. 'We'll take care of you. You're a hero, in a way. If you hadn't stolen our formula, the FL would never have targeted Tamane and lost their support, and the war would have dragged on and on. After all,' she says, as she pushes the needles in. 'That's why we let you take it.'

I meet her eyes. She's telling the truth, I realise in horror. Thousands sacrificed to bring a quick end to a long and bloody war. Children who should not have lived killed to ensure peace. I shudder as if something – some*one* – is straining to get out of my skin. As the prison collar is about to click closed around my neck, I feel the scalpel in my hand.

I slash out and Aline lets go of the collar, gripping at her wrist. I try to break the soldiers' hold on me and run, but Aline is already pulling out her revolver with bloodied hands, levelling it at my face.

A shot rings out, clean through the chaos. Commander Aline stares as blood appears on her forehead, burrowing out like a dark, shining grub. With a choke, she falls.

On the sand, the General bares her teeth in a single savage smile, before she too collapses, the pistol falling from her grip.

The soldiers draw their weapons, one of them running to the Commander. But the beating of my heart is in the air, and a roar is gathering, like an endless bellow of thunder.

I look up as – with a shriek – the first Seeker craft races across the sky, weapons blazing, sending the Accord target beams swivelling and twisting wildly. Rat and Bui throw themselves from the line of fire, scrambling for weapons, shooting at anything they can see, while Peg drags Falco towards the mare.

And *they* are there with me. At last, I feel them; they crowd up against every split-second decision, and every lucky shot, and every hesitation. They tear through the battlefield, revelling in the chaos, in the teeming potential of a fight.

A Seeker craft flies low overhead, firing directly into the flight deck of the Commander's ship. Fire blooms, glass explodes. I rip the prison collar from my skin and throw it to the dirt, kicking sand over it.

Only one of the Commander's soldiers is left standing. As I walk towards him, he fires. No use. Every shot goes wide. When his gun is empty of charge I stop, staring at him, and see myself reflected in his eyes: my bloodied hands holding a scalpel, the Seekers' mark clear on my chest, my eyes as hard as a bird of prey's.

'Run,' I tell him.

On his heels, and all around us, *they* dance, plucking at the tangled strings of our choices, blurring the paths between realities on this, *their* moon; the last stop before the Void.

•

The ranch house is tucked into a fold of the ragged foothills, alone and softly glowing, like a firefly cupped in a weathered palm. The surgeon steps out onto the porch and takes a deep breath of the cool, blue night. The wind whisks the smell of blood and antiseptics from his apron.

'Quite the day's work,' he says.

I smile wearily. For hours I've helped the surgeon and his husband stitch and swab, sterilise and cauterise, dose and hope. Inside, Silas lies reeling from a concussion and four broken ribs. Falco slumps on the cot next to him, demanding morphine for the wound that almost took off her leg. And the General...

'How is she?' I pass over a basin of water for the surgeon to wash his hands.

He laughs dryly, rubbing at the cracked skin of his knuckles.

'What?' I ask.

'Just the irony of it. The Accord are spread so thin that half of these moons are falling apart, and yet, some things they built to last.' He glances at the house. 'Like her.'

'She'll live?'

'The extra-dermal membrane they installed beneath her skin bore much of the brunt, and if she recovers from the blood loss, and the damage to her lung she may, yes.'

'And her illness?'

He raises a shoulder. 'Whatever they did to make her what she is, it goes deeper than blood and bone. More than I have skill to treat. It may be that, to remain stable, she will need the Accord's drugs for the rest of her life.' He catches my eye. 'But I don't think she's dying. At least, not from what they did to her.'

I drop my head. *Can't think of many who lived long enough to learn a different way to be*, Falco had said. Would the General, now that she has a chance?

Water drips as the surgeon wearily washes his face. I look over at him, lit by the steady solar lights. No tattoos on his temples, just two small scars upon his neck.

'Were you in the FL?' I ask.

'I joined up for a time. Before they lost their way.'

Beyond the ranch house the wind rushes down the slope of the foothills like water. Exhausted, I lean upon the railing, feeling every bruise and laceration, wondering how my body is still holding itself together.

'It is quiet here,' I say.

'A good spot,' the surgeon agrees, taking a pipe from his pocket, and a tin. He nods to the small, metal-sided vegetable plots. 'The shade of the hill keeps the earth from drying out too much.'

'You get no trouble?'

'The gangs know we treat whoever arrives at the door, no questions asked.'

'And the Seekers?' I stare at his face, at the deep lines of his cheeks as he lights the pipe.

He doesn't answer straight away, instead takes a long drag. 'They know I follow The Way. I think they respect that, see it as something similar to their own beliefs about the universe.'

He meets my eyes and smiles, an expression as worn and thin as an old scalpel.

'Is this peace?' I ask.

'No.' He looks into the night. 'It's life.'

•

The morning after our escape, Pegeen and Rat and Bui, all of them patched and bandaged, come riding back up to the ranch on borrowed mules and mares, dragging the damaged *Charis* on a makeshift truck behind them. When she sees the ship's hold, Falco lets out a shout of laughter. It is stuffed full of plunder: panels and components and chips and power cells, the inner workings from the Iron Slug and the downed Accord fighters.

We sit on the porch with the surgeon and his husband Marti, sipping on cups of precious, watered-down tea, watching the

G'hals calculate their profits.

'If we can shift even half of this off-world, we'll make a fortune,' Peg says.

'We'll need a good smuggler.' Falco's eye narrows, bright with morphine. 'How about it, flyboy?'

Silas starts to laugh, then winces in pain, holding his torso. 'Only if you stop calling me that,' he wheezes.

'The thing I don't get,' Rat says, picking at her teeth. 'Is why the Seekers left any of this behind. They usually strip ships and bodies to the marrow, right?'

'They helped themselves to some, definitely to the bodies,' Bui points out. 'Maybe it was too much for them to carry?'

'No,' Peg says, frowning. 'Some of this stuff was piled up, portioned almost, like it had been left deliberate.'

I meet Falco's gaze.

'Whatever the reason,' she says. 'We earned it.'

We stay at the surgeon's for two days, while the General lies silent, hooked to the medical man's cobbled together machines, and Falco curses us out and laughs at us in equal measure, and Silas groggily asks me to keep him company on the pallet bed.

Peace, I think, as I lay with my head on his shoulder, careful of his chest, listening to him breathe. Could it look like this for me?

I can't remember another time like it, on Factus. While the G'hals work on their takings and Silas painstakingly assesses the *Charis*'s damage, I limp around helping the surgeon with his supplies, watching Marti tend his garden of medicinal herbs and prized vegetables. Later, we sit down together at the scratched metal table, to cricket soup flavoured with ferocious home-grown chillies and fried greens and proteinmeal dough rolled out so thin it almost tastes like noodles. We drink tea and listen to Falco's plans for expanding the bar and her hold on Landfall with her new-found wealth, Silas's tales of deals-gone-awry on the satellite stations, Bui's and Rat's gossip from the settlements.

A rare day, all the more cherished for being transitory. Away from the surgeon's ranch, the reality we inhabit churns on, and we will have to step back onto its path, sooner or later. So, as dark falls, and Silas and Marti scrape the dishes with sand, Peg and I help the surgeon rig up his wire transmitter, Rat turning the handle furiously to make enough extra power to receive the latest bulletin.

When it arrives on the sheet, we crowd around the scratched, grey screen, watching the text appear:

AIR FLEET COMMANDER BEATRICE ALINE DEAD IN TRAGIC WRECK

It has been reported that Air Fleet Commander Beatrice Aline perished in a wreck that took place on Factus between Drax and Landfall Five. Commander Aline was escorting two captured fugitives to justice in Landfall, when a navigational error sent her craft off course, into an area of electrical turbulence above the Air Line Road. Tragically, it seems that neither her ship nor those of her

> escorts were able to regain control before the resulting
> crash. The fugitives, it has been reported, also perished.
>
> Accord scouts were able to recover the bodies of
> Commander Aline, the prisoners and her escorts from
> the site by nightfall on the same day.

Peg sits back with a smirk. 'All hail the Accord. Spinning a story like a wheel in sand.'

'"Electrical turbulence",' Silas reads incredulously. 'Who's going to believe that?'

Falco winces, rubbing her leg. 'Accord barely have a grip on these moons. They can't afford to look weak.'

Marti spends a minute or two flicking through the resulting correspondence on the black-market tangle. 'Seems like most folk think it was a Seeker attack,' he says. 'People are saying it was Hel the Converter, reminding the Accord who *really* runs Factus.'

My neck prickles, and I raise a hand to make sure the mark on my chest is covered. The surgeon must have seen it when he treated me. When I glance his way, he meets my eyes, and says nothing.

Falco thumps the table. 'Even better for us. Sounds like no one knows we were there. And if they did, they won't say.'

Rat laughs, slapping her boss on the shoulder.

I stare at the bulletin, my head odd and light. *The fugitives also perished.* How many times could I die?

'Hey,' Silas takes my arm, 'don't you see what this means? You're safe. If they've reported you dead…'

'They have reported me dead before.'

Silas smiles. 'But it said no survivors. And who is there to tell them different?'

I remember the young soldier, staring at me in horror as I told him to run.

'No one,' I murmur.

'Well then.' Silas squeezes my hand. 'You're free.'

Free. The word plagues me as we sit around the stove and talk and smoke and share sips of mezcal long into the night. It plagues me when I look in on the General as she sleeps, her small, scarred face hiding so much. It plagues me as I lie beside Silas, his arm warm on my shoulder.

Finally, after hours of sleeplessness, I ease from the blanket, and step outside.

It's deep night, and the wind is in full voice, singing of the darkness between the stars, of the invisible threads that bind worlds – that bind us all – together. I close my eyes and listen.

The change comes gradually, creeping like frost on a window, like heat through metal. This time, *they* don't rush or tear or claw, they simply are. I open my eyes. Beyond the last solar light at the edge of the ranch, a figure waits. A woman with grey hair and eyes like the darkness.

All is silent as I ease the door closed behind me some minutes later. The skin on my chest prickles in the cool night air, my shoulder gives a stab of pain as I pick up the pack, and make my way quietly down the steps.

As I reach the vegetable plots the ranch door squeaks. I stop, knowing that if it's Silas, the desire to stay might be too much, might stop me from doing what I know I need to. Slowly, I turn.

The General stands on the porch, her feet bare beneath the faded linen gown, her hands pressed to the wound on her torso.

'You're leaving,' she croaks.

I stare, remembering the grief on her face as she pressed the gun to my head, the look of triumph as she watched Aline fall.

'Yes.'

She shifts, obviously in pain. 'You promised to keep me alive.'

'The surgeon says you will live. For a long time, I hope.' I try to smile. 'Falco is going to ask you to join the G'hals. She said you have a home there, if you want.'

'As if I'd join a bandit crew,' the General murmurs, but a smile pulls at the very corner of her mouth. 'They'd treat me like a kid.'

'You are a kid, Gabi.'

She looks at me, lost.

'Where are you going?'

'Out,' I say softly. 'To the Seekers.'

'Aren't they monsters?'

'I don't know. I only know that they have answers.'

After a long moment, her face crumples, tears catching at her breath. 'Low—'

I shake my head to stop her, feeling tears gather hot in my own eyes. 'It's alright.' When I trust my voice again, I take a breath. 'I left a letter, for you all. But… Silas. Tell him I am sorry.'

'He won't understand.'

'I know. But I have to do this. There was a price, and I chose.'

At the edge of my vision, I see movement; the woman with grey hair, waiting. I wipe my eyes, and turn to leave.

'Traitor?'

'What is it, General?'

'I'm not a General, anymore.'

'And I'm not a traitor.'

I meet her gaze. For an instant, she looks beyond me and her eyes widen. 'May your thoughts be clear,' she whispers.

I walk away into that singing night, out towards the Edge, towards the vast unknown.

And *they* walk with me.

ACKNOWLEDGEMENTS

ERE'S WHERE I can open a bottle and raise a glass high to all the people who have brought *Ten Low* to life:

George Sandison, not just for snatching this book out of the air and patiently cleaning it up, but for championing many a weird and wonderful work of speculative fiction.

Tasha Qureshi, for eagle-eyed editorial skills and for fearlessly stomping the gas on the manuscript. *Egészségedre*!

The whole team at Titan, for giving Ten and I a home.

Ed Wilson, for buying the first round.

Hélène Butler and Emily Hayward-Whitlock, for being on board from day one.

RJ Barker, for words of encouragement when they were needed.

Lavie Tidhar, for help and hard liquor.

My parents and family for all their support, and Dave, for being a fan.

My sister – as always – for riding shotgun and helping me navigate through the dark.

Nick, for being the best co-pilot I could ask for.

ABOUT THE AUTHOR

S TARK HOLBORN IS a novelist, games writer, film reviewer, and the author of *Nunslinger*, *Triggernometry* and *Ten Low*. Stark lives in Bristol, UK.

Want more *Ten Low*?

To read an exclusive story, visit starkholborn.com/factus

For more fantastic fiction, author events,
exclusive excerpts, competitions, limited editions and more

VISIT OUR WEBSITE
titanbooks.com

LIKE US ON FACEBOOK
facebook.com/titanbooks

FOLLOW US ON TWITTER AND INSTAGRAM
@TitanBooks

EMAIL US
readerfeedback@titanemail.com